SCORING BIG

KELLY JAMIESON

NATE

"There's one more thing we can try."

My ears perk up like a puppy being offered a treat. "I'm up for anything. What is it?"

"PRP Therapy."

No, I'm not talking to a woman about bedroom activities, sadly.

I look blankly at the doctor.

"Platelet-rich plasma therapy is a new procedure for treating knee injuries. We get a small sample of your blood from your arm, process the blood in a centrifuge, and then inject the concentrated platelets directly into your knee."

"Jesus."

"It uses your body's own healing blood cells, the platelets, to stimulate the natural repair process."

I purse my lips, nodding. "Okay."

"We're using it on a lot of professional athletes," Dr. Perez says. "I think it's worth trying before we go to surgery."

Dr. Perez is a specialist who I've been seeing about my knee. It's been bugging me for months, since last season. During the playoffs it got worse, but I was determined to play as far as we could go. The team doctors weren't happy about that, but hey, I'm a hockey player; we play with broken bones and fresh stitches.

At the end of last season, they told me rest and rehab might help, so I've been doing everything I'm told. I've been at the gym faithfully four times a week, doing the exercises they tell me to do, strengthening my quads, avoiding squatting and pivoting, definitely not running. I've been swimming a few times a week. I ice my knee when I do too much, rest it, take the anti-inflammatories they tell me to, but I worry about taking them too much.

The bad news is, my meniscus tear isn't healing.

"Yeah, I'd rather not have surgery."

"Right. This is minimally invasive, with a faster recovery period than surgery. There's low risk of infection. That said, it doesn't work for everyone."

"Oh."

He gives me more details including some stats, but he doesn't have to convince me. It doesn't sound like there are big risks, only that it might not work. "What's the recovery time?"

"It takes about two to three weeks before healing."

"That's nothing."

He nods. "You'll need to restrict yourself to light activities after the injection, then we'll gradually work back up to exercise. Usually physical therapy along with PRP will have a better result."

"I can do that. Okay. I'm in. Let's do it."

He smiles. "We'll schedule another appointment for it."

"I need this fast. I need to be in shape for training camp in September."

"I think we can squeeze you in next week."

I don't even want to wait a few days, but I guess I can if I have to. "Okay. Perfect."

I zip from the doctor's office over to my ex-wife's place in Lincoln Square to pick up my daughter.

Quinn is the best thing in my life. My ex and I have a deal that she keeps Quinn during the season when I'm playing hockey and traveling, and I take her when I'm off for the summer. Right now, we're sharing custody until school ends.

"Daddy's here!" Brielle calls to Quinn when I walk into her apartment. "How was the appointment? Good news?"

"No."

"Oh. I'm sorry." She eyes me sympathetically.

We're on reasonably good terms. When I started playing for the New York Bears, I got caught up in the big city, pro-athlete lifestyle and dating a gorgeous actress made me feel like I'd really made it. She got pregnant and we got married. Then she fell for someone else—a billionaire who finances Broadway shows.

I met the guy a couple of times. He's everything I'm not—educated, polished, sophisticated. She talked about him all the time, and it bugged me, so when she told me they'd fallen in love I wasn't completely surprised. It still fucking hurt, though. But we both love Quinn more than anything and that's enough motivation for us to work together and make sure her life is everything it should be.

"Daddy!" Quinn bounces down the hall from her room. "Can we go to the beach this afternoon?"

"Hmm. It's kinda late today. How about we go to Central Park on the way home?"

"Can I ride the carousel?"

"Sure."

"Yay!"

I grin. "Okay. Let's go, pop tart."

I smile at Brielle as she bends to hug Quinn.

"See you tomorrow night," Brielle tells our daughter. "I'm off."

I nod, remembering the schedule. Brielle has a role in a Broadway play that's doing really well. Yes, financed by her husband.

I take Quinn's hand and she skips along beside me as we enter the park. Trees provide green shade from the heat of the sun and it's so pleasant and peaceful here in this oasis in the middle of the big city, the skyscrapers rising up at the edge of the park a reminder of the world outside the green space.

Quinn attempts to chase a squirrel across the grass, then we ride the carousel not once but twice, followed up by ice cream. My knee is aching and I need a rest so we find a bench to sit on.

There's a woman sitting on a bench next to us. She has a notebook and pen in her hand, but she's staring into space. Long golden-brown hair in messy waves is held back by a headband with a pink bow on it, showing off big eyes and high cheekbones. Her lips are full and rosy, a mouth made for kissing and sucking and...well, the rest of her looks incredible too, although her outfit is...interesting. A short flouncy pink skirt shows off a long length of fantastic leg, and a tight black tank top hugs her top curves. Chunky black boots complete the ensemble.

The woman turns and her eyes meet mine as I complete my once over. Jesus. Is she crying?

I frown, resisting the urge to jump up, stride over to her, and demand, *who hurt you?*

The woman's gaze lands on Quinn next to me. She takes in Quinn's red and silver face mask and bright red cape. And she smiles. Wow. That smile illuminates her face even more, lighting up her green eyes, something so attractive about her my breath stalls in my chest.

"Are you done your ice cream?" I ask Quinn.

"Yeah."

I clean her up with some paper napkins then walk to the trash bin, which means walking past the woman next to us. I drop our garbage into the bin but as I turn back, I forget to not pivot my knee. It locks. I stumble and hit the grass. "Shit!"

Oops. Language.

The woman jumps up. "Are you okay?"

Great. So impressive, sprawled on the ground in front of a beautiful woman. Heat runs up my neck into my face. Even my ears feel hot. "I think so." I try to gather my composure and get my legs under me to stand.

She extends a hand. Christ. I take it and try to save face. "Do you have a Band-Aid?"

Her eyebrows slope together, her gaze moving over me searching for blood. "Are you hurt?"

"I think I scraped my knee falling for you."

After a startled beat, she bursts out laughing. I grin sheepishly.

Quinn turns to look back and sees me sitting on the ground holding the woman's hand. I let her help me up, putting my weight on my good leg, and dust off my jeans as Quinn skips back to us.

"Your beauty must have made my knees weak," I add to the joke.

"Oh, that's bad," she says, but she's smiling.

"Daddy, what happened?" Quinn asks. "Is it your knee?"

"Yeah. I'm okay." I meet the woman's eyes. "Minor injury."

She gazes at me with concern. "Do you need any help?"

"No, I'm good."

"Hi," Quinn says to the woman.

"Hi." The woman's gaze softens into an almost wistful expression. I have no idea what that's about, but the fact that she likes kids…*my* kid…is hugely attractive. "I like your cape."

"Thanks. I'm Clover. From Harmonia."

I doubt this woman has a clue what she's talking about.

"Clover is my favorite," she replies seriously.

My bad. She does know. Harmonia is a comic book series about girl superheroes that's become hugely popular and is now turning into a whole universe.

"Me, too! And we went on the carousel. Twice!"

"Did you?" the woman replies. "Lucky you. I love the carousel."

"Me too. My favorite horse is the white one."

"Because Clover has a white horse."

"Yes!" Quinn jumps up and down.

"Hmmm. I don't have a favorite. It's been a long time since I was there."

"You should go," Quinn says. "Then we got ice cream. Strawberry shortcake."

"Oooh, I love those. You really *are* lucky." She shoots a smile my way. "Now I want ice cream."

"You can get one right over there." Quinn points.

Damn. This would be the perfect time to say, *I'll go get you one,* but I'm here with my daughter, not trying to pick up chicks.

I love my daughter. But she's a bit of a cock blocker.

Ugh. *Sorry, Quinn.*

That sounds like I'm on the prowl, but I'm really not. I mean, not anymore. When the season ended, I went on a sex bender. Actually, I've been doing that for years, but this year it didn't feel right. Maybe I'm getting old, but I want something more than hookups. Something real. And this woman is hot, but doesn't exactly give off "long term relationship" vibes.

"What's *your* favorite kind of ice cream?" Quinn asks the woman.

"Hmm. I do love strawberry. I used to go to a place that had strawberry cheesecake ice cream. It was amazing. I don't know if they're still around."

"I love strawberry, too. That sounds good."

Great, my daughter has so much in common with this woman. And all I want to do is get rid of her.

Kidding.

I repress a sigh. "We better get home, pop tart. You need dinner before bed."

"Daaaad. It's summer."

"I know. But I also know how you like to stall at bedtime and we need to start early if I want you asleep by midnight." I send Quinn's new friend a wry glance.

She smiles back. "A bedtime staller, huh."

"Daddy says I'm a kickass staller."

My face heats. "Quinn." We've talked about her language, but I take full responsibility for the extent of her profane vocabulary. I'm working on it.

"I don't know if that's something to brag about," I add, although I do sometimes admire her creativity. "Okay, let's go."

Quinn ignores me. "I love your headband."

"Thanks." The woman touches the pink bow. "I like bows."

"It's really pretty." Quinn eyes it covetously. "Daddy doesn't know how to do pretty hairstyles."

I grimace. It's true. Styling hair is definitely not one of my strengths.

"A headband is easy peasy," the woman says. She pulls it off, and motions Quinn closer. She slips the band over Quinn's head and uses her hand to smooth Quinn's blond hair back. "See?"

Quinn shoots me a longing glance.

"We can buy you a headband sometime," I say.

"Keep this one," the woman says gently. "It looks good on you."

"Really?" Quinn fingers the bow.

"Sure." The woman smiles at her.

"You don't have to do that," I say.

She lifts one delicate shoulder. "I know. It's fine."

"What do you say, Quinn?"

"Thank you!" She twirls. "Thank you, thank you, forever and ever!"

"Okay, let's go," I try again.

"Can you make it home okay?" the woman asks with a glance down at my knee.

I take a few steps. "I think I can." I hope. "Thanks, though."

"Okay. If you're sure."

If only I was alone. I'd be milking this for everything I could. The good thing is, I appear to have distracted her from whatever she was sad about.

Quinn takes my hand. "I'll help you walk, Daddy."

The woman smiles. "Hold onto him."

"I will."

We turn away from her, me limping. Dammit.

By the time we get home, my knee is hurting like a bitch. I'm going to have to ice it after all that walking. I can't even keep up with a fucking seven-year-old. I've had enough of this shit. That niggling worry about my knee is always there in the back of my mind. Because if I can't play hockey, I don't have much else going for me. Well, besides Quinn, obviously. She's the best part of my life.

2

CARLY

That guy is hot.

I watch him limp away with his cute-as-a-button blond daughter, who's wearing my favorite headband. She's holding his hand like she's helping him. So sweet.

Also he has a great ass.

I like how his longish dark hair falls in silky strands around his face, and an attractive stubble shadows his jaw and upper lip. His nose with a bump on it, a small scar on his chin, and fearless brown eyes the color of espresso give him a tough, kind of badass look. His height, inches above six feet, adds to the imposing air, and he has a bold energy. And yet, that contrasts his expression and gentle manner toward his daughter, and he has a quick sense of humor, making fun of himself by turning his fall into a joke. He made me laugh, and that's a sure way to win me over.

I also like how he bends toward his daughter, letting her "help" him, listening to her chatter, and the love in his smile when he looks at her.

Crap.

One look at a kid and I'm a puddle of hormones.

I sigh and look down from watching him walk away. He has a

daughter, although no wedding ring, and I'm definitely not looking for romance or even a hook up.

I'm back in New York, the Big Apple, the city that never sleeps. I should be out clubbing and partying and going to museums and Broadway shows. Instead, I'm sitting here on a park bench all by myself moping and feeling sorry for myself.

I need to find a job. I'm not completely broke, but my meagre savings won't last long, and I can't couch surf with my friend Gianna forever. I glance at my phone to check the time and see the email from the Maddens I was reading earlier. A wave of longing swept over me so intense it brought tears to my eyes. I press my fingertips to my mouth as I read it again.

Dear Carly,

We miss you a lot I wish you came with us to Montreal. Our new house is really big and we have a pool. Mom says maybe we can get a dog I want a King Charles Spaniel like the Lacroix family had. Remember Coco? I miss them too. I hope you are doing okay and having fun in New York maybe sometime I can come visit.

Love

Amaris

"I miss you, too, Mare," I whisper.

She attached a picture of her, her little brother Daniel, and their baby sister Belle in front of their new swimming pool. I study their precious faces.

Amaris was seven when I started working for the Madden family as their au pair. Now she's almost eleven. There's a big difference between a seven-year-old and a ten-year-old. And Daniel—he was four and now he's seven. Baby Belle arrived while I was part of the family and she's almost walking now. Baby Belle. That's what I called her.

My arms ache to hold that sweet baby, to hug those little monkeys. I loved those kids like they were my own. Leaving them was like having my heart ripped out. The Madden family was a joy to work for. They're not perfect; Lois Madden was loud and talked way too much and could be a little overwhelming, but we connected in a way that was special and they told me often how lucky they were to have me.

Only, when it came time for them to move again, they didn't need me to move with them.

I rub the pang behind my breastbone and pull in a long breath. I have to get over this.

I send a quick reply, sounding as cheerful as I can, telling her I miss them too! Then I get up and start a brisk pace back to Gianna's place on West 74th. I can't wait until I can find my own place, but wow, that's not easy in New York. Especially without a job.

I've never had a place of my own. My bedroom at home in Buffalo doesn't count—I was a kid. My dorm room at Columbia was pretty sparse. And the bedroom I had in the Madden home in Paris still wasn't really mine since it was in someone else's home.

I let myself in with the extra key Gianna gave me. It's a tiny two-bedroom apartment in an old brownstone which she shares with three other girls. There's barely room for the four of them, never mind five with me, but they're kind enough to put up with me.

I sit at the small dining table with my laptop. I tried to do some work today for the first time since I've been back. I'm almost finished the article I'm writing, which an editor at Moxie Magazine is interested in. I need to get it done and hopefully sell it and make some goddamn money. I've already asked for one extension; I can't do that again.

I open the laptop and tap the keyboard, leaning back in the uncomfortable wood chair. What I wouldn't give for a nice ergonomic desk and chair. My neck and back would thank me. But beggars can't be choosy. I'm happy to have a roof over my head.

Tomorrow. I'll start looking for a job.

I open my article. Actually, I mostly stare into space. I only need to write another five hundred words. This should be easy peasy. But I'm distracted not only by Amaris's email but by that encounter in the park with the big gorgeous dude and little blond girl.

I sigh.

What am I even doing? I'm obviously not capable of being a writer.

I hear Gianna's key in the lock and I save and close my article.

"Hi!" She breezes in, dropping keys on the small table near the door, tossing her purse onto a chair. "You're here! Finally I get to see you!"

"I'm here." I smile at her.

"I've been so busy the last few days. I feel like a terrible hostess."

"That's okay! You don't have to entertain me. And I've been trying to get over jet lag and reorient myself. It's all good."

She sits at the table and studies my face. "What's wrong?"

I don't want to whine to her. She's nice enough to put me up here. "I got an email from the Maddens. It kind of bummed me out."

"Ah." Sympathy warms her dark eyes. "I'm sorry. I know you loved working for them."

"Yeah."

"Who would've thought? I remember when you wanted to get out of New York and Jody suggested moving to Europe to be an au pair and we all laughed."

"Right?" I'd been so desperate to escape I would've done anything.

"We need wine." She jumps up and crosses to her fridge in the tiny kitchen. A moment later we have glasses of pinot grigio in hand and have moved to her couch.

"So...I've been meaning to ask," she says. "Does Jeff know you're back?"

"God, no! I haven't communicated with him since I left."

Jeff. My ex-boyfriend, Jefferson Mills, former portfolio manager at Affiniti Dividend, Interest & Premium Strategy Fund who, just over three years ago, was charged by the SEC in a massive scheme to defraud investors, along with two other guys he worked with.

I don't even like thinking back to that time. A lot of it is a fog, no doubt my brain trying to help me cope by erasing those horrible memories. But I remember enough to shudder. I take a gulp of wine.

"He's still in jail," Gianna says.

"In one of the cushiest prisons in the country."

Gianna makes a face. "True. But it's not like he's at risk of going out and murdering someone."

"I guess not. Ugh."

"I can't believe that happened."

"I know. I was an idiot."

"How were you supposed to know what he was doing?"

"I should have known he had no morals and ethics." I'm not submerged in sadness at the thought of how much I loved Jeff, like I used to be. The passage of time has eased that, although I do still feel a twinge of heartache and betrayal at how things ended with us. There was also a long time when I questioned my judgment about people and whether I could trust them.

"He fooled a lot of people, not just you."

"Yeah." I shake my head. "I felt so sorry for the people who'd lost millions of dollars because of his deception. Thank God the judge ordered restitution."

"Too bad Jeff didn't have to pay it all himself."

"The company paid a shit ton of money. But Jeff had to pay some too. I assume he's broke now, but who knows, criminals are gonna crime."

She laughs. "Enough about him." She waves a hand. "Tell me more about the hot French dude you were dating."

"Ah. Gabriel."

"You even say it with a French accent." She sighs.

I grin. "Gabriel was a sweetheart but not ready for commitment."

"You don't seem heartbroken."

"We had fun together and the sex was amazing, but I was more disappointed that I'd lost my companion. I went out with a few other guys, but it's just as well I didn't get serious about anyone since..." I extend my arms at my sides. "Here I am."

"You didn't want to stay in Europe?"

"It's not that easy without another au pair job right away. And honestly, I don't want to work as an au pair anymore. Ever again. It hurt so much to say goodbye to those kids." My throat squeezes and I try to keep my voice steady as I add, "I miss them."

"Aw. I'm sorry. You must have gotten so close to them. You were there for years."

"I'll survive." I smile brightly.

"Did it feel like what happened with your sister?"

I pout, that memory still tender. "Yeah, sort of."

When I was seventeen and my sister was sixteen, she got pregnant. She decided to keep the baby and try to finish school. My mom traveled a lot in her job and was hardly ever home, which meant I looked after Sophia, and then I also looked after Ayla. I took a gap year after high school that turned into two so I could look after them. Then Sophia graduated, took off for college in Chicago, and told me she didn't want me to come with them because she wanted to raise her daughter herself. Apparently, she felt I was taking over. That fucking destroyed me, and it still hurts.

"Are you going to keep writing?"

"Yeah. But I'll have to find something else." I rub my forehead. "I have no idea what. I didn't finish my degree when all that shit with Jeff went down, so I have a bunch of gender and sexuality courses that are pretty much useless."

"Maybe you should go back to school and finish your degree."

I tilt my head. "Hmm. I could do that, I guess. But still—I need to support myself."

"I'm sure you'd qualify for some kind of aid."

I tap the table. "That might be worth looking into. Although I'm not sure gender and sexuality was the best idea for a major."

"What else do you think you'd like to do?"

"I don't know." I stare glumly at my wine. "I like writing my ranty blog posts. And my less ranty articles."

"I like your ranty posts. That one you wrote about 'boys will be boys' was fantastic."

"Thank you."

"It just exonerates them from bad behavior," she adds. "And I never realized it. It seemed lik a cute phrase, but when you look at in a broader context, it's really toxic."

"And it reinforces the assumption that boys are wired to be a certain way and can't change that."

"Yes! I also loved the post you wrote about how you're a feminist but you love men."

I smile. "Thank you. I do love men." I hesitate, almost telling her about the book I started writing while I was in France. But I keep it to myself. Because it seems so unlikely that I'll ever a) finish it, b) publish it. I don't want to set myself up for the humiliation of the inevitable failure. "I guess I have to sort my shit out," I finally say with a sigh.

"If I hear of any job leads, I'll let you know." Gianna works in marketing for a big tech company. "You'll find something," she adds with more confidence than I'm feeling.

"Well, let's catch up on gossip. Tell me what happened between Mark and Brian. I heard they split up."

3

NATE

Quinn's at Brielle's tonight and I'm in my kitchen getting things ready. Some of my teammates who are still in town are coming over for poker and bourbon. I picked up lots of snacks and fried chicken is being delivered later.

My buddy Brando arrives first. Probably because he'll be the first to leave. He's a "newlywed," with a new girlfriend and a baby on the way.

"Dude," he says as he walks in. "How's it going?" He saunters in and sets a bottle of Knob Creek on the counter.

"Good. How's Lola?"

"Good. Getting a little bump."

I remember back when Brielle was pregnant. We didn't plan the pregnancy, but we thought we could make things work. It was actually a fun, exciting time. "Is she having weird cravings? Brielle wanted Chinese takeout, like literally every day. Especially egg rolls."

Brando laughs. "At least that's not weird. Lola wants tuna. All the time. Cans and cans of tuna."

"At least that's healthy."

"Actually her OB/GYN is worried about her mercury consumption."

"Jesus."

"I know, right? Also, she craves dill pickle chips and lemonade."

"She's into the salty stuff."

"Yeah. What makes them want strange stuff all the time?"

"I think it's hormones."

A couple more guys arrive and I go let them in.

"We were just talking about pregnancy cravings," I tell Hellsy (Josh Heller), Cookie (Owen Cooke), and Millsy (Easton Millar).

"Sounds like fun," Millsy drawls. "Thank God I'm not worrying about that yet."

"How about you, Hellsy?" I pour drinks. "Now you're married, babies are probably on the way."

"I don't know. We're not in a rush." He accepts the glass of bourbon from me.

"A more important question we should be discussing is why men have nipples." Millsy takes a sip of his drink.

We all stare at him.

"Why should we discuss that?" Brando asks.

Millsy shrugs. "Don't you wonder about it?"

"No," we all say at once.

"Didn't some movie star get their nipples removed?" Cookie asks.

I wince. "Ouch. Why?"

"Because they're useless," Hellsy says.

"Speak for yourself. I like a little nipple play," Cookie replies.

I close my eyes. "What is happening here."

"There is a reason," Brando says. "It's because when an embryo forms, like before it becomes male or female, it has breast tissue. It's not until puberty that hormones kick in and make a difference."

I blink. "Okay. I guess that makes sense."

"Nothing wrong with a little nipple play," Millsy adds. "Direct link between cock and nipples."

Everyone is standing around the island with weird looks on their faces.

"I'm googling who's had their nipples removed," Cookie says, gazing at his phone.

My phone buzzes with more arrivals. "Thank Christ," I mutter. "JBo and Bergie are here."

This distracts from the bizarre conversation and when a few more guys show up we get settled around my table with drinks, food, and cards.

"How's the knee?" Bergie asks.

"They're going to do some kind of injection. We'll see."

"Hopefully that works," JBo adds. "We need you ready for training camp."

I'm starting to have serious doubts about that. I blow out a breath and study my cards. "Maybe I just should have gone for the surgery now. If I wait to see if the injections work, it'll be too close to the season."

They all nod thoughtfully.

"Tough call," Millsy says. "Nobody wants to have surgery if you don't have to."

"What does your agent think?" Brando asks.

"We talked about it. He thinks I should just have the surgery, but it's not his body."

"How about your family?"

"My mom says don't have surgery unless I absolutely have to. She says once you've been cut, your body is never the same."

A few guys wince.

"And what am I going to do with Quinn?" I shake my head. "If I end up on crutches for weeks."

"Get Brielle to take her," Millsy says.

"Ugh. I mean, she'll help out if she has to, but our deal is that I take Quinn for the summer."

"I have nanny names," Brando offers. "I can pass them on to you."

"I don't like the idea of hiring a stranger."

"Well, you have to vet them," Brando says. "I'm learning. They have references and you definitely need to talk to the people they used to work for."

We're well into our evening when Jake asks, "How long does it take women to orgasm?"

We all stare at him.

"You've never made a woman come?" Hellsy asks carefully.

"Of course I have! Jesus. It just…sometimes it takes a while."

"Like…how long?" Millsy says.

"Because it definitely takes women longer," JBo adds.

"And how were you doing it?" Hellsy asks.

"Why do we have to talk about sex all the time?" I mutter.

Everyone ignores me.

"Apparently the average is fourteen minutes," Bergie says.

"But, like, who's timing it?" Millsy says. "If you're watching the clock, you're probably not doing it right."

"It seems like an hour," Jake says.

"Again, how are you doing it? Are you talking oral? Or P in V?"

"Or anal," Hellsy adds helpfully.

"Women can't come during anal," Jake says.

We all make a loud noise of disagreement.

"Oh hell yeah, they can," Millsy says. "But you have to…you know…"

Jake squints at him.

"Like vaginal," he says. "Women need clitoral stimulation."

"Jesus." I lower my head into my hand. "Are we giving sex education classes to the rookies now?"

Bergie grins. "As your captain, I'm pretty sure sexually satisfied guys play better hockey."

"He's talking about his partner's satisfaction, though," Hellsy points out.

"I don't know about you, but I'm more satisfied when *she's* satisfied," I say. Christ. Why am I getting into this?

JBo aims a finger at me. "Solid point."

"Maybe *that's* your problem," Millsy says. "Are you focusing on *her* pleasure?"

Jake squints again.

"Dude," Hellsy says.

"If she's having trouble getting to the finish line, there are things you can do," JBo says confidently. "I'll send you a link to an article I read. Just remember—don't rush it."

"Also, lots of foreplay," Hellsy says. "*Lots.*"

"Ask her what she likes," Bergie says.

"Okay! Who watched the Yankees game yesterday?" I ask. "Anyone want more hummus?"

CARLY

I reread my last few paragraphs of my article, *Why Toxic Masculinity is Bad for Men*. Nodding, I let my thoughts continue and for a while the words flow from my fingertips.

There. I think I'm done. I sit back and regard my computer screen. Okay, I need to move things around...my thoughts were a little disjointed. But that's easier than staring at a blank page. I blow out a long exhalation of relief. Yay.

When I left my job interview earlier today I felt good, but since then I've been replaying my answers in my head and now they don't seem so great. My lack of experience became very obvious. I don't even know why I applied for a job as a personal shopper. Oh wait, yes I do. It sounded fun. What's more puzzling is why they gave me an interview.

Of course I don't get the job.

I spend more time scouring Indeed. There's a job as a receptionist for an architectural firm. I can see myself sitting at a posh desk answering the phone. Well, it sounds a little boring, but I can probably do it. Hey, here's one that pays up to a hundred thirty thousand dollars a year! And I'm qualified. But...it's dealing with people with personal debt issues. I like helping people. But they probably make that much money by pushing some kind of services on people. That's a no for me. Okay, it's a maybe.

Stock associate at Bloomingdales. Another maybe. Guest service agent at a hotel. Is that a front desk clerk? The hourly rate is good, but they want a year of hotel experience. I could try anyway. How about scanner/data entry? I could work in an office all day scanning stuff.

That sounds boring AF.

I sigh. I have to apply for everything, boring or not. I spend the rest of the day doing that. Then, triggered by a news item about a woman who was just murdered by her ex-spouse even though she had called the police on him numerous times and had a restraining order, I write one of my ranty posts for my blog. It comes easily to me when I'm passionate, and it's not long after I hit post that comments start showing up. Yes, I get the trolls, the "not all men" guys with no self-awareness, but also lots of supportive comments and some that open up interesting discussions.

I love this. A few months ago I monetized my blog by selling ads and using affiliate links, and it's starting to make a little money. But I can't rely on that.

Maybe I should be writing my blog posts under an alias. Maybe the people I'm applying to for jobs are googling me and finding my blog and then deciding not to hire me. I pause at this. Then I shake my head. It's not like I'm posting porn or advocating for killing animals. I am who I am.

I do get the idea for another article, though...so that's good. I make some quick notes. Tomorrow I'll query a few editors about it and see what they think. Now I have a few published articles, and my blog gets the numbers it does, it's a little easier to get their attention, but there's never any guarantee.

I head out for a run in Central Park. I'm enjoying the park and the exercise is definitely improving my mood. I'm sweaty and gross and about to cross Central Park West when I see the hot guy who fell in front of me at the park that day hobbling toward me. On crutches. Accompanied by his daughter, that little cutie, wearing her cape, her mask dangling around her neck.

They make it to the curb and the little girl smiles at me. "Hi, Headband Lady!"

"Hello again, Clover." I eye the guy's crutches. "Minor injury?"

He grimaces. "We're trying a new procedure. I just had an injection and my knee's a little sore from it. Shouldn't last long."

"Oh. Okay." The tight lines of his face tell me it's more than a little sore. Poor guy.

"My name's not really Clover," the girls says. "It's Quinn."

"Ah. I like that name. I'm Carly."

"We're going for ice cream," she tells me.

"Ice cream again?" I ask dramatically. "You really are lucky." I pause. "Where are you going? I don't think your dad's going to make it far."

He grunts.

I eye them sympathetically. "Maybe I could go get the ice cream for you? And bring it back here?" I nod at a bench near the stone wall of the park.

"You don't have to do that," he says, as his little girl says, "Yes!"

"It's not a problem. Go sit down." I look at the girl. "Something strawberry, yes, Quinn?"

"Yes, please!"

"And you..." I pause, looking at her dad.

"Nate. Are you sure?"

"Of course!"

He reaches for his wallet.

"No, no. Don't give me money. I could be a scam artist and you'll never see me again."

"Forty bucks isn't going to break me," he mutters. "Here."

"Okay." It's nice that he trusts me. "What kind of ice cream do you like?"

"Surprise me."

Eeeek. "Okay. I'll be back in a few."

"Get something for yourself!" he calls after me.

Ice cream right after a run? Why the hell not.

Remembering the place I used to go when I lived here in college, I cross Central Park West, jog down another block and around the corner. Yessss! It's still there and cute as ever. And they still have my favorite, the strawberry cheesecake. I order two of those and then ponder what to get for Nate. I know nothing about him except he's big and brawny. I end up ordering a flavor called Heavy Rock—vanilla with fudge, brownies, and cookie dough.

They're still sitting on the bench when I get back, the crutches propped at Nate's side. He smiles when he sees me.

I like his smile.

"Here you go!" I give him his change, then hand out treats along with spoons and napkins. We sit beneath the shade of big trees, a sea of yellow cabs streaming past us along with bicycles and pedestrians enjoying the weather. I admire the stone construction of the church across the street.

"Do you like the ice cream?" I ask Quinn.

"It's my new favorite!"

"Where is this place?" Nate asks, looking at the cup. "Sugar Shack."

"A couple of blocks away. I used to go there in college. They have amazing flavors. How's yours?"

"Awesome." He digs his spoon in again.

"It's called Heavy Rock."

He grins. "Okay." He takes another spoonful, and I catch myself watching him slide the spoon out of his mouth. I drop my gaze quickly to my own ice cream. "I can't believe I didn't know about the Sugar Shack."

"We have to go there, Daddy!"

I grin. "Now you can't un-know it."

He meets my eyes, amusement dancing in his. "Yep. Thanks for that." He takes another spoonful of ice cream. "So what do you do for a living, Carly?"

I sigh before I can stop myself. "Nothing, at the moment. Between jobs, I guess you'd say. I'm looking, but I'm also doing some writing." I finally sent in my article to Moxie. "That's not enough to pay the bills, though." I see curiosity on his face and force a smile. "It'll be fine."

"Of course." I look at Quinn. "Are you on summer holidays?"

"Yes. I love summer holidays. But I like school, too. And I miss my friends Jada and Hazel."

"Are you going into second grade?" I ask.

"Yes!"

"What's your favorite subject?"

"I like math."

"That's great. That was *not* my favorite subject."

"What was yours?" Quinn asks.

"English. I also loved social studies."

Quinn nods. "Daddy hated all subjects. He says he fucking hated school."

I blink.

"Quinn." The warning tone of her dad's voice has her dropping her gaze.

"I didn't say the F word. *You* said it. I just said that you said it."

Nate sighs. "I wasn't much of a student."

"Obviously you're more of an athlete," I comment.

"Yeah."

He seems confident and fearless. He definitely has a very physical presence, and not just his size but his energy. Even with a bum leg. I'm interested in this man. As in, intrigued. Okay, also attracted. But we're sitting here with his daughter.

Quinn chats more with me. She's very bright. She reminds me of

Amaris at that age—so open and eager to learn about the world. A pang of sadness beats in my chest. I still miss those kids.

When Quinn is finished, she hops up and goes to try to peer over the wall.

"Thanks for doing that," Nate says. "I hate letting her down."

"I understand. She's very sweet."

"She's amazing." The warmth and pride in his voice tugs at something inside me.

"Her mother…?" I ask carefully.

"We're divorced. We share custody."

"Ah. What do you do in the summer? Camps? Daycare?"

He shakes his head. "I'm off for the summer too."

"Oh. Because of your knee?"

"No, no. I play hockey. Our season was done in May, and we don't get back to it until September."

"Oh." I blink. He plays hockey. "You're a professional hockey player?"

One corner of his mouth lifts. "Yeah. What, you've never heard of me? Nate Karmeinski."

I bite my lip.

"I guess I'm not that famous," he says sadly.

I laugh. "Sorry. I don't follow hockey."

"I play for the Bears."

"Oh wow. I've heard of the Bears. Everyone in New York has heard of the Bears. I grew up in Buffalo where hockey's pretty popular, too. I just never got into it."

"How long have you lived here?"

"I went to college here, then I left for a while and came back." That's pretty vague. My leaving and coming back are depressing topics.

Quinn returns. "I can't climb the wall. Clover would be able to climb the wall." Frustration furrows her little brow.

"You just need a little help." I jump up and lead her to the wall. I give her a boost and she clambers up to the top and hangs on with tiny arms, her cape hitting me in the face.

"I can see over! Can I sit up here?"

I cast an uncertain glance at Nate, who's watching from the bench. I'd better not do something risky with a child I don't even know, although I totally get how fun it would be to sit on that wall. "Maybe not today." I give her another moment, then say, "Down you come. Put your arms out!"

She extends her arms and I swoop her down to the ground as if she's flying.

Nate's smile is affectionate as we return, Quinn running with arms extended and her cape flying out behind her.

"Okay pop tart, we better get you home." Nate reaches for his crutches. Quinn jumps to help him.

My heart!

"Can I help?"

"No, I'm good. Thanks again for getting the ice cream." He bestows a smile on me that makes me feel like I'm melting ice cream inside.

"Not a problem."

"Are you coming, Carly?" Quinn asks, standing close to her dad. "Where do you live?"

I'm homeless. But I don't say that. "I'm staying with a friend on 74th." I gesture vaguely.

"Ah. We're just down the street here." Nate points.

I hesitate, eyeing his crutches. I don't want him to fall again. "I can walk that way with you."

We wait for the light to change and traffic to come to a stop before setting out across the wide street. I slow my pace, but Nate is pretty good on the crutches.

His building is close and he halts out front of the charming old structure. A driveway curves around a green space with a few small fountains and arched windows glow above the front doors. "This is us."

"Ah. Nice building."

"Thanks." He meets my eyes and I see the flicker of hesitation. "Would you…like to go for coffee some time?"

I hold his gaze. I would. I really would. He's so attractive. And it's nice to know he's interested, too. But… "I don't know. Probably not a good idea," I say regretfully. "I just moved back here and I don't have a job or anywhere to live, even, and I should probably deal with that before I…" I trail off. "Bad timing."

"Yeah. For me, too." He jerks his head toward the crutches.

For some reason that strikes me as funny, and I start giggling. "You asked me to go for coffee, not run a marathon with you."

His lips twitch, the disappointment on his face turning to mirth.

I know I shouldn't, but… "Okay. I'd love to have coffee some time."

His smile…wow. "Okay. Tomorrow? Quinn is going over to a friend's place for the afternoon."

I lift a shoulder. "It's not like my schedule is packed. One o'clock?"

"Make it one-thirty. There's a bakery on Columbus—Queen of Tarts. We could meet there."

I haven't heard of it, but I like the name. "Sounds good."

"I'll give you my number," he says. "You don't have to give me yours, but just in case…" He reels it off and I enter it into my phone.

"Okay. Thanks." Our eyes meet again and a little shiver works down my spine. "See you tomorrow."

"Yeah."

Heat dances over my skin. "Goodnight." Then I call out, "Night, Quinn! No stalling!"

Quinn laughs and Nate shoots me a grin as he follows her up the driveway.

Damn. I like him. And I like his daughter. I like how they communicate, with obvious love, and how they take care of each other, even a seven-year-old girl. I like Nate's matter-of-factness about his profession and self-deprecating comment about not being that famous. He's confident but not cocky, vigorous but not aggressive. I want to know more about him.

Gah. But that's not what I'm here for. I'm definitely not looking for a relationship. I need to figure my own life out before I get someone else involved in it.

It's just coffee.

4

NATE

We arrive at Queen of Tarts at the same time. Carly lifts her hand in a small wave as she approaches me from the opposite direction, her smile beaming. Christ, she's pretty. Today her long hair is flying silky and free, unlike yesterday when it was sweaty and scraped up into a high ponytail. She's wearing black shorts, a black and white striped T-shirt, the same boots, and carrying a fluffy orange purse that my gaze catches on. Wild.

"Hi!" We stop face to face in front of the bakery. "How are you?"

"Great." I move to the door but she's there first, holding it open for me and my stupid crutches. I hop inside and pause in front of the display cases full of tempting baked goods. "Have you been here before?"

"I have not. It looks amazing." Her gaze slides over the offerings, eyes wide.

"They have more than just tarts. Their cupcakes are good, too, and their brownies."

"Strawberry rhubarb tart. That's what I want."

"You got it." I order that for her and an English toffee brownie for myself, along with coffees. I'm annoyed that she has to carry the things to our table for us. I'm so ready to ditch these crutches.

"They even have savory pies." She eyes the menu. "Chicken and leek. Steak and mushroom. Have you tried those?"

"Oh yeah. They're an easy dinner."

"Not much of a cook?" She turns her attention to me and picks up her steaming mug. Her right hand is adorned with a silver and diamond ring in the shape of a bow.

"Nope. I try more when Quinn is with me. During the season I have some meals delivered for me—healthy shit that my personal trainer makes me eat."

"Oh. Wow."

"Quinn's not fond of quinoa and sweet potatoes."

She laughs. "She'd probably acquire a taste for it. I wouldn't eat sweet potatoes when I was a kid, but my mom sliced them up and told us they were giant carrots, so I ate them. And they're delicious!"

I grin. "Genius. I need to lie more to my kid."

"There's a time for it."

She cuts into her tart with a fork and scoops up some of the fruit. "Mmmm."

I like the sound of that. I'd like to be the one making her moan.

I swallow hard and focus on my brownie.

"This is amazing. Yours looks good, too."

"Want to try some?"

"Yes."

I grin at her directness and push my plate closer to her. She takes a bite-size piece.

"Oh wow. I'll definitely be coming back here. Does Quinn like it?"

"Of course. Cupcakes are her favorite food."

"More than ice cream?"

"Hmm. Could be tight. Also anything from Dylan's Candy Bar. She loses her mind when we go there."

"Definitely not quinoa and sweet potatoes. I see the problem."

I laugh. "Yeah."

"How's the knee?"

"Not bad. I can lose the crutches tomorrow, probably, if it doesn't hurt too bad."

"How did you hurt it, anyway? Sex injury?"

I choke on my coffee. My head snaps up and I meet her eyes. She bites her lip, trying not to laugh.

"Yeah, that's it," I say. "I like it rough." I give a salacious wink.

"That doesn't surprise me. You *are* a hockey player."

"Ha. The truth is, I hurt it playing hockey. But you knew that."

"I figured so." Her grin is so goddamn delightful.

"So…you vaguely told me what you're doing here in New York," I say slowly. "Did you just come back?"

"Yeah. I've been living in France for the last three years."

"Wow. Okay. That's cool."

"It was wonderful." She gives a half-hearted smile. "I was working as an au pair for a lovely family. Three little kids." The smile turns wistful. "But they moved back to Canada and didn't need a nanny anymore. So I came home."

"Ah."

"I don't know many people here anymore. I'm staying with a college friend until I can find my own place."

"So, you went to college here…where are you from originally? Oh wait, you said Buffalo."

"Right. You?"

"Erie, Pennsylvania."

"Ah! Practically neighbors!"

"Yep."

We start talking about our favorite beaches and summer memories and trips to Niagara Falls. Our pastries finished, we set our plates aside and focus on our coffees.

"So you have one brother?" she asks.

"Yeah. James. He's two years older than me."

"Does he play hockey, too?"

31

"Nope. He was too smart for that."

She laughs.

"I'm kidding. He did play hockey as a kid, but he didn't have the talent to go pro."

"Ah."

"How about you? Siblings?"

"I have a sister. Sophia. She lives in Chicago with her daughter Ayla. We're not super close." A feel a pinch of regret in my chest. "She went to college there and stayed there."

"Hey, James went to college in Chicago, too."

"No way! That's so funny. What does he do now?"

"He's an economist at the Bank of America."

"Whoa. Still in Chicago?"

"Yep. How about you? You said you came here for college. What did you study?"

"I was majoring in gender and sexuality."

My chin jerks down. "Uh. Okay."

She grins. "I know, I know. You wonder what the heck someone does with a degree in gender and sexuality."

"I didn't even know there was such a thing. But..." I tilt my head. "You have me curious..."

"Don't jump to any conclusions. It's not about learning sex work."

"Hey! I never thought that."

"Maybe not sex work, which is nothing to be ashamed of, but you were definitely thinking of sex."

"I always think of sex," I answer honestly.

She laughs, thankfully. "I kind of like thinking about it, too."

Well, then. I feel an inconvenient stirring in my southern region. "Does a degree in sex make you good at it?" I ask casually.

"*Very* good." She gives my salacious wink right back to me. She doesn't take me seriously, and I fucking love that. "It's more learning what it means to be a man or a woman. Or neither. And how gender and sexuality arise from networks of power and social relations."

"Uh." I'm not educated and never considered myself smart, but I'm intrigued. "Doesn't gender arise from...well..."

"Sexuality and gender are actually socially constructed concepts," she says. "And they can vary through someone's life and in different social settings."

"Okay." I nod, thinking about that. "I guess I can get that."

Her lips curve into a smile full of appreciation and goddammit if it doesn't make me feel like I'm ten feet tall. "I didn't actually finish my degree." Her faces scrunches up briefly. "Some shit happened and that's when I moved to Europe."

"Well, that's got me curious. What kind of shit? Oh, wait. You don't want to talk about it."

"Eh."

"That means it was a dude."

She rolls her eyes. "Okay, yeah. It's fine, it was years ago. I was involved with this guy who I thought was 'the one'..." She makes air quotes. "He was a portfolio manager at a big investment house. Turns out he was defrauding investors. He's still in prison."

"Jesus." I gape at her.

"Yeah." She sighs. "Ah well."

I shake my head. "That must have been a shock."

"It was. I had no idea. I still don't know how I could have been such an idiot."

"I'm sure he didn't want you to know what he was doing."

"True." She pauses. "And what about you and your ex-wife? How long were you married?"

"Five years. Five years too long." I give a dry chuckle.

"Can I ask what happened?"

"It wasn't dramatic. She fell in love with someone else. She didn't cheat on me, at least. She was honest about it." I lift one shoulder. "We were never really suited."

"Ah."

"We thought we were. I thought it was sick, living in the big city, lots of money in my bank account, dating a Broadway actress. Well, *now* she's a Broadway actress. At the time, she was doing off-Broadway stuff. We got married because she was pregnant with Quinn."

"Ah." Her faces softens. "I'm sure Quinn makes it all worthwhile."

"Absolutely. Quinn's the best thing in my life." I pause. "That sounds pathetic."

"No." She slowly shakes her head. "No, it doesn't. She's your daughter. She *should* be the best thing in your life."

"Yeah. I really miss her during the season, although I do see her. Just not as much. I guess…it's been a while since I've been single and lately…" I trail off. I barely know Carly. How to scare off a woman on your first date: tell her you're looking for something serious. I keep my mouth shut. "Well, I'm lucky to have her."

"I agree. She's a sweetheart."

"Thanks. She wants a tattoo like you have." I gesture at her delicate ankle, but the boot hides the ink. I noticed the swirling script on a ribbon tied into a flowing bow yesterday.

Carly glances down. "Oh."

"What does it say?"

"C'est la vie."

She says it with what sounds like a perfect French accent.

"I wanted it to say 'shit happens,' but my friend convinced me I'd regret that."

I grin. "Quinn would definitely want a tattoo that says 'shit happens.'"

"Um, yeah, I noticed she has a bit of a trucker vocabulary."

I lift a hand. "All my fault. I've tried to watch my language around her but fuck, it's hard. I'm a hockey player."

She gives me a mock-reproving glance. "Come on. It can't be that hard."

"I'm getting better at it. But she's picked up a few things. Anyway, the tattoo is nice."

"I got it done in France. It's a reminder to me that stuff happens, but that's life."

I nod. "Yeah." I peer at her empty cup. "More coffee?"

"Sure. But I'll get it."

"Ugh."

She smiles at my frustrated noise. When she returns, I say, "I'd suggest going for a walk, but that's not happening right now."

"That's okay. I'm sure it's aggravating to not be able to do what you want."

"It really fucking is. And it'll only be worse if I have to have the surgery."

"More surgery?"

"This was just an injection. We're trying to avoid surgery if possible. It'll take a few weeks to see if this worked but if not, I'll have to have my meniscus repaired."

"Oh. Damn."

"Yeah. And the more time that passes, the closer we get to training camp, which means I may not be able to play right away."

"What does that mean for you?" She eyes me curiously. "Would you not make the team? Would that mean you're out for a whole year?"

"No. I can start when I can play, when I get medical clearance. I just hate not being able to play. And it could mean playing in the minor league for a while." And of course worrying that I'll never be able to play again and my career could be over. Without hockey, I don't have much else going for me, so that's a little unnerving. Okay, terrifying.

But I don't lay all that on her.

"Understandable," she says.

"On the other hand, it might work out for the best if it's when Quinn is back at school, because then she'll be back with her mother and I won't have to worry about looking after her."

"True. I'm sorry you're going through that."

"Eh. It happens." I pause. "C'est la vie."

We share a smile and damn, she's so pretty and caring and she gets my weird sense of humor and I'm really having fun. It's different talking to someone other than Quinn or my teammates and I want more of it.

5

CARLY

For dinner, I eat the steak and mushroom pie I picked up at Queen of Tarts before I left earlier. Lexi, Imani, and Lorelie are all home, making the tiny kitchen crowded. I don't even know these women, I only know Gianna, and they're nice enough, but I can tell they're frustrated by me and my stuff being around. This gives me a feeling of pressure. I have to get out of here. I guess there's always a hotel. I really need a job first.

I have an interview tomorrow for a dispatch position with a portable toilet company. I don't know why they offered me an interview; I don't have any dispatch experience. But they offered me an interview and I need to go, even if just for the experience. I can get ready for that.

But I keep thinking about Nate.

I really like him. I'm really attracted to him. I agreed to see him again, although we didn't set an exact time.

Huddled into a corner of the couch that is also my bed, I try to make myself small and unobtrusive as I apply for more positions, then look for rooms for rent. I could get a room in a four-bedroom apartment shared with others. Maybe I should go have a look and see what it's like.

I make that arrangement for the day after tomorrow, then go back to the new article I started. I sent a few queries but haven't heard back yet. Somehow I manage to focus on work until Gianna gets home.

"How was the coffee date?" she asks.

"It was…really great."

She pauses and gives me a look. "Really. You didn't sound very sure last night."

"I know." I blow out a breath. "I don't want to make too much of it. Because the last thing I need right now is a relationship. And I'm still kind of leery. Because of Jeff. Like, I don't know how to judge people anymore."

"I guess that's understandable."

"And I didn't come back to New York to find a man." I came back because…because I had nowhere else to go.

Pathetic.

I need a purpose in my life. I need to find out who I am, on my own, responsible solely for myself.

"I should be working. Writing. Job hunting," I go on. "Why would someone like him be interested in me? Homeless and unemployed, with an ex who's in prison."

Gianna laughs. "You won't be homeless and unemployed for long. And your ex being in prison has nothing to do with you. You're a smart, loyal, determined woman. Plus you're beautiful. Why wouldn't he be interested in you?"

"Aw, thanks." I make a face. "I guess I'm feeling a little doubtful about myself."

"Well, you shouldn't. We all have ups and downs in our lives, and I know you, you won't stay down for long."

I smile at my friend. "I appreciate the kind words. And you're right." I square my shoulders. "I applied for more jobs and Thursday I'm going to look at an apartment. And Nate asked to see me again. And I'm going to."

"Good! That's exciting!"

When Gianna's in her room and I'm tucked into my makeshift bed on her couch, I pull out my phone. I have Nate's number but we haven't communicated yet. I type in a text message.

CARLY: *Hi Nate, this is Carly. I have a job interview tomorrow and I'm looking at an apartment on Thursday, so maybe we could go out Friday?*

I send it. Then add, *If you're still interested.*

Shit. I add another message. *And if that works for you.*

Now he'll think I'm an idiot. I close my eyes, my phone on my chest. I start when it vibrates. I pick it up and peer at it.

NATE: *Definitely still interested. Let me see what I can work out.*

Right, he'd have to find a babysitter for Quinn.

CARLY: *Sounds good.*

I set my phone on the table and turn the lamp off. I settle into my bed with my usual shifting, adjusting, sighing, and turning over. I'm just starting to drift to sleep when my phone buzzes again.

I should ignore it. It's bedtime.

Do I ignore it? No, I do not.

I stretch an arm out to grab it and read the message.

NATE: *Okay we're set for Friday night. I can pick you up or we can meet nearby.*

I smile, a little rush of pleasure running through me.

CARLY: *I can meet you in front of your place.*

NATE: *Perfect. How about 6:15*

CARLY: *See you then.*

I have a date with a hot hockey player. No job. No home. No problem!

The job interview goes okay. The apartment viewing, not so much. It's in Harlem, which is okay except I have no idea where I'll be working, but I guess that doesn't matter. The place itself is fine but there's only one bathroom so I'd have to share with three other people. I'd also be sharing the kitchen and living space. The couple the apartment belongs to use the main bedroom and there's a female tenant in another. The room comes with a bed and a desk and chair. It would be perfect except that the while the woman showed me the place, her partner walked out of their bedroom in his tighty-whities and a motorcycle helmet.

I blinked a few times at him as he walked into the kitchen, shoved his hand down his underwear to scratch, then opened the fridge *with that hand* and pulled out a beer.

I don't even want to think about why he needs a motorcycle helmet.

I just don't know if I can do it.

I left with a non-committal response and started looking on my phone as I took the subway back to Gianna's. I'm not going to be able to be choosy, but surely there's something better.

I spend Friday looking at a few more places—Brooklyn, Hamilton Heights, one in Astoria that was actually pretty nice but expensive. None of these places will rent to me without a job, though.

Then I get ready for my date. I'm not in the best mood. My search for a job and a home is depressing me. I almost think of canceling, if only for Nate's sake, but hopefully going out will cheer me up.

I dress in loose jeans, a blue and white sleeveless shirt with a wrap waist that I tie into a big bow, and pointy-toed red flats since I'm walking. It's gorgeous summer evening so I add my sunglasses and a small cross body bag.

Nate is sitting out front on the low wall around the garden and fountains, looking at his phone. I apparently dressed appropriately, because we sort of match—he's wearing jeans, a button-down blue and white striped shirt and brown leather loafers. He looks up as I approach and smiles. "Hey."

"Hi." I stand in front of him smiling like a fool. Jeez. I'm already cheered up and I've only just laid eyes on him.

He stands and looks at his phone again. "Our Uber should be here any second."

"Hey! No crutches!"

"I ditched 'em."

"Is that okay? How's your knee?"

"It's okay. I'm not sure if the treatment has helped, though." He makes a face.

"Oh. How long will it take until you know?"

"The doc said two or three weeks. Next week I start physical therapy."

Our car arrives and we climb in.

"Where are we going?" I ask.

"Chelsea Piers."

"Ooookay."

"For a jazz cruise."

My mouth falls open and my eyes pop wide. "Seriously? That is awesome."

"I hope so." His smile widens as his eyes move over my face. "Then dinner after."

"I'm excited!"

He tips his head, still smiling. "Good. Me too."

The car slogs through Friday evening traffic to Chelsea Piers, where we make our way to the dock for the cruise. I take my complimentary glass of champagne and we find a place to sit near a window. The boat is beautiful, all gleaming light wood with glass tables and green upholstered booths. The low sun gilds everything and glints off the brass saxophone of one of the musicians.

"I've never done anything like this," I tell him as we glide out into the harbor. "When I lived here before, I was a broke college student." I pause. "Now I'm a broke adult."

He laughs. "I haven't done this either."

"Where is Quinn? With her mom?"

"No, my friend Bergie and his wife are looking after her. They have two kids."

"Oh, that's nice you have someone who can babysit."

"Yeah."

"Is he a hockey player, too?"

"Yep. He's the captain of the team."

"Ah."

"I'm an alternate captain."

"Oooh. What do the captain and alternate captain do? Does that mean you're the best players?"

"No." He shakes his head and takes a sip of champagne, the jazz trio of sax, keyboard and drums serenading us with a Cole Porter song. "The captains are the only players who can talk to the officials, so if they call a bad penalty or miss an offside we can talk to them about it and get an explanation at least. Sometimes the team captain organizes social events or team meetings." He pauses. "It's also about leadership. Leading by example. Working hard, showing the rookies how to succeed."

"How long have you been playing?"

"My whole life?"

I smile. "How long professionally?"

"Uh…ten years. I got drafted when I was eighteen, and I played two seasons in the AHL—the minor league."

"So you're a veteran."

"I am." He grins, then rubs his mouth.

"What's wrong?"

"Nothing. I just worry about whether my knee will ever get better. I'm a veteran, which means I'm not a young pup anymore and things don't heal up like they used to."

"How old are you?"

"Twenty-eight."

"Oh yeah, you're over the hill."

"How old are you?"

"Twenty-five. I took a couple of years away from school before I started college."

"A baby."

"Oh, come on. And I'm kidding. You're not old."

"In hockey, that's ancient. Okay, I'm exaggerating. I actually feel like I've been playing my best hockey the last couple of seasons."

A jazzy piano tune starts, and I move my shoulders to the rhythm of "Mine" by George Gershwin.

"Another drink?" Nate asks.

"That would be lovely."

We cruise past the Statue of Liberty and Ellis Island, One World Trade tower, and countless sailboats on the water. As the sun lowers in the sky, it glints off various high rises, creating an amazing panorama.

"I'm in heaven," I say. "Sipping champagne, listening to jazz, looking at this beautiful scenery. I can almost forget my life is a shambles."

His forehead creases and he leans closer. "It can't be that bad."

"Now it's my turn to exaggerate." I roll my eyes. "I just feel a little lost at the moment. My job hunt isn't going well, and neither is my apartment hunt." I tell him about some of the places I looked at, but I don't want to whine and ruin our evening, so I keep it brief. "I had an interview the other day with a portable toilet company!"

He barks out a laugh. "What?"

I grin. "Hey, it's honest work. But I didn't get the job. I've applied for a bunch more, though."

"What do you want to do?"

"That's the problem. I don't know." I make a face. "My college courses don't prepare me for much. I've thought of going back to school, but I'd have to take something practical. Maybe some business courses." I shrug.

"Didn't you say you worked as a nanny?"

"Yeah. For three years. I don't want to do that again." My firm tone ends that line of conversation.

The cruise is about an hour and a half and then we disembark. "I made a dinner reservation," Nate says. "Are you hungry?"

"I definitely am."

He leads the way to the restaurant a few blocks away in the Meatpacking District.

"Is your knee okay to walk?" I ask as we stroll the sidewalk.

"I feel it a bit, but it's fine. My quads and hamstrings are powerful."

I laugh, even though I'm sure that's true.

Inside the brasserie, the lighting is dim and the atmosphere urbane with lamps on each table and Edison bulbs lining the wood beams above us. We're shown to a small booth and we both order glasses of red wine, then sip them while we look over the menu. We agree to skip the raw bar, although I feel a bit uncool doing that. Perhaps I should develop a taste for oysters and tuna poke but since Nate isn't a fan either, I'm okay with it. He orders whipped feta for us to share to start and then the prime rib, and I get roasted seabass.

Once that's all out of the way, we regard each other across the gleaming wood table. The restaurant hums around us, voices talking and laughing, cutlery clinking on plates, and shouts and bursts of flame erupting from the open kitchen. It's charming and so is Nate, smiling at me as he lifts a glass of wine to his lips.

How the hell did this happen?

I gulp my wine.

Just enjoy it.

"So…didn't you say you're a writer?" Nate asks.

"Oh. Yeah." I grimace. "Sort of."

He smiles. "What do you write? Please tell me it's porn."

I choke on a laugh. "No! Sorry. Nothing wrong with porn, just…" I pause as if thinking. "Maybe I should try that."

He laughs too.

"It could be profitable," I muse. "I have a blog. I write about stuff I'm passionate about."

He tips his head. "Huh. That's cool. Like what?"

"Like the patriarchy."

His jaw loosens. "Oh."

I grin. "That always shuts down conversation with a man."

"No, no. I'm interested."

"Really?"

"Yeah. Does that mean you're a feminist?"

I eye him warily. "Yes."

"Cool." He shrugs.

"I write about inequality, obviously. Domestic and intimate partner violence."

"Cheerful things."

I smile because his tone is gentle, not mocking. "Sometimes, yeah. While I was living in France, I started submitting articles to different publications—usually women's magazines. I've had a few published."

"Hey, that's great."

"And..." I pause and drop my gaze to the table. "I've been working on a book."

"Wow." He blinks. "You must be really smart."

I laugh at that, but then see he looks perturbed. "Um...is that a problem?"

He huffs a laugh and shakes his head. "Of course not. I love women with big brains."

"My brain isn't that big," I say wryly. "The other day I was having a bath and my friend's faucet stuck on and I freaked out because the tub was going to overflow. We were yelling back and forth through the door and the water was getting near the top of the tub and finally she yelled at me, 'Pull the plug!'" I pause. "Genius."

Nate cracks up.

I smile. "I do stuff like that. Like talking to someone on the phone and walking around looking for my phone so I can check email."

"Ha. I've done that. I also told a reporter after a playoff game 'that was a big two points for us.'"

I stare blankly at him.

"There aren't points awarded in the playoffs," he explains. "It's like a tournament. You have to win the most games to advance."

"Ohhhh. Haha. Okay, I get it."

He grins. "I just use that line too much. It slipped out, but I got shit about it for months."

"It must be hard to be interviewed after you lose a game."

"Definitely not as much fun as when you win. It's really hard when you've fucked up bad."

"Have you? Fucked up bad?"

"We all make mistakes. Last season, one of our top players did a dumb thing and hit another player late and injured him. He was fucked up for weeks over that."

"Oh wow." I bite my lip. "Hockey's a dangerous sport."

"It can be."

Our whipped feta arrives, served with chewy, crusty bread, and we both dig in and continue to talk. I watch Nate, fascinated by almost everything about him—his smile, his hands, his strong forearms, his self-deprecating humor, his quick wit. Watching him spread cheese onto a piece of bread is almost...erotic.

Yikes.

"Do you have a life motto?" I ask him, attempting casual.

"Hmmm. I don't know...do you?"

"My tattoo." I nod toward my leg.

"Right. C'est la vie."

I nod.

"I guess mine is...I licked it so it's mine."

A laugh bursts from my lips. "Okay, good one. I approve."

He gives me a slightly evil look that makes my girl parts tingle. "Good. This is from one of my buddies: an orgasm a day keeps the worries away."

I collapse into giggles again. "Oh my God."

"Seriously, though. I guess my motto is—life is an adventure; take the risk."

"Hmm. I'm not much of a risk taker." The only impulsive thing I've ever done is drop out of college and run away to Paris.

"Sometimes you should. Life's an adventure."

Our eyes meet and I feel a tingly buzz of attraction and connection.

Take the risk. I don't know if I can live by that motto. But I'm definitely tempted.

6

NATE

I want to take Carly up to my place and fuck her like her douchey criminal ex is living in the apartment below me.

She's hilarious and sweet, optimistic, and authentic. And sexy as fuck. Tonight her caramel brown hair is in messy waves, her lips are stained a deep red, and her eyes are rimmed with dark shadow that makes them look huge and seductive. Tension twists low in my gut as I turn to her in the darkness of the back seat of the Uber. "Come to my place?" I ask in a low voice.

Our eyes meet. And hold. Her lips part. "Quinn?"

"She's having a sleepover."

"Ah." She smiles. "Okay, then—yes."

Reaching for her hand, I swallow a groan. I give her hand a quick squeeze and keep my fingers curled around it as we make our way through Manhattan, through traffic, lighted signs, and glittering skyscrapers.

In the driveway in front of my building, I jump out and hold my hand out to help Carly. She slides out too and we enter the brass and glass doors to the lobby. I wave at Felipe, the doorman on duty, and lead the way to the elevators.

"Nice building," she murmurs.

"Thanks. It's convenient. Close to the arena but also it's easy to get to our practice facility. A bunch of guys live in this area." I'm babbling a bunch of nonsense, trying to be cool and casual. Meanwhile my blood is sizzling through my veins and hot need builds in my groin.

Moments later we're entering my tenth-floor apartment.

Carly crosses the dining room and living room window overlooking the park. "Lovely view."

I walk up behind her. "Yeah." I brush the hair off the back of her neck and bend to press my lips there. Soft. Careful.

She shivers.

"Would you like a drink?" I murmur near her ear. The scent of her hair is like warm flowers with a hint of peaches. It makes me even harder.

"Um. I guess that would be more mannerly than heading straight to your bedroom?"

I laugh softly. "I'm okay with straight to the bedroom." I kiss the side of her neck. "But I don't want to rush you." Another kiss. "Or pressure you." I slide my tongue over her skin. "We can sit and have a drink and make out a little first."

She chokes on a laugh. "All right."

I actually bought wine earlier in hopes that this might happen. "Have a seat." I wave at my big couch along one wall. "Red wine okay?"

"Absolutely." She sits as I hike to the kitchen. "Do you have three bedrooms?"

"Yep." It's a screw top bottle, yay, so I quickly pour two glasses and carry them back.

"That's amazing. My friend's apartment is so tiny and with four other women there, I feel a little crushed. I've been sleeping on the couch and living out of my suitcase. It's getting to be an ordeal."

"Jesus. I didn't know that." When she said she was staying with a friend I assumed she at least had a bed.

49

She takes the wine. "Yeah, it's not ideal. Hence the apartment hunting. I wish I could afford something like this."

"I guess I'm lucky. It's expensive to live here." I sit next to her. "It's good having a room for Quinn and a spare room for visitors."

She lifts an eyebrow.

"Not that kind of visitor," I say dryly. "Believe me, you won't be sleeping in the spare room."

"I probably won't be sleeping," she replies in a flirty tone.

"Definitely not." I lean closer and touch my nose to hers. "I hope you know we're gonna break my bed."

She chuckles. "Ooooh. That sounds promising."

I sip my wine, close enough to smell that erotic fragrance again, close enough to see the amber glints in her green eyes and the smooth texture of her skin.

"You're looking at me..." she murmurs.

I smile. "Yeah."

"Stop." She's smiling, too.

"Stop being so gorgeous."

"Ha."

"How about I kiss you? I'll close my eyes."

Her eyelids lower and her bottom lip strays from the top lip. "Okay. That'll work."

I tilt my head and lean in. The first touch of my lips on hers is firm but closed-mouthed. Heat and pressure spiral inside me. She turns her head just slightly, lifting her chin to move into the kiss. I kiss her again, letting my tongue slide over her bottom lip, then opening on her mouth. She parts her lips eagerly and we sink into each other. I lick into her mouth, more heat buzzing through me. Blindly I set my glass on the coffee table, luckily not missing, and slide my hand around the back of her neck, into her hair, bringing her closer still.

She makes a soft noise in her throat as our kiss deepens. I kiss her again. And again. Then I shift away, take her wine glass and drop it next to mine, and go in again. Now her hand is free, it rests on my shoulder, fingertips digging in through my shirt.

"Making out is fun," she says against my lips.

I smile, the curve of my lips matching hers. "Yeah. I like kissing you." I drop another light buss on her mouth. "I knew I would." And then I go deep again, starving for more of her taste, more of her feel. Our kisses are long and wet, lots of tongue, and goddamn, I'm as hard as a hockey stick. I'm in pain.

I stroke the soft skin of her neck then let my hand drift lightly down over her shoulder, her collarbone and then...her breast. She inhales sharply but doesn't stop me and I cover her soft tit and gently squeeze. Oh yeah...fuck yeah...full and firm, her hard little nipple prominent beneath her shirt and a bra that's barely there.

She arches her back, pressing into my palm, and I drag my lips over her cheek, the delicate line of her jaw, the side of her neck. Her head falls back and I suck so gently on thin skin, eliciting another sexy noise. As I feel up her tits, she grabs the back of my neck and caresses me, her fingers sending cascades of electricity down my spine.

We both part at the same time, staring into each other's eyes. Hers are deep green and heavy lidded. She parts wet, swollen lips and the air around us thickens and electrifies. "Fuck," I mutter under my breath.

I'm burning up, heat rushing through me, excitement pounding in my veins. Holding her gaze, I study her shirt. It looks like it ties up, so I tug one end of the bow and loosen it. Her tongue touches her bottom lip, then her teeth sink into it. I'm giving her time to object, and she doesn't, so I keep going, until the shirt is open. I tug the sides and part it, revealing a skimpy, sheer beige triangle bra. Her tits are round and perfect, the nipples coppery and puckered. Jesus. My mouth literally waters.

"There's not much to this bra," I say, tracing the edge of the cup.

"Is that a bad thing?"

"Christ, no." I groan and brush my fingertips over her nipple. She lets out a tiny whine. "Like that?"

"Yes. More."

"Mmm." I push up the elastic band of the bra and let her naked flesh fill my palm. "Christ. Beautiful." I kiss her again as I plump and squeeze and let my thumb circle her nipple.

"I love having my nipples played with," she breathes. "Love it…"

I lift my hand to her mouth and slip my thumb inside. Her tongue swirls and she sucks and then I return my wet thumb to her nipple. I rotate it over the tender tip and she shudders hard against me.

We both dive in for more long, deep kisses, straining toward each other. I play with her tit and she slides her hand into my hair, her nails on my scalp sending sparks cascading down my spine. I lift my hand to her throat and cover it so gently as I devour her mouth, my other arm sliding behind her back, holding her there.

"Can I take off your shirt?" I mumble long moments later.

"Yes. If you take off yours, too."

"Deal." I don't bother with the buttons, just reach behind my head and yank it off. I think a button pops, but I'm not sure and I don't care.

"Oh." She studies my torso with appreciative heat that makes my dick even harder.

I toss the shirt aside then turn my attention to hers, pulling it loose from her jeans, unbuttoning it the rest of the way, and pushing it back off her shoulders. She helps get it off and I'm so desperate to taste her, I shove her bra above her tits and lean in. I think my dick is about to explode as I lick over a nipple.

She sinks back into the couch and holds my head as I bend over her and play and tease and then close my lips around the nub. Jesus. Sweet. Perfect. I suck harder and she gasps, fingernails scraping my scalp again. "Okay?"

"God, yes. Yes."

She has another tattoo trailing along her ribs beneath her right arm that I vaguely take note of before I move to the other tit. She stops me for a moment to unfasten her bra and I grasp it and fling it away. She slides deeper into the couch cushion, giving me access to her toplessness and holy fuck, it is amazing, gorgeous smooth skin, lush curves, stiff little nipples.

I feast, losing myself in her scent and taste, pressing my face into her cleavage, licking around each globe, sucking and marking her. I move to kiss her again, my hand once more covering her throat in a claiming, possessive gesture.

I licked her so she's mine.

Okay, getting ahead of myself here, I'm all drunk on hormones or something and not thinking clearly, but this is amazing and so fucking good, and I'm not even inside her yet.

Please, let me get inside her. I'll weep with disappointment if that's not how this ends. But in the meantime, I want to pleasure her and make her feel as fucking high as I am.

She's sprawled out next to me and I glide my hand down over her stomach, over the zipper of her jeans, slowly...then between her legs. I can't feel much through the denim besides damp warmth, but I cup her firmly there and her hips lift into my touch.

"You want it?" I murmur near her lips. "You want me to touch you here?"

"Yes."

"Do you need to come, baby?"

"God, yes." Her low groan inflames my senses even more.

I press the heel of my hand just below her mound and she lets out another moan, then reaches for me. Her hand brushes my aching hard on and I grit my teeth. Then she covers my cock and applies firm pressure. "You're big."

"Ah. I sure as hell am right now. Christ, Carly."

She smiles, her eyes hazy, hand rubbing. "I like it."

"Can I take off your jeans?"

"Y-yes. Please."

I flick open the button and lower the zipper, then slide off the couch to kneel between her legs as I work the snug jeans down hips, thigh, calves, and off. Now she's in only a minuscule sheer thong. I lean forward and breath in the scent of her arousal, *fuck*...it's like drug hitting my veins. "Pretty." I press my mouth to the triangle over her mound. The sheerness reveals bare skin beneath and I'm excited beyond belief to see her, to touch her there, taste her there. *Patience.*

I jump back onto the couch for more of those luscious Carly kisses, my hand roaming over her from tits to pussy, squeezing her so gently, then rubbing over the bump of her clit. Somehow she gets my jeans open and my eager dick springs free. When her fingers close around me, the top of my head nearly splits in two as a bolt of white-hot electricity sears up my spine.

"Mmmm. Wow." Her head is back, eyes closed as we fondle each other on the couch like freakin' teenagers, and it's so goddamn hot I'm losing my mind. "You feel good."

"Christ." A groan rumbles in my chest. "So do you. Touching me. Yeah...squeeze a little...aw, fuck. And here..." I cuddle her pussy with my palm. "So good." I dare to slip my hand beneath the panties and we both stop breathing when my fingers graze soft, bare flesh. The softest. I trace plump lips then find her mouth in another hot kiss as I explore deeper with one finger... "Wet. Christ." I slide my finger around her juicy cunt, unbearably turned on.

Her hand stills on my cock when I trail a wet fingertip over her clit. "Ahhhh God..." Then she slowly jacks me while I finger her and we kiss. And kiss. And kiss.

The room is spinning. I'm dizzy and dazed. "Can I fuck you, Carly?" I whisper. "I have a condom."

"If you don't, I'll die." She curves her hand over the sensitive head of my cock. I'm so primed I could come with a couple more strokes. "Please, Nate. Fuck me."

"Here? Or..."

"Right here."

I launch myself up. I dig around for the condom then shove

down my jeans and boxers. She wriggles out of her panties and I sit back down beside her and lift her, turning her onto my lap, straddling me.

She gives a breathless laugh mid-air. "Eeeep."

I smile with wicked enjoyment. "Baby. You are so fucking hot. Look at you."

She smiles down at me, on her knees in front of me. Her eyes are sultry, her mouth a dream, and my cock is stiff and at attention between us. She holds out a hand for the condom and I give it to her and watch with dirty anticipation as she opens it, then rolls it onto my shaft.

"Jesus." I close my eyes and grind my back molars together. But I want the visual, so I crank open my eyelids and watch her lift herself above me, holding my cock, then lowering herself... slowly...onto me.

The head of my cock notches into her opening and even through the latex I feel the heat and slickness. She watches my face as she takes me inside.

"Fuck, that's gorgeous," I groan. "Look at you...all smooth and pink...taking me...take it all."

"I want it all." She sucks in a breath and takes me deeper, her eyes flickering.

I grip her hips. "Slow, baby. Nice and easy...there..."

She blows out a breath, her lips forming a tiny o, then inhales again. Her inner muscles are snug and slippery, squeezing me. "It's... good. I'm okay. You're filling me so deep."

"I like that. Okay?"

"Yeah."

Then we're there. All the way. Her hands flat on my chest, she sits on my cock, pulsing around me, and our eyes meet again.

"Ohhhh. Wow."

"Yeah." I bite my bottom lip, trying to stop myself from bucking up into her like a madman. Then I gently lift her hips.

She moves with me...up...back down...up...long, smooth, slick glides of flesh, nerve endings prickling. My balls draw up tight.

She moves faster, riding me hard, her tits jiggling, a rosy flush spreading from between them up into her face. She leans down to kiss me and our tongues tangle, teeth clicking, lips smashing together, both of us crazed with the need to fuck and come.

I hold her tits, pinch her nipples, lose myself in her sweet pussy milking me. So close, so goddamn close, but she has to come first.

So I grab her waist and lift her off me. She gasps as I spin her down to her back on the couch and climb over her in a smooth move.

"Whoa."

I grin as I take my cock in my hand to enter her again. I penetrate deeply, watching her face go lax. She pulls her knees back and I sink even deeper into her.

"Oh God. That's amazing."

I study her, gloriously messy and flushed, one of my hands pressing to her lower abdomen, the other finding her clit. I circle it and her breathing hitches, and when I press more firmly on her stomach I feel myself moving inside her and she cries out. "Jesus!"

Her clit is swollen and I slick up more of that sweet nectar and smear it around, and around.

"Just...a little..." She shifts her pelvis and my finger slips left. "There... oh yeah...oh God...oh *God!*" Her back arches, her abs tighten and the blush on her skin deepens. She contracts around me so tightly I nearly lose it. So close...

I stroke her until her head is tossing, then stretch out over her between her legs and rock my hips, fucking into her in fast hard strokes. Her hands move up and down my ribs, over my shoulders, my neck, my hair. We bite at each other's lips, my stomach grinding against her, my thighs quaking as tension torques and builds at the base of my spine then explodes outward in ecstatic, hard waves.

I collapse over her, gulping for air, my heart wild. Holy shit.

Holy fucking shit. When I can move, I shift to the side, drag my eyes open and look at her.

Our eyes meet. The world slows and narrows. "What the hell, Carly."

Her big eyes gaze back at me, pupils blown. "Yeah. What the hell."

7

CARLY

"I'll walk you home."

I smile at Nate. "Okay, thanks."

I don't need to be walked home, but it turns out I like being with him.

I take a last look around his apartment. The whole place is color-coordinated in shades of gray and white and charcoal—the living room with pale gray furniture (one chair sporting a pink stain that appears to be fruit juice), the sleek kitchen with *two ovens*, his bedroom with a big charcoal upholstered bed, and the bathroom that's all shiny white and silver and Carrera marble with subtle gray veining. The floors are all a light wood and big pieces of modern art in similar shades hang on white walls.

"Thanks for a fun evening," he says as we walk. "I had a really good time."

I smile up at Nate. "I did too. Thank you."

When we arrive at Gianna's building, we stop on the sidewalk out front. "I'd like to see you again." His eyes move over my face.

Yessss. "Me too."

The corners of his lips lift. "I'll call you."

"Okay."

He bends his head and brushes his lips over mine, then deepens the kiss. I could get lost in it all over again. Never mind the cars passing by or people walking their dogs. All there is, is his mouth, his scent, the heat radiating off his hard body. Damn.

He pulls back with a smile that crinkles his eyes. "Bye."

"Bye."

I climb the steps to the door and watch him stride confidently away.

Then I sigh and float into Gianna's apartment.

She looks up at me and grins. I texted to let her know I wouldn't be home last night. "Hey."

"Hey." I drop my purse on a chair and throw myself onto the couch beside Imani. "I'm so tired."

"No sleep?" Imani accompanies the question with an exaggerated wink.

"Not much." I smile.

"Tell me everything," Gianna says.

"He made me breakfast."

"Nice."

"I really like him."

"And his wang?"

I choke on a laugh. "Oh my God. Let's just say it's...satisfying."

"Excellent."

"We went on a jazz cruise," I tell her dreamily. "Then dinner. Then back to his place. His daughter had a sleepover. Did I mention that I really like him?"

"This is so great!"

"Well, let's not get too excited. I don't have a job or a place to live. I need to focus on that before I worry about finding a boyfriend."

"You can do both."

"Maybe? I need a nap. But I have to go look at a few more apartments this afternoon."

"Okay. Want me to come with you?"

"Sure! That would be great, if you have time."

"My Saturday is open. And you can tell me more details about your sleepover."

"Ha."

I go shower and change, then head out with Gianna. My steps are dragging, but I don't regret a moment of last night.

"Tell me more about this man," Gianna says on the subway. "He's divorced?"

"Yes. But it sounds amicable. She fell for someone else but at least she didn't cheat on him." I shake my head. "That sucks, though. And he really loves his daughter."

"That's awesome."

"He was amazing," I tell her. "His body is perfect; he's strong and physical, but also considerate and generous. I'm melting into a puddle of lust all over again just talking about him." Ten minutes later I realize I haven't shut up about him. "God, stop me," I say with a laugh.

She grins. "It's kind of cute. But I'll change the subject. I'm thinking of having breast reduction surgery."

I gape at her. "What?"

She shrugs.

"That was quite a shift. Why are you thinking about doing that?" Well, I don't really have to ask. Gianna is curvy everywhere, and she does have large breasts.

"The usual reasons. I'll be more comfortable. My back and neck hurt and I have big dents in my shoulders."

"Well."

"Also the skin under my boobs gets irritated." She sighs.

"It's expensive, isn't it?"

"Yes. I have the money saved up. I told myself if I could do that, then I should go for it. But now I'm hesitating."

"Why are you hesitating?"

"I don't like pain. Having surgery for something that technically isn't needed—like, in a life-saving way—seems masochistic."

"It's not masochistic. I get that surgery involves pain, but you're in pain now."

"True."

"I guess there are always risks."

"Yes, and I've thought at length about every one of them."

"I bet. Um, what does Isaac think about it?" Isaac is her boyfriend.

She slants me a look that's a bit amused and a bit chiding. "They're not his breasts."

I scrunch my nose up. "Of course they're not. It's totally your decision. I just wondered if he's supportive."

"Ah. Well, he is. He loves my boobs, but he's in agreement that it's my body."

"That's good. Do you have a doctor you'd go to?"

"Yeah. I did a lot of research and I've been for a consultation. He has a good rep and seemed to know what he was doing. He explained everything very clearly."

"Well, I think you've done everything you can to make sure it's as successful as possible. And if it's something you want, you should go for it. Imagine yourself doing things that are uncomfortable now, like..."

"Running. I'm so jealous every time you go for a run. Even with the best sports bra, it's uncomfortable for me."

"There you go. We can run together when you're ready."

"You're the best."

"Aw, thanks. And don't worry about after the surgery. The other girls and I will take care of you. Although hopefully I'm not actually living there anymore."

She laughs.

It's good having her there with me to look at apartments. She immediately nixes one based on the outside of the building, and gives me her honest opinions of the others. And she keeps me focused on apartments instead of reliving exciting moments from last night.

We pick up dinner on our way home and it eat on the couch, watching TV with Lorelei. I'd give *anything* to have my own space and be alone for a while. The places we saw were all crap. I'm beginning to think the apartment with the guy in his bike helmet and underwear wasn't so bad. I repress a sigh and settle into the couch with my laptop do some research for my book. I'm doing this.

To Be a Man.

No—Be a Man.

Hell yeah! Finally I have a title. That just flashed into my head. My research around gender and traditionally defined masculinity is coming together. I need to interview some men about some of my ideas around strength and vulnerability, relationships, body image, sex and sexuality, racial justice, fatherhood and...

Nate has a whole hockey team full of men.

Nah, I barely know him. I can't interview him.

I've already asked Isaac if I can interview him and his friend Andres, who's Black. I want to talk to diverse men. I talked to Jim Madden about fatherhood before I left Paris and I have my notes from those conversations. I'll find other men.

Wow. I feel like I'm actually making progress with this idea.

Nate

"How was the date last night?"

"Fucking fantastic." I grin at Bergie. I'm at his place to pick up Quinn, but she's still outside with Mandy and the kids.

"Got some action, huh."

"Maybe."

He laughs. "Coffee?"

"Sure." I follow him into the kitchen where he has a pot of coffee already brewed. He pours me a cup and we sit at the big island.

"How did you meet this girl?"

"We met in the park. Quinn started talking to her."

"Ah. Using the munchkin as bait."

I snort. "As if. Nothing happened that time. Other than my knee gave out and I fell on the ground right in front of her."

Bergie laughs uproariously. "Seriously?"

"Oh yeah." I make a face. "I thought I'd never see her again. Then we ran into her again when we were going for ice cream. I was on crutches and she took pity on us and got the ice cream for us."

"Kids and crutches. Work every time."

"Jesus." I shake my head.

"Are you gonna see her again?"

"I hope so."

"Hmmm. That's...different for you."

"I know." I stare at my coffee for a moment. "I'm tired of just hooking up all the time. I'm..." I pause. "I'm kinda lonely. And horny."

He laughs again. "I get it."

"I think I want someone around for more than just one night. And Carly's the first woman I've met that I feel like it could be her."

"Wow. Never thought I'd hear this from you."

"I know. What's happening to me?"

"You're getting old."

I don't take offense, because it's true.

"Growing up, maybe," he adds. "I know Brielle did a number on you, but that was a long time ago."

"It wasn't just Brielle," I mutter. "There've been a lot of women who I thought were interested in me. Turned out they were interested in hockey players. Parading me around to expensive places. Posing for pictures or taking selfies. Ugh."

"When you're young, you don't even care that they're interested in you because you play hockey. You're just happy to get to tap that."

"That's how I got involved with Brielle," I agree ruefully. I rub my chin. "Not doing that again."

"So you think this girl...what's her name?"

"Carly. Carly Corrigan."

"So you think she's not like that?"

I consider that. "I don't think she is. She seems pretty genuine."

"That's cool, then."

Quinn rushes in and jumps at me. "Daddy! We slept in sleeping bags last night! And had popcorn. And root beer floats! Do you know what a float is? It's called a float because the ice cream floats in the root beer. It was vanilla, but that was okay, it was delicious."

I grin at her. "Sounds great."

"Did you have fun with Carly last night?"

"We had a good time. We went on a boat."

"Ohhhh! I want to go on a boat!"

"We can do that sometime. The boat went right by the Statue of Liberty."

"Let's go do that now."

"Not today, pop tart. We have important things to do."

"Like what?" She frowns suspiciously.

And she's right. "Laundry! So exciting."

"Ugh."

"Go get your things," I tell her.

She huffs and trudges out of the kitchen.

"She knows about Carly?" Mandy asks in a low voice.

"Yeah, I told her we were going on a date."

"It seems...early in the relationship for that?"

"I know. I don't usually talk about my dates with her, because she'll likely never meet them. But she knows and likes Carly." I pause. "Also, it feels...different with Carly."

"He's catching feelings," Bergie says to his wife with a smirk.

I roll my eyes, but I don't deny it, because I definitely have some kind of feelings for her.

"Oooh. This sounds promising." Mandy's practically rubbing her hands together. "We need to meet her."

"Maybe some time, yeah. That'd be great."

"Wow." Mandy looks at Bergie.

"I know, right?"

I shake my head.

"How's your knee?" Mandy asks. "I heard you tried some new procedure."

"Yeah." I tell her about it briefly. "I have another appointment with the specialist next week." I screw up my face. "I don't feel like things are much different. So I'm kind of pessimistic about it."

"Oh, darn. That's too bad." She gives me a sympathetic look. "Does that mean surgery?"

"Probably."

"It'll be fine. The team only uses the best doctors."

"I know. This guy's really cutting edge." I pause. "Ha. Good pun."

They both laugh.

"What about Quinn?" Mandy shoots a quick glance down the hall. "Don't you have her all summer?"

"Yeah." I rub my mouth. "I've been thinking about that." Actually, I know the perfect solution to that problem, but I don't want to say anything. Maybe it's a cocoa bananas idea, but it's been floating around my head. "I'll definitely need help. I'll figure it out."

Quinn bounces into the room with her backpack and I finish my coffee. "Okay. I guess we should get going. Thanks for having Quinn last night. I really appreciate it."

"Any time," Mandy says. "She's a sweetheart."

I guess that means Quinn didn't tell anyone to fuck off last night. Whew.

8

CARLY

Over the next few days, Nate and I text back and forth. Then I don't hear from him for a whole day. Or the next day.

Damn. Is he ghosting me? That's disappointing. And depressing. I'll send him one more text; there's no reason I have to wait for him.

CARLY: *Hey, haven't heard from you for a few days, everything okay?*

I wait a few minutes for reply, then give up. I finished my pitch email for the "Bitch Please" website yesterday, so I go over it to polish it before sending it off to distract me from Nate. I feel good about the article about why "politically correct" is the wrong name for that concept.

After I hit "send," I sit back, then reach for my phone.

NATE: *Sure everything's great, killer, kickass*

I purse my lips and reread the message. I'm not sure what to make of this. I don't know the guy that well. I think I'll take this as a sign to back off. Again—disappointing. But I don't need drama in my life; I have enough problems.

CARLY: *Sorry to bother you! Take care.*

I drop my phone and shake my head. I'll go for a run in the park. It's cool and overcast today, so I should take advantage of that. I change into my running gear, pop in my earbuds and find my favorite playlist, then set out toward Central Park West and the nearest entrance to the park. I shouldn't think about Nate, but it's hard not to. I mean, I can sleep with a guy and not get all romantically involved. That's not the problem. Really. It's just...disappointing.

Okay, okay, you're disappointed. We got that. Get over it, Carly. There are lots of guys in New York City.

I let the upbeat music fill my head, lift my mood, and fuel my run, my feet pounding the pavement into the park where big trees stretch their branches above me. Every time, I've been running a little further. I'm really getting into this. I did a lot of walking in Paris taking the kids out and lost weight while I lived there, and I don't want to gain it back. I pat my belly.

Fuck Nate. He'll never see my belly again.

That's supposed to cheer me up, but it doesn't really. Oh well.

I've just turned to head home when my phone beeps in my ear. I'm getting a call. That doesn't happen very often. I tap my Bluetooth earbud to answer.

It's the portable toilet company. They have another opening and want to offer me a job.

Yay.

Honestly, I'm not thrilled. Hands on my hips, I try not to pant as I listen to the HR woman give me details. I need this job. I shouldn't be so picky. But I find myself asking for a day to think it over.

Music playing again, I keep walking, sorting things out in my head. It's a job. If I take it, I can keep looking. I won't have as much time to write, but it's what I have to do to get an apartment. I really need to take this job. Then I'll call the underwear dude and see if the room's still available. And I'll be all set.

I resume my run at a light jogging pace.

I should feel happier.

I round the corner onto 74th and see a man walking toward me. A man and a little girl wearing a glittery mask and a red cape. My heart bumps and I slow to a walk, eyes on them. He spots me and lifts a hand, then stops in front of Gianna's building and waits for me.

Huh.

"Hi," he says as I pull out my earbuds. "We dropped by to see if you want to come for ice cream with us."

His expression is stiff, his eyes unhappy. I study him, switch my gaze to Quinn, and smile. "Hi, Quinn."

"Hi, Carly!" She bounces. "Strawberrrrrry iiiiice cream!"

I laugh. "I have to stop eating ice cream after my runs."

"Why?"

"Er... good question." I look back to Nate cautiously. "Are you sure?"

He gives a terse nod. "Yeah."

I look down at myself, all sweaty and gross. Well, he's seen me like this before. Not to mention sweaty and naked. "Okay. Let's go."

Quinn skips ahead of us. Under her cape she's wearing a red and pink flowered sundress and her hair is held back by my headband with the pink bow.

"Your text earlier was a little...cryptic," I say.

"Yeah. Sorry." He rubs his face. "I was in a shitty mood. Your text..."

I wait.

"Sounded like a brush off."

"*Your* text sounded like a brush off. Or maybe a fuck you." I keep my voice low.

"Shit. I'm sorry. That wasn't what I intended. That's why I'm here. I wanted to straighten things out."

"Is something wrong?"

He sighs. "I went to the doctor this morning. The specialist. The PRP injection didn't work. So I have to have surgery."

"Ohhhh. I'm sorry."

"It's not like it's life threatening." He rolls his eyes. "I'm just being a big baby."

I laugh softly. "Oh, okay. But seriously, nobody wants surgery.

Especially a pro athlete. It's understandable that you're upset." I pause. "But you don't need to be a dick about it."

After a startled beat, he bellows a laugh. "Yeah. You're right. I really am sorry."

"Okay. You're forgiven."

Quinn has paused in front of the window of a stationery store decorated with huge colorful flowers and bumble bees. We catch up to her.

"Look, Daddy, isn't it pretty?"

"Yeah."

"Can we come here before school starts? They have school supplies."

"Maybe."

"THEY HAVE HARMONIA SCHOOL SUPPLIES!" Quinn presses her face to the glass. "Look! Holy shit!"

I bite my lip to stop my laugh, inspecting the colorful supplies with the Harmonia world design and the girl heroes of that world, Clover, Etana, and Minka. Amaris, one of my sweet charges in Paris, loved those stories.

"Let's make a deal," Nate says. "If you don't say any swear words before school starts, we'll come back and get you Harmonia school supplies."

Quinn blinks at him. Her small mouth puckers then she nods and says, "I'll try."

We continue walking, turn the corner and then we're at the Sugar Shack. This time we eat our ice cream seated at one of the little wrought iron tables in front of the shop.

"Daddy has to have an operation," Quinn says. "He won't be able to walk. But I can look after him."

Nate's expression turns troubled, but he smiles at Quinn. "Maybe you'll be a doctor when you grow up."

She considers that and it's so damn cute. "No, I want to be a super hero. Or maybe a hockey player."

"Do you know how to skate, Quinn?" I ask.

"Of course." She looks down her little nose at me. "Do you?"

I bite back a smile. "I do, but not very well."

"Daddy can teach you. He taught me. Next year I'm going to hockey camp. And we can go skating in Central Park in the winter."

I nod.

"Well, hockey player, doctor…you have a while to decide," Nate says.

A sudden breeze blows my hair back. The sky is darkening and the wind is picking up. "Looks like a storm is coming."

"Yeah. I guess we should go."

"Can we walk Carly home?" Quinn asks.

"Of course."

"You don't have to. What about your knee?"

Nate waves a hand. "It's fine."

As we walk, Quinn skips ahead and I ask him, "Are you worried about the surgery?"

"Honestly? I'm more worried about what I'm going to do with Quinn."

I tip my head. "Her mom won't take her?"

He grimaces. "I floated the idea past her, but she's auditioning for some big role and our agreement is that I have Quinn right now. She said to find a babysitter."

"Oh. Damn. Do you have any ideas?"

"I asked a couple of my teammates who have kids. They interviewed nannies and they gave me some names, but I tried contacting them and they all have other positions now, and honestly, I don't like the idea of leaving her with a stranger."

"Oh." I sigh. "Like me and my damn job search." I pause. "I did get a job offer today."

"Oh."

"It's with a portable toilet company."

"Jesus."

I laugh. "I know. But it's a job."

"Look. This has been burning a hole in my brain for a while. You need a job and a place to live. I need a nanny. I'll hire you and it'll solve both our problems."

"Ummmm…" I turn to him. "What?"

He regards me with growing enthusiasm. "It's a great idea! I have a spare room you can move into."

"Are you serious?" I frown and go very still. I feel the bump of my heart in my chest.

"Hell, yeah."

My insides tighten and go cold. Slowly, I shake my head. "Quinn is adorable, but I can't do that."

"I'll pay well," Nate says. "It's just temporary, until I'm mobile again. You can keep job hunting."

A couple of large raindrops splat onto my face and shoulders. "No."

The corners of his eyes tighten. "Again…why not?"

Why not? Because my sister thought I was stealing her daughter and took her away from me. Because the Maddens didn't need me anymore and I lost those kids, too. Because even though Nate has a gorgeous apartment and a sweetheart of a daughter, I'd rather work for a portable toilet company than go through that again.

Thunder rumbles in the distance as we reach Gianna's place. I meet Nate's eyes. "I'm sorry. I just can't."

9

NATE

We make it back to our place just before the rain gushes down, running the last half block. Fuck, now my knee's sore but Quinn loves it, laughing and turning her face up to the wet stuff.

I'm distracted as I make dinner—my specialty, sloppy Joes—but I manage to listen to Quinn talk about Harmonia school supplies and headbands with bows, and respond appropriately. I hope.

We play a game of Taco vs Burrito and then I get her to bed. As usual, she has multiple requests—for a snack, for juice (I give her water), for more bedtime stories. I'm about to put my foot down when she says, "Daddy, is your knee going to be okay?"

I sit on the edge of her bed and smooth back her hair. "Of course it is."

"But you have to have a surgery."

"Yes. But that's to fix it."

"Will it hurt?"

"Well, not when they do it. They'll give me medicine that helps stop it from hurting too much. But it might hurt for a while after."

"Are you scared?"

I smile at her. Christ. I want to be confident and ease her fears.

But I have to be honest. "Sure. But it's natural to be scared about something like that."

"Maybe you'll get a popsicle after. My friend Leo had his tonsils out and he got a popsicle."

I nod seriously. "I hope I get a popsicle."

"What if they operate on the wrong leg?"

I blink. "I'm sure they're very careful about that." *I hope.* "For a while after the surgery I won't be able to do all the things I usually can. So we'll have to find different ways to have fun together."

"I can look after you."

I gaze into her blue eyes, her expression so earnest and serious, and my heart squeezes tight. "Thank you, pop tart. That would be great."

Finally, she's tucked into bed and I have a beer in my hand.

I guess I should have talked to Quinn about the surgery sooner. It's totally normal that she would have questions and fears about it. I hope I said the right things.

I hope they operate on the right knee.

Jesus. Okay, I'm a little worried about it. Not so much the surgery itself, but the outcome. I need my knee to be better. I need to be able to play hockey. What if I can't? What if I try, but it's still a problem? What would that mean for future contracts? What if this is the beginning of the end of my career?

I guzzle down some beer.

Okay. *Get your shit together, Karmeinski.* This is a routine, relatively minor surgery. I want to be able to play for the start of the season, but if I can't, I just want to be able to play, period. It'll be fine.

My thoughts turn to my conversation with Carly. My job offer seemed genius—a win-win. She needs a job. I need a caregiver.

But she flat out turned me down.

It didn't seem like *that* crazy of an idea.

I admit I'm a little peeved. I don't get turned down by women very often.

"Well, that's a douchey thought," I mutter out loud. I slide a hand into my hair and push it back off my face. I need a haircut.

I lean back and take a pull of my beer.

What happened with the family she worked for? I may not be the brightest bulb in the chandelier, but I have a good imagination and crazy thoughts about abuse or an affair start swirling. Maybe the father came onto her. Maybe the mother! Or maybe Carly did something wrong and something happened to one of the kids... ugh. That would be awful.

It kills me not knowing.

Fuck, it's not my business. I asked, she answered. *Let it go, asshole.*

I still have a couple of agencies I can contact about getting some help. It should be no problem. I don't need Carly.

Maybe she needs me, though.

Nope. Apparently not. She'd rather work for a portable toilet company than look after my kid.

Jesus. I knock back more beer.

Carly

The girls are having a party tonight. Yay.

I like a good party and it'll be great for me to meet people in New York. So I'm going to have fun tonight! I hope.

I've helped make food and clean up, trying to hide my belongings so the living room is clear. Isaac is the first to arrive and takes charge of music, so I finish cleaning the bathroom to Tiësto's "The Business." The music definitely helps.

I wish Nate were here.

No. I sigh. First of all, we've only been out twice. Second, he just offered me a job as a nanny, to which I freaked out and bolted. So much for a couple of great dates with a fantastic guy. I just blew it.

Not to mention a job offer that should be the answer to my prayers. But I'm scared.

Forget about it. It's party time!

Guests start arriving, drinks are consumed, the music gets louder. Most people here are couples, but that's okay, I'm not looking for a man! I drink wine, talk to people, dance a little in the tiny space we have, and drink more.

I'm in the kitchen refilling my wine glass when one of our guests joins me. I saw him earlier, but we haven't been introduced. "Hi, I'm Carly." I smile. "I'm staying here temporarily, Gianna's a friend of mine."

"Nice to meet you, Carly." He shakes my hand with a delicate shake that does not appeal to me. "I'm Ian."

"Hi, Ian." I sip my wine.

He moves closer and smiles. "I have a girlfriend, but she says it's okay if I make out with other girls."

I stare. I draw back. "Okay, good for you. Have fun!"

I scoot back into the living room and position myself next to Isaac and Gianna.

"Water is not wet," Isaac says.

I frown.

"Yes, it is!" Gianna's eyes flash fire.

"It's not. It makes other things wet, but it's not wet itself."

She heaves a sigh and looks at me. "Is water wet?"

"I have to go to the bathroom." I make a quick getaway.

Great party!

I take my time in the bathroom, only because I'm weary and I'd rather just stay here. I didn't sleep well last night after Nate's ridiculous job offer and today I went for a long run and applied for a bunch of jobs. But I can't stay in the bathroom all night.

I emerge just in time to see Ian climb onto the coffee table in the living room and whip down his pants. He thrusts his arms in the air and yells, "Who wants some of this?"

I close my eyes. Maybe I *can* stay in the bathroom.

I eye the couch sorrowfully. That's my bed. I want to go to bed. So much. But people are sitting there, and more people are walking in the door. This party is never going to end.

After a couple more glasses of wine, I can't do it anymore. My eyes are gritty and heavy. I stumble into Lorelei's room and fall onto her bed. She'll wake me up when she needs it and I'll move to the couch.

I don't know how long I've been passed out for when I'm jostled awake by the bed moving. At first I'm not sure where I am. What is happening? Am I dreaming? Then I remember the party. I'm in Lorelei's bed.

But why is it moving?

"Oh baby, yeah, that's it."

My eyes pop open wide.

"Deeper," Lorelei says. "Fuck me."

Oh Jesus.

I don't know who she's with, but he grants her wish. The bed starts bouncing.

"Yeah," the guy groans. "You like that?"

"Harder."

"Spread your legs wider, babe. Yeah…like that."

I've had enough. I scramble up.

Lorelei shrieks.

"What the fuck!" the guy yells.

"Sorry!" I crawl down to the bottom of the bed. "So sorry."

"Who is that?" the guy says.

"I don't know!"

I glance back and in the dim light I can see the pale bare ass of a naked guy on top of Lorelei. "It's me, Carly. Sorry, sorry. I'm leaving."

I lurch out to the living room. It's quiet and dark now. I guess most people have left. Except for Ian. He's passed out on the couch. My bed.

I want to cry. I slump for a moment while I debate what to do. I just want to sleep. Horizontal. I grab a blanket from the cupboard in the hall and climb into the bathtub. Better than nothing.

I'm so tired, but now I can't sleep. I'm pissed and I'm morose. But it's not even my apartment, so how can I be angry? I really, really need my own place.

Oh God. I know what I have to do.

NATE

I get the text message Saturday morning.

CARLY: *When are you having the surgery?*

Hmmm. What does this mean?

NATE: *They've scheduled it on a priority basis for next week, Monday.*

I set the phone on the counter and return to helping Quinn make chocolate chip cookies.

"Can I eat the cookie dough, Daddy?"

Yikes. Brielle got mad at me for letting her do that. Apparently it's dangerous. I don't want my daughter to die, but how bad can it be? I've eaten a lot of cookie dough. My whole life I've enjoyed taking risks, but the last thing I want to risk is my precious girl. "Just one little taste."

She dips in with excitement and pops a spoonful of batter into her mouth. "Yum."

My phone buzzes.

CARLY: *And how long will you need help with Quinn?*

A slow smile tugs at my mouth. I enter my reply and hit send.

NATE: *I don't really know, but it'll be at least a few weeks.*

We scoop dough onto the cookie sheet. Neither of us is very

good at this, so our cookies are all different shapes and sizes. Whatever. They'll taste good. Then we pop them in the oven.

CARLY: *If you still want me to help, I can do it.*

I grin. I don't know what changed her mind, but I'm not going to question it. This works out for both of us. And having her right here in my home...I have to admit the appeal of that. After the other night, I want more of her.

NATE: *That would be great. You can move in this weekend.*

We text a few more times and arrange things for Sunday. "So guess what?" I say to Quinn.

"What?"

"I'm going to need help after my operation on Monday and Carly is going to come help."

Her eyes pop wide. "Really? Cool!"

"Yeah. She's going to stay in the spare room."

"I told you. I can look after you, Daddy."

"I know you can. But she'll help. I'm a big guy and I don't think you can carry me around."

She snorts. "Carly can't carry you either."

I laugh. "True. I'm kidding. But it'll be good to have another adult here just in case."

"Okay! We should go buy strawberry ice cream so we have some when she gets here."

My kid. "That's a great idea."

"And let's save some cookies for her."

"I don't know if I can do that. I want to eat them all."

"Me too." She makes a cute face. "We can make more."

"Yeah, we can."

Sunday can't come soon enough. I want to see Carly again. I want to ask her to go out tonight. But I'll be disciplined. I can wait until tomorrow.

I pick her up in my car to transport all her stuff, which is actually minimal. Two big suitcases is it. Considering that's her life's possessions, it's kind of…sad. But she was living with another family for those years in Paris, so I guess she didn't need furniture and shit like towels and sheets. She's really starting over.

Quinn tries to help with one of the suitcases, wrestling it out the apartment door, but I pick it up to carry it out the front door and down the steps to the sidewalk. I'm double parked on the narrow street with my flashers on, so we can't take long.

"My friend Gianna wants to meet you," Carly tells me. "She's worried I'm moving in with a serial killer."

I laugh. "I get it." I follow her back inside and she introduces me to her friend, a dark-haired beauty who scrutinizes me with narrowed eyes. "Nice to meet you, Gianna."

"You too. I googled you."

"Of course you did." I smile. I have nothing to hide. Other than a few fighting penalties and the time I let Philly score on our empty net in game seven of the playoffs. "This is my daughter, Quinn."

"Hi, Quinn." Gianna's smile is friendlier for her. "Has your father ever been arrested?"

Quinn blinks.

"She's kidding," I say, shooting Gianna a mildly reproving look.

"I am," she agrees.

"My dad's never been to jail," Quinn says. "But sometimes he fights."

Gianna's eyebrows shoot up.

"In hockey games," I say. "Not off the ice."

"Good to know. Do you have any problem if I drop by to visit Carly? Unannounced?"

My lips twitch. "Not at all. Any time."

"What one item would you save in a fire?"

Huh. After a beat of surprise, I say, "My daughter, obviously."

"Good answer."

"Do I pass?"

"I guess so."

Carly lets out an exasperated laugh. "It'll be fine, Gianna."

"It better be." She gives me a pointed look. "Okay, let me know if you need anything. *Anything at all.*"

"I will."

They hug and we head back out to my car. Quinn gets in the back to sit in her booster seat and Carly slides into the front passenger seat. It's a quick drive to my place. I park in the underground garage and we take Carly's things up to my apartment. I have a key for her, so I hand that over, and then show her to her room. It's minimally furnished but it has the necessities—bed, dresser, nightstands, lamps.

Quinn excitedly shows Carly around the rest of the apartment including the linen closet where towels are and my room, which Carly has already seen. I try to catch her eye in amusement, but she doesn't look at me.

"This is where we keep the toilet paper," Quinn says seriously.

I groan.

Carly nods, equally serious. "That's important information."

Then Quinn drags her to her bedroom.

"This is my room," she announces. "I cleaned it up because Daddy said it was a fucking mess."

"Quinn!" My exasperation is no doubt evident in my tone and the hand I shove into my hair.

"You said that!" she protests again. "Remember, it doesn't count if I'm just telling what you said."

"Okay, I guess we weren't entirely clear on the rules," I say. "No F words at all."

"If I can't say them, you can't say them." She folds her arms and eyes me mutinously.

"I'll try, too," I mutter.

"Come see my Harmonia stuff!" Quinn grabs Carly's hand. From the door, I watch her excitedly chat about the toys, and I watch Carly listen with serious attention.

"This one is really nice," she says, running fingertips down the doll's hair.

"It's my favorite. Also I love Storm." Quinn holds up the white horse. She lowers her voice. "I sleep with her."

Carly doesn't bat a long eyelash. "She's beautiful."

"I have all the horses. I like to have contests where they race and jump."

"I bet Storm is a good jumper."

"She is, she is. And look! Daddy bought me another hairband." She bounces over to her dresser and brandishes the brightly-colored strip of fabric.

"Oh, pretty!"

"Do you know how to do beachy waves?" Quinn asks. "You must know. Your hair is wavy."

"Yes, I know. Do you want me to do your hair like that?"

Quinn clasps her hands together in front of her chest. "Oh yes. I would love, love, love that. Daddy doesn't know how to do beachy waves."

No lies detected.

"He had to watch a YouTube video to learn how to do a braid," Quinn shares.

Carly's lips twitch.

Then Quinn turns to me. "Can we have ice cream, Daddy? We got it for you," she adds to Carly. "Strawberry."

Carly smiles at my daughter and my heart does something funny in my chest. "Oh wow. My favorite! Thank you!"

"Can we have some now?" Quinn asks again.

"Nope. It's too close to dinner time," I say. "We'll have that for dessert."

Quinn wrinkles her nose but accepts my answer. "I'm going to work on my panda." She pauses. "It's a latch hook kit," she adds for Carly's benefit. "I love pandas."

"Cool."

Carly follows me down the hall to the kitchen. I smile at her. "So...what changed?"

She sighs. "The portable toilet company called and offered me a job. I knew I should take it, but I just couldn't do it. And I was ready to rent the room from the guy with the bike helmet and underwear. I figured it couldn't be that bad, right? I'd just buy lots of wipes and clean everything before I touch it. But..." She puckers up her mouth. "That wasn't really appealing either. And then the girls where I'm staying had a party and since I sleep on the couch I couldn't go to bed, and I was *so* tired. I ended up crashing on Lorelei's bed, but then she and some guy came in and started boinking on the bed right beside me. It was dark and they didn't know I was there. So. Here I am."

I try not to laugh at her story. But I have to say this. "I'm glad you're here, obviously." I search her face. "But I need to make sure you're here because you want to be."

She sighs. "We both know I'm a little desperate. But I love Quinn. So...yeah, I want to be here."

Relief slides through me. "Okay, good."

"And it's only a few weeks. Right?"

"Right." She's never going to find a job and an apartment in a few weeks. "But you can stay as long as you need to," I say. "I don't want you to feel pressured to find something else. Find the right job. The right place."

She's silent for a few beats, then quietly says, "Thanks."

"So. We didn't talk money."

"Right." A look of discomfort passes over her face, then she squares her shoulders.

"The companies I was looking at were charging nearly a thousand dollars a week, which is for forty hours, but since you'll be here twenty-four seven, I'll pay you three thousand a week." I hesitate. "Is that enough?"

She gapes at me. "Jesus. Yes. That's too much, Nate. I won't be working twenty-four seven. I have to sleep."

"Oh. Right. Well, that's okay, I don't mind paying you to sleep."

She lets out a strangled laugh. "You don't have to do that."

"Look, I'm just relieved I have someone here. And it won't be just Quinn, I might need someone to bring me pain meds for the first few days."

"I...I..."

I wave a hand. "Deal. Obviously meals are included. You might have to shop for food. I guess we should talk about duties. You have experience at this. I don't."

"Okay, yes, it's good to be up front about expectations."

We go over things. I already have a cleaning lady, so I don't expect her to clean, but laundry would be helpful, maybe some cooking right after my surgery. "Or ordering takeout," I add. "I'm good with that too."

"I can handle that," she says dryly, holding up her phone. "What about discipline?"

I blink. "Oh. I'm not really into that kind of kink."

"What?" She frowns. "No! Not me! Quinn."

I bark out a laugh and swipe a hand across my forehead. "Right, right." Christ, I have a one-track mind with her. "Well, Quinn's pretty good. I'm a believer in consequences."

She nods. "No spanking."

"God no!" I stare in horror. "I'd never hit her."

"Good."

"The most trouble I have with her is at bedtime."

"Oh yeah." She smiles.

"I haven't been consistent about bedtime during the summer," I confess. "And she *hates* going to bed."

We talk a bit more about Quinn, then I move closer to Carly and murmur, "I'm glad you're here." I bend to brush a kiss over her soft mouth.

She steps aside. "Er, that's another thing we need to talk about."

I blink. "What?"

"Us." She waves a hand back and forth between us. "Now that I work for you, we can't...our relationship needs to be employer and employee. Nothing more."

My jaw slackens and I stare at her. What?

"You have a daughter," she adds in a rush. "And it just keeps things clear and simple."

"Right." I clear my throat. Thoughts bounce around in my head. I didn't think of this. *Why didn't I think of this?* Probably because I didn't want to. But she's right. I guess. No, she is. But...*damn*. "Well. This is just for a few weeks, though. Right?"

She bites her lip and fuck, that's so sexy, my groin tightens. I remember what her mouth feels like. Tastes like. "Right."

"So...after...when this..." I wave my hand like she did. "...business relationship is done, we can pick up where we left off."

Her eyes are big and shiny, her lips pouty. "Maybe?"

Shit.

"If we're both still interested," she adds, her voice sounding a little squeaky. She swallows.

"Well, *I'm* still interested," I say assertively.

"Let's just put that aside for now." She pushes her hair back and nibbles her lips again. "Just business."

Fuck. I press my lips together. Finally, I say, "Just business."

11

CARLY

Well, my new job starts right now. I'm picking Nate up at the clinic where he just had his arthroscopic surgery. Quinn and I spent the day together, going for a walk in the park, getting lunch at Queen of Tarts bakery, and now we're here.

Nate is woozy and a little pale, hopping on crutches, his knee bandaged beneath the hem of his shorts. Tucked beneath his arm is Shadow, Quinn's stuffed horse. She gave it to him so he wouldn't be afraid.

"Call us if you have any questions." The doctor's assistant hands me several pages of post op instructions and pain meds. "Pain medications were injected into his knee during the surgery. They'll wear off in about eight to twelve hours. He can take one of the pain pills then. And Dr. Perez will see him back here in two weeks. There's a card with date of the appointment in the envelope."

"Thank you." I give her a quick smile and help Nate out to the car. We maneuver him into the front seat and I zip around to the driver's side to get him home as quickly as possible.

"Does it hurt, Daddy?" Quinn asks from the back seat.

"Nah." He rubs his mouth. "I'm good. Just need to rest a bit."

I give him a sideways glance, then focus on New York traffic. It's been a long time since I drove here, and that was minimal. I manage to get us to his apartment without cracking up his BMW, thank God, and then get Nate into bed.

My heart squeezes, seeing this big, fit guy tense with pain, closing his eyes as he stretches out on his bed. I resist the urge to touch his forehead and smooth back his hair. I work for him.

Nate is prepared and I use the bolster he bought to elevate his leg. Then I hasten to the kitchen to get the ice packs. "Every two hours for twenty minutes," I tell him as I arrange the packs, ignoring the muscles of his legs and the dark hair dusting his skin.

"All righty," he mumbles.

Quinn climbs onto the bed to lay beside him. "This is for you, Daddy." She hands him a colorful folded paper.

"Careful, sweetie, don't jostle your dad's knee."

"I'll be careful." She eases closer. "I love you, Daddy."

Oh, my heart.

"What is this?" Nate asks, taking the paper and unfolding it.

"It's a get well card. Carly and I made it for you."

He reads her words, USE YOUR SUPERPOWERS AND GET WELL SOON, and studies the picture of Clover and Shadow she drew. His expression turns misty and he leans over to kiss her forehead. "Thank you, pop tart. I love it."

My heart expands even more.

I sit in the chair in the bedroom and study the information we were given. He could feel nauseous or even throw up. I gnaw on my bottom lip as I read. "Do you want anything to eat or drink?" I ask. "It says clear liquids are okay, and soup or Jell-o."

"We bought Jell-o," Quinn says. "Strawberry! I made it yesterday."

"Perfect. You're a great helper."

"Water," Nate says.

I fetch that and he has a drink, then sinks back into the pillows.

"Might sleep a little." He closes his eyes.

"Yeah. That's probably a good thing. I'll check on you in a bit. Quinn, do you want to stay here?"

"Yeah."

But it's not long before she joins me in the living room.

"Daddy's asleep," she says. "Can we watch TV?"

"Sure, let's do that."

I make dinner for Quinn and I. Nate doesn't want food, but he eats a little Jell-o mostly to please Quinn, I think. I keep checking on him, bringing ice packs and fresh water. I check the bandages on his leg. There's a little blood, but that's supposedly normal.

Quinn is a sweetheart about going to bed. I expect when she gets more comfortable with me she might make a fuss, but tonight she's great. Then I check on Nate again.

He's awake now and his jaw is tight as he shifts on the bed.

"Need the good pain meds?" I ask lightly.

"Fuck. I don't want to take that shit. People get addicted to it."

He's right. But he doesn't have to suffer. "We'll be careful," I say. "You can take Advil between these, and we'll gradually stretch out the time between the narcotics."

"Okay," he grudgingly agrees.

I get him a pill and a glass of water.

"I'm bored," he grumbles after swallowing it down.

I sit in the chair. "What do you want to do? Watch TV?" He has a big screen television on the wall and the remote is nearby.

"Eh. I don't know." He pauses. "I want a steak."

"Seriously?"

"No. Well, yeah, but no."

"I can get you some soup."

He agrees to that and even wants a few crackers with it.

Ten minutes later, he barfs it up.

He makes it to the bathroom on his crutches. My stomach hurts listening to him. Damn, I actually don't mind looking after people, it comes kind of naturally, but I don't like it when they're sick or hurting.

He hobbles back to bed and I help him get settled again.

"Well, so much for picking up where we left off," he mutters, eyes closed. "That was pretty sexy, huh?"

I laugh. This time I let myself smooth his damp hair back from his forehead.

He sighs.

The poor guy. My throat aches and I want to climb onto the bed like Quinn did and snuggle with him.

But I can't. He's my boss.

"Maybe you should take another pain pill," I say tentatively. "I think you might have lost it when you threw up."

"Ugh. Right. Okay."

We do that and he lies back again. "I think your friend likes me."

I lower my chin. "Gianna?"

"Yeah."

"Where did that come from?" I grin at the randomness.

"I don't know. Is she your best friend?"

"Yeah. We went to college together here. My childhood best friend still lives in Buffalo. I had a friend in Paris—Elise. She's going to come visit some time."

"Do you miss her?"

"Yes." I pause. "Who's your best friend?"

"Brando."

"Brando?"

The corners of his mouth lift, eyes still closed. "Brandon. Brandon Smith. We call him Brando."

"Ah. One of your teammates?"

"Yeah. He plays right wing."

"What position do you play?"

"You don't know? You googled me."

"Gianna googled you."

He opens one eye. "Really."

"Okay, I did google you. But I don't remember what position you play."

He heaves a sigh. "I'm crushed. I play defense."

"Ah."

"Brando has a girlfriend now. They're having a baby."

"That's…nice?"

"It is. It wasn't planned, but they're really happy. It's good. Quinn wasn't planned either, but she's the best thing that ever happened to me." A small notch pinches between his eyes, then he relaxes. "She's wonderful."

"She is." He's silent for a moment and I think he's fallen asleep when he asks, "What's one of your guilty pleasures?"

I give my head a small shake, smiling. "I don't think people should feel guilty about pleasure."

"Oh. That's a good answer. I *like* that. I like pleasure."

I know he does. My skin heats. "I do feel guilty sometimes about binge watching Real Housewives."

I love the smile that spreads across his face. "That, you *should* feel guilty about."

"Hey."

"Kidding. Whatever razzles your berries."

I crack up laughing. "Oh my God. The meds are making you so funny."

"This is my natural humor."

"Okay."

"I wish I didn't puke in front of you."

"Don't worry about it, big guy. Do you want some juice?"

"Yeah. Apple juice. With ice."

He guzzles that down and I take the empty glass. "I'll let you sleep."

He grabs my hand. "I don't want to sleep. I slept all day. Oh. You probably want to go to bed."

Gulp. He can't say things like that without me thinking about the last time I was in this room. With him. In bed. "No, I'm good. Do you want to ask me more random questions?"

"I do."

Shaking my head, I sit again. "Wait, tell me what *your* guilty pleasure is."

"Junk food. I love burgers and fries. During the season I try to eat healthy, so I feel guilty when I go to Shake Shack, but I love it."

"I love it, too."

"We'll go there. As soon as I can walk."

I smile.

"If you won the lottery, what would you do first?"

I tap my chin. "Hmmm. Since I'm currently homeless, I'd buy a home. Maybe a condo like this."

"You're not homeless. *This* is your home."

"This isn't *my* home. I'd like my own place. I've never had that."

"What? How can that be?"

"I lived in a dorm in college. Then I moved to France and lived with the Maddens. Now I'm here."

"Huh. Okay, I get it. A lot of guys on the team rent apartments because we never know if we'll be traded. But I wanted to own a place."

"It's probably been a good investment." I wrinkle my nose. "I guess getting traded is part of the pro sports life."

"Yeah. Some guys move around a lot. They call them 'rental players,' even. Brando's played with a bunch of different teams. But I've been here in New York my whole career. Well, I played a couple of seasons in Connecticut. For our farm team."

What would happen with Quinn if he got traded? That would be awful if he had to move away from her. Living the rich, famous pro athlete life seems so glamorous until something like that happens. Yikes.

"What would *you* do if you won the lottery?"

"Pay off my mortgage. Then take Quinn to Disneyland."

"Oh, come on. She hasn't been to Disneyland?"

"She's been to Disney World. She loves it. But I'd like to take her to Disneyland. I'd take her there every day. They're building a

Harmonia Park. Don't tell her; if she finds out we'll never hear the end of it."

She laughs. "Oh, she would love that! But you wouldn't quit playing hockey."

"Eh. I don't know. I've probably only got a few years left."

I tilt my head. "What will you do after that?"

"Good question. Ask me when I'm not on narcotics. Right now I want to be a pilot."

I choke on a laugh. "Because you're high."

He gives me a slightly loopy grin. "Good one."

We chat a little longer, then he does fall asleep. I turn off the lamp but leave the bathroom light on. Pausing at the door, I look back at him, stretched out on the beg, leg elevated, face relaxed.

This isn't what I expected to happen between us after our first date. Or second. And even though I'm uneasy about my ability to keep things strictly business when I'm still so attracted to him and I know how good he is with his hands and his mouth and…well, everything, I'm glad I'm here.

I check on him around three in the morning, peeking into his room. He's taken off his shirt and shorts and is lying in his boxers, still on his back, leg still elevated. But he's sleeping, so that's good. In the dim room, I take in his shape again, all that skin, the hair on his lower belly that trails down under the elastic band of his boxers that is so freakin' hot, the thickness of his thighs. Wait, I'm supposed to check his bandages. I move closer to peer at them. They look okay, so I back out and go back to my own room.

I hear him moving in the morning and I jump out of bed to see if he needs help. He's sitting on the bed, his bandaged leg straight out in front of him, still wearing just boxers.

"How are you doing?" I ask.

He looks up at me and I'm suddenly aware that I'm only wearing my nightie, a short cami style in black with ivory lace at the cups. His gaze moves over me. "Goddamn, I wish I wasn't nauseous and in pain."

"Oh no. Do you need more pain pills?"

"Yeah, I guess so." He rubs his face.

His water glass is empty so I refill it in. When I get back, Quinn is on his bed with him in her red Harmonia PJs. "Good morning," I say to her cheerfully. "You're here to help look after your dad already?"

"Yes." She sits cross-legged. "What do you need, Daddy?"

"These." He swallows the pills. "And I need one of those." He gestures to a bottle on the nightstand.

That's not one of the meds the doctor gave him, but I reach for it, shake one out, and hand it to him. He swallows it, too. Curiosity has me glancing at the small bottle as I set it back on the nightstand —Concerta. I don't recognize that name.

"Breakfast?" I ask. "How about you, Quinn?"

"I'm hungry." She slides off the bed.

"What do you feel up to?" I ask Nate. "Do you need to take a Gravol?"

"Nah. It's not that bad. Maybe some Jell-o."

"I can get you that!" Quinn bounces out of the room.

I follow Quinn and we get her a bowl of cereal which she eats on Nate's bed while he spoons strawberry Jell-o into his mouth.

"That was good," he says when done.

"You must feel better."

"A little. I need a shower."

"You can't get your bandage wet," I remind him.

"I know. I got some things they recommended. There's a plastic cover. It's in the bathroom."

"Okay." I fetch it, noting the chair in the shower. "Let's get this on you and then I'll help you shower."

Nate and I look at each other for a moment as heat shimmers around us in the room. He's sick and wounded and still there's this crazy chemistry between us. How am I going to help him shower without wanting to put my hands all over that hard body?

12

NATE

This sucks. I've got a hot babe living with me. She's going to help me shower. And even if I could get it up, which due to the pain and the vague feeling I'm going to barf again I sincerely doubt, I can't touch her because she works for me.

Be careful what you wish for, I guess.

And oh yeah, my daughter is here.

I like the feel of Carly's fingers brushing over my skin as she covers my bandaged knee. She focuses on her task, then lifts her head. "Okay. Hopefully that does it. You have a walk-in shower, so it shouldn't be too hard for you. But I'll stand by in case you need help." She hands me my crutches.

She starts the water for me then leaves, the door half open.

"Where are you going?" I call.

"I'll just wait out here!"

"I thought you were coming in the shower with me."

Silence.

Then, "Um. Do you need me to?"

"Kidding. I'm fine."

I'm not so sure of that, actually. I can't put any weight on this leg. And I can't bring the crutches in. I'm prepared with a shower chair, the bag, and a long-handled scrub brush. Sure I'd like her wet, soapy hands all over me, but it's kind of embarrassing to feel so weak and helpless. So I'm doing this on my own, even if it kills me.

I sit my bare ass on the plastic chair and shampoo and wash up. Standing on one foot, I grab the towel hanging next to the shower, rub my hair, drag it down my body, then wrap it around my hips before picking up my crutches to hobble out.

"I feel like a new man," I announce to Carly.

Her gaze tracks down my torso to the towel. She blinks away, her cheeks pinkening.

Cute.

"Good," she croaks.

I rub my chest where a water drop trickles down, then hop farther into my bedroom. At the dresser, I pull open a drawer and lift out a pair of boxers. I let the towel drop to the floor, giving Carly a back view. I hear a faint choking noise behind me and my lips kick up into a satisfied smile.

Then I try to put on the boxers. "This isn't going to work," I mutter. "I need to sit." I turn to the bed.

"Be careful," Carly says with what sounds like a moan.

I'm an evil shit because I like that.

"I will." I sit and pull on the shorts, then glance at Carly whose cheeks are even pinker as she gazes out the window. "You've seen it all before, hon."

She presses her pretty lips together and gives me a reproving look. "I know, but this is different."

I sigh and settle myself on the bed, shoving the bolster under my leg to keep it elevated. Weariness floods my body and I close my eyes. "Wow. That tired me out."

I hear a soft huff, then her hands are adjusting my pillows. "Do you need anything?"

"Not right now."

"I'll check on Quinn."

"Thanks."

She leaves me alone and quiet falls all around me. Faint voices float from the living room and I'm so damn grateful Carly's here to look after Quinn because I feel like a big helpless baby right now. I fucking hate it.

Later, I start my exercises, which are ridiculously simple but enough to keep some mobility—ankle pumps, straight leg raises, heel slides. I have to keep moving so I can do the more intense rehab sooner.

On day three after the surgery we change the bandages. Quinn is surprisingly squicked out by this, so Carly helps me. She inspects the small incision and the bandages with stoicism. "It looks pretty good," she says. "I think we can just put a couple of Band-Aids on now."

"Great. Let's do it. It feels good without all those bandages."

"Still pain, though?" She gently smooths the plastic strip on my skin.

"Yeah, but not too bad. I think after today I can stop the narcotics."

She glances at me. "Don't be a hero. If you need them, take them."

"We'll see." I don't want to take them more than I have to. Hopefully the Advil will be enough.

That night I hop out to the living room where we get my foot propped on the ottoman with some cushions, and we all watch a movie. Carly even makes popcorn for us, which makes Quinn happy and that makes me happy. When the movie's over, Carly gets Quinn into bed. I switch to a sports news show and watch some baseball.

Carly returns and perches on the arm of the couch.

"You're really trying to keep her to a bedtime routine," I say.

"Yes. That should help with the stalling. Maybe." She makes a face. "I guess I'll go to bed, too."

"It's early," I say. "We could watch another movie."

"Uh…"

"Oh. You probably want some down time. I get it." I'm a shitty patient but I'm trying to be a decent boss.

She smiles. "Do you want company?"

I have to be honest. "Yeah."

"Okay." She sinks into the corner of the couch.

"We can watch something more adult," I say enthusiastically. We run through a few choices and settle on a fairly new adventure movie neither of us has seen. Before it starts, she gets us drinks and cheese and crackers. "I've never enjoyed a piece of cheese this much." I pop another hunk into my mouth.

"Any problems with constipation?"

I close my eyes. "Jesus. As if I want to talk about that with you."

She laughs. "Sorry, but it's a side effect of the pain meds."

I sigh and rub my face. "And so sexy."

She rolls her eyes. "It's not like you're up for action right now anyway."

"I know, but come on...my fragile male ego is being wounded here."

"Actually, I'm impressed with your willingness to accept help, even from Quinn."

My head turns to look at her. "Yeah?"

"Yeah. In Western society, we expect men to be tough all the time."

I grimace.

"Stoic," she goes on. "Self-sufficient. Unemotional."

"Are you saying I'm not those things?"

She smiles. "No, I'm complimenting you on your courage to be vulnerable."

"It's not easy," I admit. "I feel like a weak baby. I hate it."

"I know." One corner of her mouth hooks up. "But I don't think your masculine identity is all that threatened. You know this is temporary. You know this doesn't really impact who you are as a man. Right?"

I think about it because it's a damn good question. "Yeah."

"That's good. Remember I said gender roles are socially constructed?"

"Right."

"So they can change. Men don't have to be all tough and closed up to be masculine." Her eyes soften. "I can't believe I'm telling a hockey player this stuff."

I nod slowly. "You know, there are a lot of um…masculine stereotypes in hockey."

Her eyes widen and she leans forward. "I bet there are."

"I feel like you want to conduct research on me now."

She laughs. "It's intriguing!" She taps her chin. "I bet there are links between perceived masculinity and violence in the sport."

"Ugh." I know only too well there are problems in the sport. I love hockey and I hate criticism of it, but it doesn't help to close your eyes to it.

"Is there a perception that more violence—I mean, tougher players—are better players?"

I have to think about that, too. "For sure. Especially in lower levels. But it's changing. There's a lot more emphasis on speed and skill now."

"Yeah?" She tilts her head. "This really is fascinating. I'm going to do more research."

"Great." I make a face. "We all love it when someone tells us to be more sensitive."

She laughs again, not taking offense. "That's not what I'm saying at all."

"You should talk to Hellsy, Millsy, and Morrie. They started this project to help men talk about mental health and their feelings."

"Really?" She straightens. "Wow, this is more and more interesting."

"I'll ask them about it. They love to talk about that shit."

She studies my face. "Really?"

"Sure. Once I'm a little more recovered." I pause. "You know, once Quinn fell when she was learning to skate and she started crying."

She waits, eyeing me with gentle focus.

"And my first instinct was to tell her to get up and stop crying." I tip my head back, remembering. "But she was scared and she hurt her arm and...it didn't seem right to just disregard how she was feeling."

Carly's eyes warm. "Yeah. Would you have done the same if you had a son?"

Her forthright question deserves an honest answer. "Probably not. But I would now."

A smile tugs her lips and I answer it with one of my own as we share an extended moment.

"That's great," she says softly.

"What did you say?"

I'm on the couch, my leg straight in front of me. I have my earbuds in and my phone rests on my chest. I think my ex-wife just told me she's moving to L.A. Like, two days from now. That can't be right. I'd think it's the narcotics, but I've been done with those for a few days now.

"It's an incredible opportunity, Nate. We talked about this."

I sigh. Yeah, we did. Years ago. Brielle's been making a name for herself on Broadway, and now she's been offered a role in a TV series. In Los Angeles.

Quinn. What about Quinn? My stomach jolts. "Are you taking Quinn to fucking L.A.?"

Thankfully, Quinn and Carly are out picking up groceries.

"No." Her voice is calm. "I want her to stay here with you. The school year's about to start. It's a great school, her friends are there. It would be better for her to stay here."

"Thank Christ." I blow out a breath. I don't see Quinn as much as

I'd like during the season, but if she was in L.A. I'd *never* see her. And I can't handle that. "But...Brielle...I'm on fucking *crutches*."

"I thought you hired a nanny."

"Yeah. But it's temporary."

"Well, make it permanent."

It's not that simple, but I'm not going to explain it to Brielle. I sigh.

"I know it's bad timing," she says. "I'm sorry. I can't do anything about that. And I can't say no to this offer." Her tone becomes pleading.

"Of course not." I shove a hand into my hair. We agreed when we got married, Brielle pregnant with Quinn, that I'd support our family while Quinn was small, but Brielle was clear that she intended to pursue acting and there might come a time where her career would have to take precedence.

That happy day is here.

I'll be on the injured list for...who knows...six weeks? My knee will get better, sure, and I'll be able to do more with Quinn. Until I start playing again. Then I'll really need a nanny—someone who can stay overnight with her.

Someone like Carly.

"I'm sorry! I want to do this."

I nod, the corners of my mouth slipping down. "I know. You have to do this." I'm happy for her. Our marriage ending wasn't fun, but we've stayed amicable for Quinn's sake, and over the years I've gotten over being butt hurt that she fell for someone else while married to me.

"Thank you. I think we should tell her together, okay?"

"Yeah. That's a good idea."

"I'll come by tomorrow."

"Sure." Christ. I scrub a hand over my face. "I won't say anything to her until then."

I end the call and stare up at the ceiling. Is Quinn going to be okay about this? She loves her mom. I've been careful to never, ever criticize Brielle in front of Quinn, and honestly Brielle's a good mother. Quinn is going to miss her like crazy.

Can I convince Carly to stay? Being a nanny isn't what she wants to do. She's so smart it's scary, with the research and writing she does. That's what she wants to do; not look after someone else's kid. Even though she's really good at it. Even though my kid worships her.

I think it through, going over things in my mind about how it would work. I guess I shouldn't tell Carly before we tell Quinn, but I need to talk to her about this.

Now.

13

CARLY

"Is your knee hurting?"

Nate scowls back at me. "No. Why?"

"You seem on edge."

His jaw sets. "Brielle called."

"Oh. Bad news?"

"Depends how you look at it." He forks his fingers into his hair and shoves it back, glancing toward the bathroom where Quinn is right now. We just got home from the store and I'm putting things away in the kitchen. "She's coming over tomorrow."

"Okay." I'm mystified about what's going on, but I guess it's not my business. "I'll go out while she's here."

"You don't have to do that."

I don't need to be a part of their discussion, whatever it is, so I'll either hide in my room or go for a walk. I'm not sure I even want to meet Brielle, so going out is the better choice.

I misjudge that though, and by the time I've put on a sweater, shoved my phone in my purse, and pulled on my boots, she's here.

Quinn lets her in with an excited squeal. "Mommy!"

I hesitate in the hall, watching them hug. Clearly they love each other. I get a little pang in my heart seeing Quinn with her mom.

Brielle straightens, her smile surprisingly teary. She's gorgeous—tall, slender, honey-blond and blue-eyed. "I miss you, honey," she says thickly. Then she looks up and sees me hovering.

Nate has hopped from the living room to the foyer. "Hey, Brie," he says. "This is Carly, our...nanny. Carly, this is Brielle, Quinn's mom."

I smile. "Hi, it's so nice to meet you."

Brielle looks me over, her face expressionless. "You too. I've been hearing so much about you from Quinn."

I don't blame her for assessing me. I'm taking care of her daughter. It has nothing to do with Nate, I'm sure. But then she glances at him with slightly narrowed eyes and I don't know what she's thinking.

Oh well.

"I'll be back in a while!" I say brightly, edging past Quinn and Brielle. I set a hand gently on Quinn's head.

"Don't rush," Brielle says. "I'll get Quinn to bed tonight."

"Come back when you want," Nate says firmly, sliding Brielle a look. "We're not kicking you out."

His words warm my chest. I meet his eyes and we both smile. "I know," I say softly. "See you later."

I'm having lunch with Gianna tomorrow, so I don't call her to meet up. I have my laptop so after I wander through Bloomingdales looking at clothes I can't afford, I head to a café and do more work on my resume.

Of course I can't help wondering why Brielle is there and what Nate was so upset about. It hasn't been three weeks yet, but he's a lot more independent now. In fact, he barely needs me now. Maybe that's why Brielle is there. Maybe they don't need me anymore. My stomach swoops.

Well...c'est la vie. Right?

I stare glumly at my resume. I don't even know whether to add this job. It's real employment, but more child care work experience doesn't help me in getting the kind of job I want. Except, I still don't even know what kind of job I want.

I open my manuscript and read through what I wrote yesterday. It's pretty good. I'm making progress on this. I get some writing done and then finally when I can't put it off much longer, I head back to Nate's apartment. I can sneak into my room and hang out there.

I can't sneak past Nate, though. He's sitting in the living room with the TV on, but he sits up and clicks it off as I walk in. "Hey."

"Hi. How was your visit?"

"Fucking awful." He pinches the bridge of his nose. "Can we talk?"

"Sure…" Yeah, he's definitely going to tell me I'm fired.

"In the kitchen." He gestures and we head in there, him on his crutches. He perches his fine butt on a stool, his jaw clenched, eyes pinched at the corners.

"What's going on?" I set my purse on the counter, concern for him rising inside me along with my anxiety about the job ending.

He takes a breath. "Here's the deal." He keeps his voice low. "Brielle has gotten a fantastic part in a new Netflix series."

I nod.

"In Los Angeles," he adds.

My eyes widen as implications hit me. I cover my mouth with both hands. "Is she…taking Quinn?"

"No." He gives his head a forceful shake. "She wants her to stay here. With me."

"Ohhhhh." I let out a breath. "That's good."

"Good for me. Sort of." He swallows. "Quinn's not so happy her mom is leaving."

"Oh no. Poor baby. Of course she's not." I rub my upper arms, my stomach knotting. I hate Quinn being sad.

"It's also not great timing," Nate adds. "I hope to be training soon. I doubt I'll pass the physical at training camp, but maybe I can be playing by the time the season starts."

"When is that?"

"Mid-October."

I bite my lip. "That might be pushing it."

He grimaces. "Maybe. Still, I'm going to be doing rehab and working out, and skating soon, then when I am playing, we're on the road a lot." He meets my eyes.

Heat prickles in my chest and then spreads through my body. "You're going to need a nanny."

"Yeah." He holds my gaze steadily. "You. I need you."

Okay, this isn't what I was expecting. Strangely, I feel relieved, even though I didn't want to take this job at first. But staying even longer...? "Nate..." I pull in a long breath. "I can't do that."

"You still don't have a job. Or an apartment."

"I know. But...I'm working on it."

"But you don't have to. I mean...if you were looking for your dream job, I'd never suggest you give that up, but the jobs you're looking at are all crap."

I wince. "They're honest, paid employment."

"I know, I know. Sorry. I don't mean to be demeaning. I guess being a nanny isn't much of a step above that, for you. I know you have goals with your writing. But think about it." He leans forward, his forehead creased earnestly. "Quinn's in school during the day. That could be your time to write. She'd need to be picked up from school—I can take her, once I get mobile again—and then she goes to some activities a couple of times a week. If I'm home, that's all there is to it. If I'm away, you'd need to take care of her at night and get her to school in the mornings."

"I don't know." I wrap my arms around myself and lean on the counter, my legs a little wobbly. My thoughts are jumbled. "I don't know."

"It's a lot, I get it. Think about it. Brielle's leaving tomorrow, but I won't be going for intense rehab and working out for a while yet. Okay?"

I look back at him and the warmth and imploring in his eyes has my heart fluttering.

I can't care. I already care too much about Quinn, and I especially can't let myself care about Nate. I know what happens when I leave my heart unguarded.

But I do care. Just a little. I hate that Quinn's unhappy. I hate that Nate's stressed and worried. But as much as I love helping people, I have to protect myself. I have my own goals and dreams and…it's too much right now.

"I'll think about it," I manage to choke out.

"Thanks." Nate stretches his hand out and lays it on my arm, giving me a gentle squeeze. The heat and strength seeps into my skin and an overwhelming desire to move into his arms for a hug, to feel that heat and strength everywhere, nearly takes me down. The longer I stay here, the more I have to fight the cravings I have to touch him. To be touched by him.

I jerk back. "I'm going to bed."

"Okay. Good night."

"Night, Nate."

I barrel down the hall to my room and shut the door, closing out Brielle's and Quinn's soft voices coming from Quinn's room. I hope she's okay.

I clutch my upper arms again. Why am I so disturbed by this? It's not that big a deal. I just need to settle down and think things through.

"I don't know, Carly." Gianna eyes me over her coffee cup in the little restaurant where we're having lunch. "It might be worth considering."

I glare at her. "I don't want to be a nanny my whole life!" Why do I feel like I'm being trapped into looking after people forever? And then losing them. I can't keep doing it.

"I know that. Nobody's saying it has to be forever."

"I only did this because it would be a few weeks. Because it would give me time to get my shit together."

"Get your shit together living at his place. That's going okay, isn't it?"

"Well. Um." I fiddle with a fork. "It's going okay, yeah."

"What's the problem? If he's a bad man, just say so and we'll get you out of there, somehow."

I let out a dry laugh. "He's not a bad man. He's a very good man, I think. I really like him." I glance at her up through my eyelashes. "And I'm really attracted to him."

"I know that."

"But...we agreed that while I was working for him, we wouldn't go there. It's a business relationship now. And it would be awkward with his daughter there."

"Well, shit. But yeah...that makes sense. So you thought that after you're done working for him, you two would spend a week in bed together."

"Ha. Something like that." I flash a taut smile. "It's a little uncomfortable at times because there's this crazy chemistry between us and I just want to jump him, and I get the feeling he'd jump me if he wasn't on crutches, and we're both resisting it because we agreed, but..." I sigh. "If I stay working for him, it solves my housing and job problem. Yes, I don't want to spend my life as a nanny, but on the other hand I'm not thrilled about answering phones for a cleaning service or working in a grocery warehouse."

"So if you have to do something temporarily, you might as well be a nanny."

My mouth twists into a wry smile. "I suppose."

"You could keep looking for something else while you're working for him."

"Yes."

"Except you still don't know what you really want to do."

"Actually...I sort of do."

Her eyes widen. "What? Go back to college?"

"No. I want to write."

"Your blog?"

"And articles. I pitched another idea and sold it. And I've been working on a book." I've only ever shared this with Nate and I'm reluctant to tell Gianna. I don't know why; I don't think she'll mock me for it. It just seems so personal.

"Oh wow! That's awesome! What kind of book?"

"It's non-fiction. I had this idea about masculinity and the anxiety and pressure men feel to meet societal expectations. I started working on it in France, actually. And I got even more excited about it when Nate and I were talking about hockey players and masculinity, and he mentioned his teammates who started this initiative to get men to open up more about their feelings. I've already outlined the whole thing and written eight chapters."

She gapes at me. "That's amazing, Carly. Do it!"

I shrug. "I don't know if it'll ever be published. And I don't know if I can make enough money writing articles. But I want to do it."

"I think your blog and your articles give you a good platform for publishing a book. And you're a good writer."

"Thank you." I smile, touched by her words. "Anyway, Nate pointed out that during the day when Quinn's at school, I could write."

"Oh yeah! Even more perfect! Come on, Carly—this is a no brainer."

"You think?"

"I do."

"I'm afraid," I blurt out.

"What are you afraid of?" she asks softly.

"I'm afraid of how much it will hurt when things end. When the job ends. Like it did with the Maddens. And like it did with my sister and Ayla." My voice catches.

"Ohhhh. Oh, hon. I'm sorry." She reaches across the table and squeezes my hand. "I understand that."

"I already feel like I'm getting too close to them. To Quinn, I mean," I add quickly. "Last night I *hated* that she was upset because her mom's leaving. I was mad at Brielle for doing that to her daughter, but that's ridiculous. She has a career that's important to her. And if she took Quinn with her, Nate would be devastated." I bite my lip. "Divorce is no fun."

"Nope."

"And Nate and Brielle get along fine. Still, with a child involved…ugh. Anyway, that's why I'm hesitating."

"Also there is that little problem of you and Nate wanting to ride the bony express."

I choke on a laugh. "Yes. But we can handle that. We've done it this long." And the frustration over it is starting to make me bitter.

She props her chin in her hand. "I admire you both for keeping things professional, and I think he's a great dad to care about his daughter. On the other hand, parents have sex all the time."

I tilt my head. "What are you saying?"

"Where there's a will, there's a way."

"Uh…"

She laughs. "You get it."

"I don't think it's a good idea."

"It's just scratching an itch, right? You both want it. Blow off some steam. Or blow him."

"Haha." *I'd love to.*

"Just be discreet."

I tap my fingers on the wooden table.

"Okay, okay. Never mind. You're right. Sleeping with your boss definitely complicates things."

"Oh hell yeah. We are definitely not going there as long as I take the job." I rub at the feeling of heaviness in my chest. Nate's a special guy and the more I get to know him, the more I like him, and the more I want him, and…oh well. Sometimes we have to make grown up sacrifices. No riding the bony express. "Thanks for talking me through it. You made some good points."

"We have to call Mommy."

I gaze at Quinn the next morning. She's nearly in tears.

"I don't think we can," Nate says. "She's on a plane right now."

"I need to talk to her!" Quinn's voice rises.

"Okay, we'll call her and leave a message," Nate says calmly. "Then she'll call you back when she can."

"But I need to talk to her! What if she's dead?"

Oh my God.

Nate and I exchange a look. "She's not dead, pop tart," he says gently. "She's fine."

"We don't know that." Tears have started flowing.

Oh boy. Crying kids are a weakness of mine. I want to cry, too, seeing Quinn upset like this.

"Can I have a hug?" I ask softly, moving to her. "I need a hug."

Quinn allows me to pull her into my arms, burying her face against me. I stroke her hair and meet Nate's eyes. His face is tight with concern. "I need Mommy," she sobs.

"I know you do. Of course you do. She's your mom. She loves you so much. I know she does, and I know she's sad she had to leave." Quinn sobs quietly for a few minutes, but quiets as I continue to reassure her. "And your dad is here and he loves you, too. And I'm here for you right now. We care about you, too."

Finally she pulls back and wipes her face. After a final hiccup that hurts my heart she says, "I'm scared."

"Are you?" I sit at her eye level. "What are you scared of?"

"I'm scared she won't come back."

"She will." I smooth her hair again. "She will."

Quinn is supposed to go over to her friend Jada's place to play, but she refuses to go, saying her tummy doesn't feel well.

"Oh man," Nate says, when we have a moment alone. "What is up with this?"

"She's scared," I say, which he knows because Quinn already said that. "This is hard for her. Just when she's supposed to be going back to live with her mom and go back to school, this happens."

"It's not like I'm a stranger," he mutters, running a hand through his hair. "She's never done this before."

"She sees Brielle over the summers though. And she knows she's there."

"Fuck." The corners of his mouth turn down. "I'm pissed at Brielle, but I know this isn't her fault."

"Yeah." I totally get that. "We just have to keep reassuring her. One of the kids I looked after in France had a lot of anxiety, so I learned some things."

"Like what?"

I think back. "We tried to teach her to reframe her thoughts. Not in those words, just getting her to think about her fears and talk back to them."

He eyes me skeptically.

"There was a book we read to Henry," I say. "Maybe I can get it from the library."

"Buy it," he says. "Whatever you need."

I nod, making a note to go online and check where I can get it. "And I can work on relaxation techniques with her."

"She's a little kid."

I smile. "Kids get anxious."

"Jesus." He blows out a breath. "Okay. What can I do?"

"Be there for her and show her you love her." I pause, then add, "Which you always do."

One corner of his lips hoists up. "Thanks."

"She'll get through it."

He goes to Quinn's room to check on her and I open my laptop to do a search for the book I remember. I find they have it at The Strand at Columbus Avenue, but when I try to convince Quinn to go for a walk there, she doesn't want to leave her dad.

"But I can't walk all the way there," he reminds her.

"We can drive." She folds her arms.

"We can," I agree, sliding Nate a look.

"Okay, we'll all go." He looks unenthusiastic.

I drop them off in front of the store and drive around to find parking. My chest feels tight and uncomfortable. Poor Quinn. Of course she misses her mother. I don't like seeing her so upset—it's breaking my heart. I'd do anything to make her feel better. The book might help, and teaching her some ways to reframe her thoughts, and...

And crap.

I park the car and sit there for a moment, hands still curled around the steering wheel. She's already so upset by her mother leaving—how can I leave, too? I take a deep breath and climb out of the car.

I find Quinn and Nate in the children's section of the bookstore. Nate is sitting on a small chair looking ridiculous and bored but also hot, while Quinn flips through a book on a table. I find the book we want and Nate tells Quinn to pick out whatever she wants. I totally get the need to spoil her right now.

I look around the store longingly. I love bookstores. What would it be like to have my book here in this store? The idea fills me with excitement but also anxiety. I have to write the book before it can be in a store. I don't even know if I can do it.

I'd love to browse through all the offerings but Nate's giving off impatient vibes and I feel like we need to get out of here. Out on the street, Nate spots a restaurant. "Let's go have a snack."

It's a casual place with a few tables outside on the sidewalk so we sit there to enjoy the late summer weather. The food is Southern style, so we share some starters including fried pickles, biscuits and gravy, and street corn.

Quinn is quiet and doesn't eat a lot, so Nate and I chat about the bookstore and back to school and...after a while, a squeezing feeling in my chest, I meet Nate's eyes across the small table and say, "I'll stay."

14

NATE

Training camp starts next week on Thursday, and Monday is the first day of school for Quinn. I drive out to the practice facility to work out. Brando's going to be there, and a bunch of other guys. They'll be skating too, which I can't yet, but I can do my rehab exercises and upper body workout. The excitement of training camp still gets me revved and motivated.

"Holy shit," Brando says when I pick up some weights. "Look at your biceps."

I glance down at my right arm, then my left. "What?"

"They're swole," he says. "Also your delts. Jesus, man, you're ripped."

"Heh." I lift the weights and flex. "I've always been ripped."

He snorts. "Not like this."

"Well, I had to work out somehow after the surgery."

"How's rehab going?"

"Good. We've been working on strengthening my quads and hammies. The exercises are getting tougher, but I like that. Still hoping I can skate before the season starts." I do another couple of reps. "I won't pass the physical next week." I say that even though

I'm still holding out a tiny, faint hope that I might. I'm willing to work hard, endure pain, do whatever it takes to get back on the ice and back on the team. But I know that's not realistic, for next week anyway. "But I still have time before the season starts."

"Yeah."

"So…Brielle moved to Los Angeles."

"What? Seriously?"

"Yeah." I tell him about her job offer. "Too good to pass up."

"What about Quinn?"

"She's staying here. For school, and her friends."

"Wow."

"She's kind of having a hard time with it, though." I sigh. "She misses her mom. She's been super clingy since Brielle left. And she's been complaining about headaches and stomach aches. She doesn't seem like she's sick, but that always stresses me out. And she's not excited about going back to school, which she was last year. It worries me."

"Ah. That sucks. I have no parental advice to offer."

"Not yet." I smirk briefly. "Brielle's always handled the back-to-school stuff. Usually at this time of year, I'm skating and getting ready for training camp. But Carly's taken Quinn shopping for new clothes and school supplies."

"That's good."

"Yeah. Carly's really patient with Quinn's nervousness."

"Thank God she's still there."

"Yeah, no shit. She agreed to stay longer. It was only supposed to be a few weeks until I got mobile after the surgery." I frown. "The bad part is we can't get busy while she's working for me."

He frowns too. "Why not?"

"Her rule." I shrug. "I get it. It would complicate things. Plus I have to think of Quinn. But fuck, it's making my balls blue as Uranus."

His mouth drops open. "My anus is not blue."

I crack up and drop the weights, nearly falling to the matt laughing. "Jesus! I didn't say 'your anus.' I said Uranus. The planet. It's blue. Like my fucking balls."

"Shit." He shakes his head. "You're telling me you're not banging your live-in nanny who's hot as fuck?"

"Nope." I pick up the weights again. "Sadly."

"That *is* sad."

"But she's really good with Quinn. She knows how to deal with Quinn's stress." I tell him about the book and some of the things she's working on with my little girl.

"It's good Quinn has her," Brando says thoughtfully. "You're really lucky."

"Yeah." I pause. "I really am. Other than the blue balls part." I sigh as I put the weights away and grab a resistance band. I lay down on the matt and hook it around my thighs.

"You coming to the party at Barbie and Nadia's tomorrow night?"

"Yeah." They're having a party to celebrate the start of the new season. "I wish I could bring Carly."

"So bring her."

"Then who'll look after my kid?"

"Oh. Right."

"That's why she's with us," I say glumly. "But I'd like her to meet you guys."

"I wanna meet her. The woman who's got your testicles hurting."

"She's my nanny but it feels wrong to go to a party without her. It's weird. Oh hey." I spot Millsy across the room. "Millsy! C'mere."

He saunters over. "Whattup?"

"Carly's writing a book. About men."

He lifts an eyebrow. "Okay."

"Not just men. It's about…" I pause to think. "It's about the pressure men feel to meet societal expectations."

"Huh. I didn't know she's a writer."

"This is the first book she's written. She's really into it. I thought maybe you could talk to her—you and Hellsy and Morrie. You could tell her about your campaign."

He nods, lips pursed. "Yeah. I guess."

"She'd be thrilled," I say hopefully.

He and Brando exchange looks.

Brando grins. "He's catching feelings for his nanny."

A slow smile stretches Millsy's mouth. "I see that. Interesting."

I frown. "What's interesting about it?"

"You've been happily single for a long time," Brando points out. "I wanna meet her."

I start some clams, lying on my side, working my hip abductors. "Whatever."

They both laugh.

"Speaking of blue balls," Brando says.

Millsy's eyebrows shoot up. "What?"

Brando waves at me. "He's hot for the nanny, but she won't bang him while she works for him. Anyway, maybe she has pink pelvis."

Millsy and I stare at him. "What the hell is that?"

"Pink pelvis. It's the female equivalent of blue balls. When she's not getting any action she gets...discomfort in the pelvic region."

"Who has blue balls?" Axe overhears us.

"Nate," Brando informs him.

"There's a solution to that, you know," Axe says with a grin. He makes a crude whacking off gesture.

I shake my head. "Believe me, I've been doing that."

"Let's see your hands," Axe says. "Do you have hair on your palms?"

Everyone bursts out laughing. "That's a fucking myth," I say mildly.

"She's probably doing it too," Brando says. "For the pink pelvis."

Oh Christ. He had to talk about Carly masturbating. I can picture her in her bed, hand between her legs... I push that image away.

"If you're spanking the monkey on the reg and you still have blue balls you should see a doctor," Brando says.

"Look, the blue balls was an expression, okay? My balls aren't literally blue. Unlike your anus." I snicker.

He throws a towel at me.

"Holy shit." I gape at my phone the next morning.

"Nate." Carly gives me a chiding look.

Oh right. I'm trying not to swear in front of Quinn. I grimace, glancing at Quinn at the dining table. She's been doing really well with the not swearing. The lure of Harmonia merch is powerful.

"What's wrong?" Carly asks.

"The team is going bankrupt."

"Whaaaat?" Her mouth drops open. "What team? Your team?"

"Yeah. The Bears." I'm reading a news article. "'Citing losses of $42 million over the last two seasons and an inability to negotiate a more favorable lease at the Apex Center, owner of the New York Bears Vince D'Agostino has filed for reorganization under Chapter 11 of the Federal Bankruptcy Code.'"

"Whoa. What does that mean?" She bites her lip, her forehead creased.

"I'm not sure." I read on, aloud. "'This will have absolutely no effect on Bears games, on our payroll, on the club's playing schedule, or any of our hockey operations,' D'Agostino said in a statement. 'The team, our season-ticket holders and our corporate sponsors will be protected during this reorganization.'"

"Okaaaaay."

"'This is no doubt disappointing,' NHL commissioner Thomas Yang said. 'But the team ownership has committed to work to resolve their financial issues and we are optimistic that the franchise will be financially and competitively successful in New York. There are rumors that former team star Johnny Risley is planning to sue the team over deferred payments still owed to him, but this has not been confirmed at this time.'" I lower my phone. "Wow. He's going to sue the team? Jee…Jeez."

"I don't know who that is."

"He retired a few years ago. He was a great player. This is nuts." I shake my head. "I'll talk to the others at the party tonight."

"Yeah. Maybe they know more."

"Nobody's said anything, so I doubt it."

Now I'm distracted with new worries about the team. Even though they say nothing will change, I assume Mr. D'Agostino is trying to find a buyer for the team, and that definitely means changes. It's good that I'll get to talk to my buddies about it at the party tonight.

"Hey, did you guys see this?" I walk into the party, holding up my phone.

"What?" Barbie asks.

"This article on the Hockey Times. About the Bears."

"What does it say?" Brandon asks.

I read the article from my phone, like I did with Carly.

"Holy shit." Brando says.

"What the hell," Cookie mutters. He turns to his girlfriend, Emerie. She bites her lip.

The owner of the Bears is her stepfather.

"Did you know about this?" Owen asks her.

She shakes her head slowly. "No."

"What else does it say?" Brando asks.

I read more. "'This will have absolutely no effect on Bears games, on our payroll, on the club's playing schedule, or any of our hockey operations.'"

"Huh." Brando frowns.

"Risley's suing them?" Hellsy says. "Wow."

"Planning to sue them," Brando corrects. "But yeah, wow."

"So…he says it doesn't change anything," I reiterate.

"We still get paid," Barbie jokes. "I hope."

"Hell, yeah." Morrie nods.

"Hopefully they can work things out," Brando says. "It sucks that we had to hear like this."

"True. Maybe they'll call a meeting tomorrow."

"We should buy the team," Millsy says with a grin. He looks at Hellsy and Morrie. "Remember, we talked about that?"

"Ha. I remember talking about the fact that we don't have enough money to do that."

"Maybe we can get a good deal if Mr. D'Agostino is having cash flow problems," Morrie adds.

"I wonder if he *will* sell it," Brando muses. "A change in ownership might shake things up."

"And trade your ass away," I joke.

"I'm not getting traded," Brando says. "Not this time."

I smile. I'm glad he wants to stay. He's moved around a lot and finding a woman and having a baby seems to have helped him settle down and figure things out.

"Okay," I say to Quinn the next morning. "You haven't said a swear word since we made our deal, so today we're going to that store to buy Harmonia school supplies."

"Yay!" Quinn jumps up and down, clapping her hands. She does a twirl. "I'm happy, Daddy!"

"Good."

"But…" She bites her lip and leans closer. "Sometimes I say the bad words inside my head."

I roll my lips in on a smile. "That's okay. It's fine to say them inside your head, just not out loud when they could offend people."

She nods seriously. "Okay."

It turns out Carly loves stationery too, so we all make the trek to the store. It's not my kind of thing, but I wander around and look at fancy papers and cards and gifts while they pick out notebooks and pencils and stickers. Carly finds a journal that makes her so happy she presses it to her heart. I don't get it, but seeing her joy makes me happy, too.

Then I spot a package of pens. There are four—silver, gold, rose, and black—and the shape of the top is a little bow. I glance over at Carly on the other side of the store, wearing a black bow in her hair, then pick them up and hide them among the things Quinn has selected.

Talking to Brando the other day, it really hit home how lucky I am to have Carly here. She's amazing, in so many ways. I'd like to show her my appreciation in very dirty ways, but since I can't, I can do this.

I let Quinn pay for her journal first, then I take care of Quinn's things, the pens tucked into the bag.

"I think we conquered the swearing," I say to her in a low voice as we meet up outside the store.

She gives me a puckered smile. "I'm not so sure. But she clearly can do it if she's motivated."

"Do I have to bribe her for the rest of her life?"

"Possibly."

I groan. "I imagine the rewards getting more and more expensive."

"You'll be buying her a car when she's twelve."

I burst out laughing.

When we get home, I remove the pens from Quinn's bag and she scurries off to her room to admire her purchases.

"Here." I hold out the package to Carly.

She drops her gaze. "What's this?"

"For you. I saw them and I know you like bows and…"

She lifts her eyes to mine, hers round and shiny. "Thank you, Nate."

I shrug. "It's just a little thing."

She holds the package to her chest. "I love them. I didn't see these! If I had, I would have bought them." She pauses. "Thank you so much."

15

NATE

Monday morning Carly curls Quinn's long blond hair into the "beachy waves" for the first day of school, and that makes Quinn happy for a while. In her new outfit, hair done, and with her Harmonia backpack, she looks so grown up. My stomach is knotted, wondering how this is going to go. If she cries and refuses to leave me, I'll probably cry too. That'll really impress Carly.

Yeah, I care what she thinks of me. Even though I'm pretty sure if I did break down in tears, she wouldn't think less of me. She's amazing like that.

Carly suggested I talk to Quinn's teacher ahead of school starting, to let her know Quinn's been having some anxiety issues about her mom being away. I don't know why I didn't think of it, and the teacher was understanding and supportive. That makes me feel a little better about her being on her own all day.

"I want to wear my cape and mask to school," Quinn says.

I meet Carly's eyes. She gives a tiny shrug.

"It's the first day of school," I say. "Don't you want to show off your new outfit?"

"No. I need my cape and mask."

It's not that big a deal and I'm not going to make it one, so I say, "Okay."

"There's Jada," Carly points out when we get to school.

Quinn hesitates. She turns her big blue eyes up to me. I crouch down and gaze steadily into her eyes. "I'll be here to pick you up," I tell her. "Carly and I. Okay?"

She nods, clearly uncertain, but then she glances at her friends again. "Okay. Wait." She takes off her sparkly mask and cape and hands them to me. "Bye, Daddy."

I give her a hug and a smooch and she dashes off.

I watch her, an achy fullness in my chest. God, I love her so much. I think my chest might burst with the love I have for her. This has been so hard. "Maybe I should stay with her at school today. I could do that—"

"No." Carly takes my arm and starts leading me back toward the car. "That would not be good."

I sigh. "I know. I'm glad that went okay."

"Yeah. Could have been way worse, like one of my kids in France."

"*Your* kids?" I'm teasing but the droop of her lips is sad.

"Okay, they weren't *my* kids."

"You cared a lot about them."

"Yeah." She keeps her eyes focused on the car in front of us as she drives us home.

"It must have been hard to leave them."

"I didn't leave them. It wasn't my choice. They left me."

"Right." She told me that the family had moved and didn't need a nanny anymore. "I'm sorry."

She lifts a shoulder. "No need to be sorry. It was disappointing, sure, but like you said, they weren't my kids."

She's not being entirely honest, I can tell. She loved those kids. I try to divert the conversation a bit. "I appreciate how good you are with Quinn. And I appreciate you staying."

"I don't know how long it will be." She sinks her teeth into her lush bottom lip.

A sharp stick pokes at my chest. "You'll give me notice if you're going to leave?"

"Of course."

"I can keep looking for someone else. But Quinn really likes you. And..." *I really like you.* I cough. We're supposed to be hands off. Employer and employee. That was fine when it was going to be a matter of weeks. But now... "I think we need to revisit one part of our agreement."

"What part?"

"The part that keeps our relationship strictly business."

Her hands flex on the steering wheel. "No. We can't change that."

"Shit." I rub my mouth. I'm more and more attracted to her, and it's not just physical. Knowing her better, seeing her every day, watching her with my daughter has gotten inside me and deepened the attraction. She's not just beautiful. She's super smart, funny, and caring. She's always calm and capable. Always optimistic. She's a rock. I want her in my life. And not just as a nanny.

"We can't complicate things," she adds in a taut voice.

She's right. But I *want* to complicate things. This is what I wanted—to meet a woman who's not just interested in me as a professional athlete, someone who genuinely likes me, someone who's real, someone who cares unconditionally. Someone I can trust.

I've been kind of cynical about relationships for a long time. I think I used sex to fill a need for connection. But sex isn't true connection without trust and honesty and intimacy, and that's why I got tired of all that. I feel like I have those things with Carly even without sex. Well, we did have sex. And it was fucking phenomenal and I can't stop thinking about it and imagining her in my bed again, planning all the dirty things I want to do to her, for her, to make her feel good.

How the fuck am I supposed to live without that?

Obviously, I can't force her. And she seems pretty resolved about this.

Shit.

Now we're going to be alone in the apartment all day while Quinn's at school. What if I can't resist her?

Of course I can resist her. I've never forced myself on a woman and I don't ever intend to. I'd never do anything that would scare or hurt Carly.

It just seems so damn unfair that I've met the perfect woman and I can't have her.

Luckily, today's the day the guys are coming over to meet Carly and talk about their initiative to raise awareness of men's mental health. I can't wait for her to impress them with that big brain of hers.

"Before they get here, I should tell you why they started the Play Well initiative."

Carly gazes back at me. "Okay."

"Hellsy, Morrie, and Millsy all played junior hockey together in Canada. In Swift Current. One day they were on their way to a game in another town. The roads were really bad and a semi T-boned their bus on the highway."

"Oh, no."

"It was bad. I remember hearing about it. Fourteen people died in the crash."

"Oh my God." She covers her mouth with her hands, her eyes big.

"Obviously, they survived, but Millsy's dad and brother were killed. Hellsy was hurt pretty bad and had to take a year off hockey. All of them got kind of messed up from it."

"No doubt. That's tragic."

"They were friends then, but after the crash they didn't talk for a long time, and then they ended up playing on the same team. The Bears. That sort of forced them to deal with some shit. And that's when they figured it would be good for them to talk to other guys about mental health."

"I really admire that," she says slowly. "I'm glad I know. Thanks for telling me."

The guys arrive together, and of course, we have to talk about the team bankruptcy first.

"Haven't heard anything more," Millsy says when they arrive.

"Me either." Morrie shrugs.

"We're having a team meeting before training camp and Mr. Julian is going to talk about it," Hellsy says. "Maybe we'll find out more then."

"Who do you think would buy the team?" I ask.

They all lift their shoulders.

"I thought we are," Millsy jokes.

"We can't own the team we play for," Morrie says.

"Why not?"

He frowns. "How can you be your own boss?"

"It's called self-employment," I say dryly.

"Oh. Right. It just seems weird."

"It does," I admit. "You're not serious, though, right?"

"Nah. Even together we don't have that kind of money."

"Not many people do," I reply.

Carly appears, smiling. She's wearing the loose, ripped jeans and fitted black tank top she wore earlier to school, her bronze hair in its usual long waves sliding over her shoulders. "Hi."

"Guys, this is Carly Corrigan."

"The nanny," Morrie says with a smile.

"That's me." She extends a hand to each of them as I introduce them, then takes a seat in a chair. "I've heard great things about you guys."

"Of course you have," Hellsy says. "Because we're great."

She laughs. "Of course."

"Tell us about your book," Morrie says.

"Okay." She nibbles her bottom lip. "My working title is 'Be a

Man.' It's about our ideas about masculinity and what it means to be a man in today's world."

Hellsy's eyes light up. "Oh hey. That's cool."

"That's why I got you guys here," I say. "You probably have stuff to say about that."

"Maybe." Morrie nods.

"I told her about Play Well." I say. "It's been good, talking about emotions. Sometimes I don't even know what I'm feeling, never mind be able to talk about it."

"Sometimes people don't know because it's a mix of different feelings," Hellsy says. "And sometimes traumatic events can make you shut down and avoid feeling anything. I learned that in my counseling. Also some people don't let themselves feel certain things maybe because of stuff that happened in their childhood."

Carly nods. "I get that."

The crease between her eyebrows tells me she's thinking about something, and I want to know what it is, but I don't press her.

"I'm fascinated by the fact that you play such a tough sport," Carly says. "Nate and I were talking about masculinity and stereotypes in the sport."

"Yeah." Morrie nods thoughtfully. "It's a physically aggressive sport. Wow, we could talk for hours about this."

We talk about how young hockey players try to be masculine, according to society's expectations and how that often means homophobia, or fears of being seen as feminine, and how these things get perpetuated. We've all had experiences, which I rarely talk about, but these three teammates make it feel safe to share stuff like the creepy coach I had in midget hockey, like the time one of my teammates started crying and everyone laughed at him, like the cruel hazing that happens.

"And then…" Carly hesitates. "Do these expectations carry over into life away from hockey? Like…the subordination of women? Sexual assault? Violence against women?"

"Wow, you're really going there," Morrie comments.

"Sorry," she says. "Too much?"

"No, this is important shit." The guys all exchange looks. "There's no doubt that sexual assault and violence against women happens. That's not exactly what we've been focusing on, but..."

"But guys who are able to acknowledge their emotions and who don't have to demonstrate hypermasculinity may not be as likely to abuse women," I say.

They all look at me.

"What? I know stuff."

The guys laugh, and Carly smiles thoughtfully. "You definitely do," she says. "It's funny you mention hypermasculinity. Do you guys see the danger of your sport as exciting?"

I tip my head, "I definitely do, but I've always been that way. Anything physical or risky is exciting to me. I made my mom gray before she was thirty with all the stupid shit I got into. Riding on the handlebars of my brother's bike going down a hill. Throwing a hammer on the trampoline while we were jumping and trying to dodge it."

Carly gasps.

"I know, I know. We're lucky we're alive. Then there was the time I got busted for drag racing." I make a face. "I love going fast."

"How about you guys?" She turns to the others.

"Not so much for me," Morrie says.

"Me either," Hellsy says.

Millsy smirks. "I have to admit a little danger spices things up."

"We don't want to hear about your sex life," I say, earning more laughs.

"Do you see violence as manly?" Carly asks us.

Again, I give her question consideration, then shake my head. "No."

"Seriously?" Millsy asks. "No?"

"Violence isn't manly," I reply. "Off the ice? Definitely not. You don't have to be violent to solve problems or whatever. On the ice, too. Yeah, the game is physical, but violence implies there's an intent to hurt someone. I don't want to hurt people. Shit, look what we all went through last year because of Cookie's hit on Brent Schneider."

"Yeah, I agree," Hellsy says. "We don't *want* to hurt people."

"Okay, yeah, when you put it that way," Millsy says slowly.

"And what about sex?" Carly asks.

"I like it," I say.

She bursts out laughing and the guys grin, all adding their agreement.

My eyes meet Carly's and there's a flash of something between us—heat. Awareness. *I like sex with you.*

Her eyelashes flutter and she refocuses. "I mean, attitudes about sex and women. Are women there for your pleasure? To use for sex?"

The other three shake their heads. I try not to look guilty and stay quiet. I may have used women for sex, but it was always consensual. I'm uncomfortable about that right now, though.

"Sex has to be consensual," Hellsy says seriously, echoing my thoughts. "For me, anyway. I know shit has happened...our junior hockey career got messed up because of the bus crash..."

Carly nods sympathetically. "I heard."

"But we heard stories about gang bangs and puck bunnies," he continues. "It happens."

"And what's even worse," Morrie adds. "Is that it gets covered up. That kind of thing should be totally unacceptable."

"Is that the culture?" she asks.

"Yeah. Hockey's a team sport," Hellsy adds. "Which is great. But when teammates cover up for each other, that's not healthy. When the team or even the league cover it up, it's even worse. It just sends the message that kind of thing is okay, just don't get caught."

"Is there locker room talk?"

"Yeah." Millsy makes a face. "Sure. Stuff happens in the dressing room, talking about girls, parties, who you're hooking up with. And that stays in there for the most part. But sometimes it doesn't."

"That raises the question—what happens if one of the players is gay? Does talking about hooking up with women make him uncomfortable?"

Millsy closes his eyes. "Yeah. Likely."

"Point taken," I say to Carly. "Even when we keep it in the room, that kind of talk can be harmful."

She smiles at me. "Are you guys the norm?" she asks curiously.

"Jesus, I hope so," Morrie jokes. "But being totally honest, I think we know who the guys are that have that wrong kind of attitude."

"We're older, too," Millsy says. "It's tough for young guys who don't have the life experience and confidence to stand up to the peer pressure. They think they need to bang every puck bunny hanging around the arena."

"I'm fascinated by the reasons this exists," Carly says, looking thoughtful. "The bro code, the focus on winning, the lack of accountability."

"Well, a 'bro code'..." I make air quotes, "...is intended to bring guys together. Which you want on a team. But if the moral code is... well, amoral, then it's not a positive influence."

"It's toxic," Carly murmurs.

"Yeah," Hellsy says. "I knew a guy—he was a few years older than me—he got caught sharing nude pictures of a girl. It got covered up. And he still got drafted. He's still playing. He probably never learned anything from that."

"I appreciate your honesty," Carly says.

We keep talking until I realize it's almost time to go pick up Quinn. "We gotta bounce, guys," I say. "Thanks for coming over."

"I really appreciate your perspectives," Carly says warmly.

When they're gone, she smiles at me. "Thank you so much for inviting them. That was super interesting. Also, I really like your friends."

I like that. They liked her too, I could tell. Once again I'm pissed that Carly's just my nanny and not my girlfriend.

Also I have the feeling that not only did Carly learn stuff from them, but we all learned stuff from her.

16

CARLY

"This is fucking stupid."

I glance over to the dining table where Nate is helping Quinn with her homework. So much for having kicked the swearing habit.

"It's not stupid," he says, sounding frustrated. "These are things you need to learn."

"Why?"

His face scrunches up. "So you can read and write and be smart."

"I am smart."

"I know you are. Which means you can learn this stuff."

"You know what Hazel told me today?"

"What?"

"She told me her baby brother peed on her dad. When he was changing his diaper. His pee shot into the air and—"

"Yeah, that happens with boys, I hear. Let's get back to homework."

"What are you working on?" I ask casually as I stroll past them into the kitchen. I can see the tension in Nate's big shoulders and I want to lay my hands on him there and ease that tension.

"Vowels," Nate snarls.

"What did vowels ever do to you?" I tease.

He shoots me a grim look.

I grimace. Yikes.

"Okay," he says. "The word bake. Is that a short A or a long A?"

Quinn pouts. "I don't know."

"Baaaaaake," I say.

She gives me a squinty look. "Long?"

"Yes!"

She circles the answer with her pencil.

"Up," says Nate. "Short or long U?"

Quinn glances at me.

I'm not going to give her answers. "Here's a rule," I offer. "When there's one vowel in a word and it's not at the end of the word, it'll make the short vowel sound. Like lot. When there's one vowel at the end of a word, it'll make a long vowel sound, as in 'go.'" I point. "How many vowels in up?"

"One."

"Is it at the end of the word?"

"No. There's a P."

"So it's…"

"Short."

"Right!"

Nate scowls and mutters under his breath. He's not into this at all.

But the rule helped, and they keep going.

"Okay," he eventually says. "Bedtime."

"It's too early for bed!"

"Quinn. It's bedtime."

"What time did we agree is bedtime?" I ask her.

"Eight fifteen."

"And what time is it now?"

She looks at the clock on the stove. "Eight oh three."

"That leaves…twelve minutes for reading."

"Fine." She starts to leave the table, but Nate stops her. "Get your things together so they're ready in the morning."

She stuffs her homework and pencils into her backpack, then trudges dejectedly off to bed.

Nate rubs his forehead. "There's a reason I'm not a teacher."

I laugh softly. "You're doing great." Once again, I want to smooth the furrow between his brows. Kiss him there. Sit on his lap and... I swallow my sigh.

"Obviously, Brielle used to help with her homework."

"Yeah." I hesitate. "You don't like reading, do you?"

He purses his lips. "No. But I'm not stupid."

"Jesus. Of course you're not. Why would you say that?"

He lets out a gust of air. "Because I was told that a lot when I was a kid."

"What?" I stare in dismay, then sink down onto a chair at the table. "Why?"

He stares down at the table for a long moment, then mutters, "I have ADHD."

"Oh." I'm not shocked by this revelation. I noticed that he takes Concerta daily and I googled it, of course, because I'm a nosy know it all. I don't know much about ADHD, but I do know it has nothing to do with intelligence. "Did that cause problems for you in school?"

"Oh hell, yeah. I always had a lot of energy, was always impulsive."

"Hence the hammers on the trampoline," I say dryly.

"Yeah. But it was more than just a lot of energy. I was always distracted. Couldn't get organized. Didn't get my homework done. And I constantly lost things—jackets, boots, hockey sticks, you name it. Drove my mom crazy."

"Ah."

"Even after I was diagnosed and started on medication, I never was very good at school." He still doesn't look at me. "Hockey probably saved my life. It gave me something to focus on and somewhere to focus my energy."

My chest squeezes. "It's good you had that."

"Yeah. Sports actually help increase neurotransmitters in the brain. That helps reduce ADHD symptoms for a while, which helps with paying attention, staying on task, being less impulsive. And it helps with sleep. So that was a good thing for me."

"That's great."

"Research is showing that symptoms of ADHD might even *enhance* athletic performance."

"Really."

"Yeah. Sports that involve quick movements and decision-making. For some reason I can focus on hockey. And all the practicing helped me learn to stay on task and cooperate with teammates. Being good at hockey helped with my self-confidence, when it got trashed because people thought I was stupid."

Something tugs hard at my heart. "Oh, Nate." I reach out and grab his hand.

I shouldn't have done that.

I've been avoiding touching him for weeks now—staying out of his way, keeping my distance. Now I have his big hand under mine and there's a flow of warm energy from him to me, coursing up my arm and through the rest of my body. I swallow.

"You're not stupid," I tell him again. I squeeze his hand. "From the first time I met you I thought how smart you are." Now I'm remembering small things, though—his discomfort in the bookstore, the way he kept referring to my brain.

"I like to listen to audiobooks when I'm working out," he says. "I like to learn stuff, but reading is hard for me."

"That's a great way to learn."

"I don't think I can help Quinn with her homework."

"Yes, you can."

"Daddy!" Quinn's voice carries down the hall.

"Coming!" He stands. "Sorry to dump that on you."

"Hey, it's not a problem. I'm here if you want to talk more."

His eyes meet mine. Heat shimmers around us, and I can't look away. "Thanks," he says gruffly, then turns and heads down the hall. He's barely limping these days.

Oh boy. I sit and reflect on what I just learned. He's obviously hard on himself about this, even though it's a neurological condition that he can't help. Thinking about the things he went through as a kid and how it impacted him makes my heart hurt.

He probably won't come back and talk more. But still, I don't go to my room, instead going into the living room, curling up on the sofa, and scrolling through my phone.

I'm surprised when I hear him say, "Night, pop tart." And then he walks into the living room. I look up and smile. "All tucked in?"

"Yeah. Only a little stalling tonight." He sits on the couch, too. "Thanks for all you've done to get her into a regular bedtime routine. It really helps with the stalling."

My chest warms. "You're welcome."

"And thanks for listening to me earlier. And for being so non-judgmental."

"I don't think you have to thank me," I say softly. "But I know people do judge things like that unfairly."

He nods.

"Is that what the Concerta is for?"

"Yeah. I still take it. I stopped for a while once, but it made too big of a difference. I like feeling...clear. Like my mind is quiet."

"Is it a problem for the league? That medication is a stimulant, isn't it?"

"Yeah, but I have a medical exemption."

"Ah. Okay. That's good."

"Also, thanks for being there to help with the homework. Maybe you should be the one to help her."

"No."

He chuckles. "Hey. What kind of employee are you? Isn't that insubordination?"

"I guess I'm not a very good employee," I reply. "I think *you* should help her. You can do it. Mostly, it's just being there to keep her on track."

"She seemed really distractable tonight. It worries me."

I purse my lips. "She is going through a sort of trauma right now, with her mom being gone. It could be that."

"True. We'll keep an eye on it."

We. I like that. Too much, dammit. Every day I get more and more merged into this small family. I try not to care. But I can't help it. I just do.

Nate and I eye each other across the short distance between us. I take in his arms revealed by the short sleeves of his T-shirt hugging his biceps, his forearms sinewy and strong, his hands big and slightly rough. My gaze wanders over his throat, his jaw, the slide of his silky hair over his forehead. Those dark coffee eyes, liquid and warm, watching me back. Slow liquid heat drizzles through me and the air turns thick.

"Carly."

"Yeah?" I whisper.

He closes his eyes. "I want you."

I let out a long sigh. "Yeah. I want you, too."

He doesn't say anything, and I watch his chest rise and fall with his breathing. His fingers spread over the denim covering his big thighs. I want to crawl over there and lick his throat, breathe in his scent, curl up on his lap and feel those big hands on my body. On my bare skin. I want to know how aroused he is. My heart beats faster and I can hear it in my ears.

He opens his eyes. "It has to be you."

I'm flooded with affection and gratitude for this man. I've never felt wanted and needed like this. He's been patient and principled and honest. He's a good man.

And I want him, too.

Why can't we do this? Who will it hurt?

Well, potentially three of us, if things go wrong. My breasts lift with my quick, shallow breaths and I clasp my hands. The wanting is powerful and persuasive. The physical ache between my legs, the swelling of my breasts, the way my lips part hungrily all take control of my thoughts and convince me maybe we can do this.

I've never felt this intense need for someone. This pull is fierce, tugging at me, fluttering so hard in my chest I can feel it in my throat.

Maybe I'm weak, but I can't resist any longer. Maybe it's crazy, but right now I don't care.

I move, sliding closer to him.

A flame flickers in his eyes and his mouth opens.

I cup his cheek and lean in to kiss that mouth. I remember it—his firm lips, his taste, his tongue gliding over my bottom lip.

A groan rumbles in his chest as our mouths meet. "Carly…"

"Yes." I kiss one corner of his mouth, then the other.

"Are you sure?"

"Yes."

I kiss him again and his hands grip my waist as he opens his mouth and deepens the kiss.

We make out on the couch, hands everywhere on each other, exploring, fondling, mouths sliding and licking and sucking. My need for him expands and intensifies with every kiss, every touch. I'm feverish and desperate, wet between my legs, my entire body pulsing and hot.

A noise from down the hall has us both springing apart. We stare into each other's eyes for a split second, then I scramble back.

It's Quinn, going into the bathroom.

Nate breathes fast, his face flushed. He rubs the heel of his hand over his forehead. "Jesus."

"Not here. Not tonight."

He eyebrows slope down and he looks like he just took a puck in a sensitive area.

"Tomorrow," I whisper back, reaching out to squeeze his arm. "Okay?"

He takes a breath. And another. "Okay."

17

NATE

I slide a bowl of cereal over to my daughter just as Carly walks into the kitchen.

The air immediately goes hot and static.

She's wearing a silky robe over...I don't know what. Her hair is still tousled in a just fucked look, except...she hasn't just been fucked. She will be, though. Soon.

Not soon enough. My skin prickles all over as she moves around me in the kitchen to get her coffee. I watch her pretty lips as she takes a sip and our eyes meet. It's like fireworks just went off in the kitchen. And in my chest.

I turn away from her to focus on Quinn, who's chatting about school and her friend's new magic castle or something. She seems happy and back to normal after last night's homework struggle.

"Do you have your form for the field trip?" I ask.

She nods and picks up her cereal bowl to drink the milk.

"Quinn," Carly says gently. "That's not good manners."

Quinn sets it down, a milk moustache decorating her upper lip. "I know. I won't do it in public."

I roll my lips in on a smile.

Carly disappears to get dressed, emerging from her room in a pair of snug jeans and a sweater. We both take Quinn to school. The air in the car is electrified as we exchange hot looks. I've been wanting this for weeks, but after last night, I'm dying for Carly. It's all I can do to control myself driving down Columbus. My dick is throbbing.

Back home, we ride the elevator in silence, not touching, and enter my apartment. The door closes behind us and it's silent. Still.

Carly drops her purse on the table and turns to me. "I'm dying," she whispers.

Thank you, Jesus. "Me too," I groan.

And she launches herself at me. With a few fast steps she's plastered against me, in my arms, our mouths fused.

Lust pumps through my veins, hot and urgent.

I lift her feet right off the floor and she wraps her legs around me, her arms around my head, and we kiss and kiss, wet, sloppy, dirty, desperate. The small whimpers falling from her lips turn me on even more, the feel of her tits pressed against my chest sending all my blood south. My dick swells painfully, the base of my spine aching.

I carry her down the hall to my room. I haven't even made the bed. The blinds are still drawn.

"You shouldn't carry me," she gasps against my lips. "Your knee… heavy lifting."

A laugh slips out of me at her being considered 'heavy lifting'. "I'm fine."

I lay her down on the bed among the rumpled sheets and kneel over her, propping myself on straight arms. "Still sure?"

I was afraid that with time and space between last night, she'd have come to her senses. Hell, I thought *I'd* come to my senses. But I haven't. I still want this. I want her. More than any damn thing I've wanted for a long, long time.

"I'm sure."

I study her face on the pillow—the color in her cheeks, the sparkle in those amazing green eyes, her tousled hair. I touch her mouth with my index finger and drag it down over her chin, her throat, down between her breasts into the opening of the shirt she's wearing, a white cotton button-down.

Her lips part as she gazes back at me, those full, smooth lips that taste so sweet. "Are you?"

"Fuck, yeah." I close my eyes briefly, every nerve ending in my body sizzling. "I know your worries about this, but we're adults. We'll act like adults."

"Yes."

"I want to be very, very adult with you." I go back onto my knees and work open the top button of her shirt. Then the next. "I can't wait to give you an orgasm."

She shivers, eyes darkening. "It won't take much. I'm so on edge I could come if you breathed on me."

"I want to do that. Breathe on you. Breathe you in. Lick you."

She whimpers.

Her shirt is open now and I part the sides to reveal a lacy bra cupping soft, round curves. I nearly choke on lust as I trail my fingertip down between them, then down her abdomen to the waistband of her jeans. I flick another button open and draw the zipper down.

"Take off your shirt," she breathlessly orders me. "I need to see you again. Touch you."

"Hell yeah." I reach behind my head and tug my long-sleeved tee off, tossing it aside. Her hands immediately land on my pecs, and fuuuuuuck that feels good. She rubs firmly and my dick goes impossibly harder. Electricity sparks over my skin.

Curving a hand around the back of my neck, she pulls me down for another kiss and Christ, the feel of her skin against mine wipes my mind blank. I'm just instinct and hunger, devouring her mouth, moving against her, rolling her on top of me and sliding my hands inside her jeans to cup her ass.

She's just as frantic, writhing and rubbing her tits on me, pushing into me with her hips, grabbing at me.

"You want more?" I whisper against her jaw. "What turns you on?"

"You do."

"Mmm." I suck the soft skin of her neck. "Tell me exactly. This?"

"Yes," she gasps.

"This?" I use my teeth, so gently.

"Yes…"

I roll her to her back again and kiss her collarbone.

"Suck my nipples," she begs. "I love that."

"Yeah." I tug the thin cup of her bra down to bare her breast. I stare for a moment, lost in visual pleasure, then bend my head and slide my tongue over the hard tip. "Oh yeah."

"Yes…do that."

"Mmmm." I lick and tease, then close my lips over her nipple and suck.

She nearly lifts off the bed, one hand tangled in my hair. "Oh God!"

I nibble and suck, move to the other breast and do the same. I lick around the curves, take soft bites of her plump flesh, and she twists and wriggles beneath me.

"I can't wait to feel you inside me."

My dick leaps enthusiastically.

I work her jeans and panties off and she lifts to take off her bra. Then I flick open the button of my jeans and draw down the zipper.

Her eyes follow my movements. "I want to touch you. I need to."

I shove jeans and underwear down and my cock springs up, thick and ready. Definitely ready. Almost too ready. "We need to slow things down, sweetheart."

"Why? We have all day."

Hmm. She's right. "There's so much I want to do to you. It's going to take all day. It's going to take forfuckingever."

She whimpers and closes her fingers around my dick, gently squeezing, then stroking.

I let out a long groan. "Yeah. Like that." I watch her hand on me, so dirty and beautiful, my cock rudely hard and dripping. She circles her thumb over the tip and looks up at me. Our gazes collide in a burst of sparks and my chest fills with heat.

"I want to fuck you so hard," I rumble. "Right now."

"Do it."

I slip my hand between her thighs to explore. I want to take it slower and savor it, but I can't, we're both so primed we're about to explode. "Nice and wet. Are you ready, gorgeous? Are you aching for me?"

"I've been aching for you since last night."

"Aw fuck, baby. Let me grab something."

I lean over and grab a condom from the nightstand, and quickly roll it on.

"That's so hot," she whispers, watching me. "Put it inside me, please, please..."

Her words ignite a fire inside me and I knee her legs apart, exposing her to me. "So pretty, Carly." I stroke the soft outer lips, brush over her clit, and she jerks. "So pink and ready for me."

I take myself in hand, slick the head of my cock up and down through her wetness, and notch it at her entrance. I pause and our eyes meet again. It's not the first time for us, but it feels special. "I've waited so long for this."

"I know." Her eyes are glossy. "Me too."

I push into her, slowly, carefully. She's so tight, closing around me, holding me tight along the full length of my shaft and it's magnificent. Sensation pours through me in violent waves. I move over her with straight arms again, watching her face as she takes me, deeper, all the way.

"Oh my God. Yes. Keep going."

My smile is tight with restraint as I try to control myself, fucking into her in heavy strokes, harder, bouncing the bed. She holds onto my arms, her gaze fastened on mine, joining us in a way that's more than just my cock inside her. Then she slips a hand down her body and finds her clit, circling it with her fingertips, brushing against my dick, making my blood run so hot I'm burning up. "Yeah. Do that."

"I'm so close. So close...Nate..." She sinks her teeth into her bottom lip and her eyelids drift down.

"Eyes on me, gorgeous."

She blinks open and stares, the green irises hazy, and then she comes with a long wail, squeezing me, rippling around me, and I lose it. I pound into her, teeth gritted, jaw tight, and I shout too as I come, spilling into the condom in hard pulses that are nearly painful. I groan and groan and fall over her, trying to protect her from my weight, and she wraps arms and legs around me again. We stay like that for long moment, breathing hard, hearts pounding. Still hard, I rock my hips to slowly withdraw, then slide in again. And again.

"I'm sorry," I finally manage to say. "That was faster than a lizard on hot asphalt."

She chokes on a laugh, tries to stop, then giggles helplessly. This squeezes me again. I start laughing too, slipping out of her, and I roll to the side with her in my arms, both of us laughing. Then Carly laughs so hard she snorts.

"Oh my God," she gasps, burying her face in the side of my neck. "I'm sorry!"

I laugh even harder. "It's cute."

So fucking much fun. She's fun out of bed, but in bed...I've never experienced this. So much pleasure and laughter and connection.

I fucked around a lot, thinking that would be enough. It wasn't enough.

This...well, this isn't enough either. I don't think I could get enough of Carly if I lived to a hundred and fifty. But it gives me something, something gratifying and satisfying and what I've wanted.

I told her about my ADHD. I don't tell people about that. I've learned a lot of strategies over the years and the medication does help. Team management knows, obviously. Only one other guy on the team—Axe—knows, and that's because he has dyslexia and we talked about when we were rookie roommates because we had similar experiences.

I don't trust many people. Many women. They've thought I'm stupid. They've used me because I'm a hockey player. Brielle has never said that, but I believe it's why she wanted to date me. Although I have to be honest and admit I liked dating a gorgeous actress. So in a way, we used each other.

Carly still wants me, even though she knows my secrets, my shame. I told her because she never judges me. I trust her.

That's why the sex is so fucking stupendous.

18

CARLY

"So…you wanna fuck again? Or are we done?"

I collapse into laughter all over again, pressing my nose to Nate's throat. God, he smells good, like sandalwood and his skin. He's vibrating with laughter, too. "We're not done."

"Okay, good. I just need a minute."

"Just a minute?"

"Christ, I'm still hard, you tease."

I gasp. "I'm not a tease!"

"You sure the fuck are." He kisses my temple. "Walking around this apartment looking all hot and cute all the time."

"Oh my God." I'm laughing all over again. It's like I'm drunk, and it's not even ten in the morning. We're both high from that fast, hard sex.

"You love to torture me," he growls, rubbing his nose alongside mine. "Admit it."

"I do not!"

"Admit it. The other day you had on short shorts and I just wanted to grab your ass."

"Okay, the short shorts might have been a tease…"

"I knew it." His hand goes to my bare butt and squeezes. I love it.

"And you don't tease me with your bare chest all the time after a shower?"

"Ah, you noticed."

"Oh God, yeah." I sigh in surrender. "I noticed."

"You do things that make me so hot and you probably don't even know."

Intrigued, I stroke his chest. "Like what?"

"Like when you flick your hair back."

"Oh."

"When you stand on your toes to get something out of the high cupboards."

I pull my head back to look at him. "Really?"

"Yeah. Hot as fuck. Also when you're writing. You have this little groove here..." He touches between my eyebrows. "And you're so focused. Also hot."

"Wow." I'm melting like a crayon on a hot stove. "I like that."

"You like making me hard?"

Our eyes meet. "I do," I say breathlessly.

He moves, his hard cock pressing against my hip. "There you go, beautiful."

"We need another condom."

"Got it." He rolls over me in an impressive display of athleticism and reaches into the drawer for another condom. "This time I'm going slow. I want to take my time and explore every inch of you with my mouth and my hands..." His hands move down his shaft, the latex stretched thin around his girth. My mouth literally waters, watching him. He's so incredibly beautiful—his cock is broad and solid and handsomely shaped, and I want to suck him off so bad.

But I'm also happy to let him take control, moving over me, delivering on his promise to explore. His mouth moves from my cheek and jaw to my throat, where his tongue softly strokes my fluttering pulse, then between my breasts. He cups them with his hands, plumping them to his mouth, sucking in hard draws that tug a path straight down between my legs. When he lifts his head to gaze down at my hard, wet nipples, the look on his face is one of such admiration and lust I'm weak. Nobody has ever looked at me like that.

My heart speeds up, my skin heating everywhere.

"You're beautiful, Carly," he says softly.

"Th-thank you." My chest fills with a fizzy sensation and my lower belly aches.

He slowly strokes down my sides, trails his lips down my belly, getting closer to where I'm craving his touch. He pauses to nip at one hip bone, then lick over it. My clit pulses with need and my womb clenches with desire.

His big hands land on my thighs and push them apart, then caress me over my butt and over my pussy, giving me a gentle squeeze there. I'm making all kinds of panty, breathy noises.

He slides rough fingertips up over my hipbones, over my belly button, his mouth so close I can feel his breath on sensitive skin. He's teasing me, torturing me with slow caress over my lower belly. Then he looks up at me, his expression taut and blazing.

I'm dying.

He turns his head and opens his mouth on my inner thigh in a long, slow kiss, then moves to my other leg. This kiss ends with a nip of teeth that makes my body twitch hard. Centered between my legs, still watching my face, he brushes his lower lip over my pussy.

"Tease," I choke out.

He smiles and backs up, his hand moving over me again, slow and sensuous, and then I see his other hand gripping his cock. It's huge and dark and shiny and the sight of him stroking himself just as slowly and erotically as he caresses me, nearly makes me come right there.

He stops touching himself and caresses my thighs again, lowering his face, and he gives me one long, lush lick. He pulls back tauntingly, then does it again. And again.

"There we go," he murmurs. "So soft. So sweet." He nips at one thigh. "Are you ready for special kisses?" He nips the other thigh. "Special licks?"

I make an incoherent sound of assent.

He uses his fingers to part my lower lips, pulling back the hood of my clit, and bestows another lick over it with just the tip of his tongue. I shudder.

He draws back, fingers working at my flesh, and he's watching, gazing intently at me in that most intimate place. I'm hot all over, my belly burning. Then he touches the tip of his tongue to me again. I'm so sensitive, I jump and moan. I love the expression of fascination and reverence on his face.

"More. Please."

He's still moving achingly slowly, his fingertips keeping me spread for his tongue. His teasing licks become longer, the whole flat of his tongue stroking wetly over me. "Ahhh," he says as if grateful.

Then opens his mouth and goes down on me. Like, *down*, covering me, his lips pressing against my pussy then slowly sucking in a deep, intimate kiss.

I'm shaking, burning,

"So beautiful," he murmurs as he lifts his head and licks again, making rough noises of enjoyment. His fingertips press my plump flesh open and my hips are lifting to his mouth, begging for more.

He draws back as if to study me, runs his fingertips over my wet skin, then with the tips of all five fingers, he taps me there. A tiny, erotic spank. On my pussy.

I cry out. My insides squeeze hard and sparks sizzle over my skin.

"You like that?"

"Oh God. Yes."

"Harder?"

I whimper.

He does it again. Another sharp tap. Harder. Then a series of faster pats. I'm nearly crying, pleasure scalding my veins.

"Look at this beautiful pussy." He laps again, slow, then sucks, tugging at my skin in a long, pull. Holding it there between his lips and murmuring his appreciation. "So smooth."

"I can't," I sob. "Oh my God, what are you doing to me?"

"Mmm." He licks. "Mmmm. This gives beaver tap a whole new meaning."

I don't even know what he's talking about, and right now I don't care.

He stiffens his tongue and finds my clit. I shiver and jerk. "Yes!"

He toys with me with his tongue, over and over, fever building, sensation growing, taking me higher, higher…I can't stop the noises that spill from my lips as my body tightens and pleasure bursts through me, incandescent, scorching. My thighs tremble and try to close, but he keeps me spread for him, drawing out my orgasm almost unbearably, until I'm limp and liquefied.

"Holy bajesus," I gasp, eyes closed.

He gives me a few last tender licks, then kisses his way up to my mouth. I can barely kiss him back.

"What the fuck is a beaver tap?" I mumble. "Other than spanking my pussy."

He grins down at me, ardor and amusement shining in his eyes. "It's when you slap your stick on the ice to call for a pass."

"Um…"

"This one's much more fun." He kisses me again, sharing my own taste with me, his big dick brushing against my tender girl parts.

"It definitely was fun for me."

19

NATE

Training camp starts today and I'm here, reporting for duty, bright and early.

There's about fifty of us here at the practice facility, me and my teammates but also guys from the farm team, brand new draft picks, and a few guys the team has invited to try out. Everyone's nervous—there's no guarantee, no matter who you are. But it would be tough to imagine someone like Bergie, our captain, not making the cut, and our goalie Gunner is for sure in.

It's kind of like the first day of school was for Quinn—being away from it for months, then seeing all her friends and classmates new and old.

The physical testing is also anxiety-inducing. They do it in front of all the team brass, so our coaches and managers all see exactly how we're doing. I'm out almost immediately, but it's not a surprise to anyone; they're aware of my status and have my medical records. We go over my rehab plan and when I might be able to skate. "I'm hoping I can be back for the start of the season," I say. "It's still almost four weeks away."

"You're not going to jump on the ice and be at full capacity on day one," Robby says. He's the head athletic trainer.

"Right, I know."

"We'll take it one day at a time," he says. "Hopefully doc gives you the go ahead to start skating next week."

I hang out and watch some of the guys go through the paces—vertical jumps, sprints, pushups, pullups, then the V02 Max tests that measure the maximum amount of oxygen your body can utilize during exercise. Basically you run on the treadmill until you pass out. One of the rookies, Phillipe Lavoie, literally pukes when he's done. I grin.

I go over to him after. His face is red and sweaty, eyes watery. I clap a hand on his shoulder. "Hey, rookie. That happened to me too, my first time."

"Yeah?"

He's a kid. He still has peach fuzz and acne.

"Yeah. You did great." I pat his shoulder. "Good energy. Can't wait to watch you skate. I hear you're speedy."

He chokes out a laugh. "I may never be able to skate again, after that."

"You will."

"Shit. Nate Karmeinski is gonna watch me skate. I'll puke again."

Now I laugh. "There're more important people than me watching you skate, buddy. Good luck."

After that, they go on the ice and I watch from the stands as the guys are put through a bunch of sprints. Then they're done because training time is limited to three hours, so they have recovery time—using foam rollers, stretching, cooling down on a bike.

Then there's a team meeting. It's not Mr. D'Agostino, it's the general manager of the team, Brad Julian, and the assistant GM Dale Townsend. They go over what we know from the news, but don't add much more. Mr. Julian does stress that nothing's changing and we need to focus on getting the best team we can on the ice for this season. He says they'll be transparent and share news with us when they have some.

I stick around for the media availability in case anyone wants to talk to me, and they do. Even the sports reporters are pumped about the season starting. The air in the building is charged with a feeling of excitement and possibility.

I just hope I'm not so far behind that I can't catch up.

I take a deep breath and face the reporters. I'm vague about my surgery and tell them I'm doing rehab right now and we're going day by day. I answer a couple of questions about whether the injury happened last year and then I'm done.

I stay for lunch with the team, but then I head out to go to my therapy appointment. I don't have to ride a bike until I puke, but I damn near do...because I want to be in the best shape I can when the season starts. Or when *my* season starts.

"You don't even need me anymore."

I level a look at Carly. "Oh, yes, I do."

She waves a hand. We're in bed again, after getting Quinn to school. My therapy appointments are in the afternoons, so this is starting to become a routine. A very happy routine.

"Not like that," she says. "I mean to help with Quinn. You're practically back to normal."

"Almost," I agree. "For day-to-day stuff. But once I'm playing, I'll need you. I can start skating tomorrow and depending how things go, I could be playing in the season opener."

"That would be so great," she says softly, fingers lightly rubbing my chest.

"Are you bored?"

"God, no! I've been getting a lot of writing done."

She sold another article to a magazine and has a proposal out for another. "How's the book coming along?"

"Really good." I love how she gets all enthusiastic when she talks about it. "I was doing research yesterday into bullying."

"Yeah?" I stroke her hair.

"Yeah. Men are supposed to be tough. Don't cry. Don't show weakness. That has a big impact on bullying."

"It makes me hot when you talk about smart stuff."

She laughs her fingertips brushing over my beard stubble. "That's funny, because I get hot when you talk about hockey."

"Hey. You want to come to one of the exhibition games with me?"

"I guess, sure. I used to like hockey. I haven't been to a game in years."

"I guess it's not big in France."

"Nope."

I was going to watch from the press box, but I can get tickets, we all have tickets for us to use. Usually it's for my parents when they come to watch a game. It's not very often I invite a girl.

"I guess Quinn will come too?" she asks.

I swallow a groan. How the fuck did I forget about my own daughter? I'm a dick. I guess I'm just used to her being with Brielle during the season. "Right. We should do the Friday game, then. It'll be a late night for her."

"That'll be fun."

"Yeah! I'm excited. She loves going to games, but I don't usually get to watch with her because I'm playing."

I get to take both my girls to the game and share my love of the sport with them. It'll be so great.

It's a pre-season game so the hockey team doesn't have all the bells and whistles set up in the arena—all the light effects and sounds and video that they'll use during the season. There's not as much fanfare when the starting line is announced. Tonight, some of my teammates are playing but also a whole lot of rookies, giving team management a chance to watch them on the ice before making cuts. They're playing against the New Jersey Storm, who are icing a similarly inexperienced team.

I sit between the girls, dipping into Quinn's popcorn and answering Carly's questions. She has a lot of questions, but they're good questions, and answering them makes me feel like I know something.

Of course I do.

Carly hangs on my words like I'm an expert and I feel ten feet tall. I think being away from hockey is affecting my self-image more than I realized. It's such a big part of who I am. It's something I'm good at, damn good, something I'm proud of, something that gives me confidence.

It still worries me a little about what happens if I don't have hockey. If I can't do what I love, what I'm good at.

But I can't dwell on that. I'm here to have fun with my girls tonight.

Also Carly gives me confidence.

"No, Carly," Quinn says patiently. "They can't cross the blue line before the puck."

I grin. She's going to be a badass at hockey camp next year.

The Storm score and the crowd all groans, but the Bears quickly even the score with a nice goal from Lavoie, our newest draft pick. I've been watching him. He's good. I don't know how his training camp has been going but he could give Beave or Goose a run for their money if they're not sharp.

I miss being there, dammit, knowing how everyone is doing, showing the coaches what I can do. It feels like a hole in my gut, an empty hollow ache.

"You okay?" Carly asks softly, nudging me with her shoulder.

I slide her a quick smile. "Yeah. All good."

"You miss it."

"Like I'd miss my lungs."

She laughs. "That's serious."

During the first intermission, the Bears mascot Orson appears.

Quinn's excited and jumps up and waves to him. I know the dude inside the costume, so I wave too, and he spots me and comes over to give Quinn a bear hug and a high five. Then we make a quick trip to the crowded store and find a hat that Quinn falls in love with—a Bears trooper hat with bear ears on top, and long knit braids.

"I feel I should have a shirt," Carly says, perusing a rack of women's wear.

"I'll buy you one."

"You don't have—" She catches my eye and shrugs. "Okay, thanks." She picks out a grey athletic style with the Bears logo on the front and I pay for the shirt and hat.

Quinn pulls the hat on and wears it for the rest of the game. So damn cute.

In the second period, the Bears score the go-ahead goal.

"That kid has amazing hands," I say about Lavoie, who just scored.

Carly gives me a hot look, dropping her gaze briefly to my hands.

I give her an evil grin back. "I'm told I also have good hands."

Her smile is slow and suggestive.

"How old is that man, Daddy?" Quinn asks.

"Who? Lavoie?"

"Yeah. He looks like a kid."

I grin. "I think he's eighteen."

"Oh. Okay."

I guess eighteen sounds old enough to her.

"I don't want to play defense," she tells us a while later.

"Why not?"

"Because you have to skate backward a lot. I don't like skating backward."

"Hmm. That is true."

"Also I like scoring goals."

"I score goals," I protest.

"Not very many." She pats my arm and Carly chokes on a laugh. "That's okay."

In the second intermission we talk to some of the WAGS—not many who I know are here, but I introduce Carly to Cookie's girlfriend Emerie and Bergie's wife Mandy. Some of the young women here are clearly watching their partners vying for a coveted spot on an NHL roster with much excitement. It's cute.

And once again I want that with Carly—when I'm playing again, I want her here, watching *me*, cheering *me* on, supporting *me*.

20

CARLY

I'm selling articles. My blog has lots of engagement. I'm working on my book and it's going great. And I'm having sex with Nate.

Could life be any better?

This won't last. But right now, it's amazing.

I could imagine a world where this goes on forever—me and Nate together, raising Quinn, Nate playing hockey, me writing…it's a dream world and sometimes I feel like I'm living in a dream.

But dreams end. We wake up and live in the real world. What's the real world going to look like? I was nearly homeless and unemployed and that could still happen.

And I could lose Nate. And Quinn. And that scares me even more.

I sit at the desk in my bedroom looking at my computer. It's still my room. I still sleep there every night, although sometimes Nate sneaks in here when Quinn's asleep. Most of our sexy times happen during the day. But Nate is busier now with his rehab, spending every afternoon working out, and now skating in the mornings and going to the pre-season games. He hasn't skated with the team yet, but that should be soon. He's determined to get back to playing as fast as he can.

I admire him for that.

I smile at my computer as I get a little lost in thoughts about Nate and his strength and determination. I really like him. I mean, *really*. Like…I could be falling in love with him.

I lean my elbow on the desk, rest my chin on my hand and gaze at the Word document open on the screen. We like to spend time together, even when it doesn't involve a bed. We have fun hanging out with Quinn. And we especially have fun between the sheets. Or on the couch. Or the kitchen counter. That happened once when I was making us lunch and he decided to eat me instead.

This is all wonderful, but also scary. I didn't sign up for this. But what do I do about it? I feel like I'm slipping down a steep slope, getting deeper and deeper into something I didn't plan to get into. But the slide is lovely.

Okay, focus. Back to the article I'm writing about how the "boys will be boys" attitude affects all genders. I think it's good and I want to get this sent off to the editor at Flair Magazine and then do more work on my book. I've started writing query letters to agents, even though it's not finished, because I'm excited about the chance to get the book out into the world. I'm saving them in a drafts folder for the day I can actually hit "send."

I work until it's time to pick up Quinn from school. Nate does actually need me now. And soon he'll be traveling. That's going to be hard on Quinn and I'm a little worried about it. She's settling down but still has spells where she's super clingy with Nate and doesn't want him out of her sight, and nights where she can't sleep. She's a night owl and has always tried to stay up later than she should, but I made a lot of progress in establishing a good bedtime routine and things were a lot better. Now things have slipped back a bit.

We've had some good, quiet talks in the dark. I've tried to help her identify what she's feeling and what she's afraid of, and then we talk about how realistic it is that it could happen, and come up with something else she can say to herself, like, *Daddy's not going to leave me* or *Mommy still loves me when she's not here.*

Nate talked to a counselor at school because it's been a few weeks since Brielle left. They haven't seen many issues at school, so the counselor said to keep doing what we're doing and gave us a few other tips for helping Quinn to manage her anxiety. Sometimes I get angry at Brielle again for doing this, and then I feel like a shit human being.

I pick up Quinn, get her home and say, "Let's get your homework done so you can spend time with your dad after dinner."

"I'll do my homework later."

"Why not now? Then you can have fun and maybe watch TV later."

"I don't want to do it now." Her voice gets a little edge of attitude.

I set my teeth together. I'm only the nanny and she could do her homework later. Maybe I shouldn't push this. "What homework do you have?"

"Spelling words."

Hmmm. "Okay, then later it is."

"I'm going to play Paw Patrol." She heads to her room.

One hour a day of video games. Nate's more lenient on that, but I try to limit her to that without being obvious about it.

I open her backpack to get out her lunch bag and the containers from lunch. I pull out her agenda where homework is recorded and see a note from the teacher. Quinn didn't get yesterday's math homework done.

What?

That's so weird. Between Nate and I, we've been helping her every evening with homework. I check what the assignment was.

Then I remember Quinn telling Nate last night she didn't have any homework.

That little...wow. She lied to her dad.

Nate's going to be pissed.

I head down the hall and poke my head into Quinn's room.

"Quinn." My tone is firm.

She doesn't look up from the screen.

"Quinn. Turn off your game and look at me."

"I can't stop right now."

"Now." I infuse extra firmness into my voice.

She heaves a sigh, turns off the game and looks at me. But doesn't meet my eyes.

I have to be careful. She's been going through a rough time. But that's not an excuse for letting bad behavior happen.

"Quinn, I saw the note from your teacher about your homework."

"I forgot about it."

"That's not what you said last night. You said you had no homework."

"I did not say that to you."

"You said that to your father."

Quinn's caught. Her little mouth tightens. She still doesn't look into my eyes.

"Okay. You can play your game after your homework is done. Yesterday's homework and today's homework."

"What? I said I'll do it later."

"You'll do it now," I say quietly. "Then you can play your game."

"I'm not doing it now." She lifts her little chin. "Daddy wouldn't make me do it now."

She's playing us off on each other. Damn. I've experienced this before but I have to say I'm disappointed that Quinn is doing this.

On the other hand, I recognize that she's comfortable enough with me to act this way. I guess I've been lucky as the new nanny that she's been on good behavior with me. Now she's more used to me. I almost feel like smiling, but keep my face serious.

"Come on," I say. "Now."

"No!"

I walk over and unplug her game console.

"What are you doing?"

"I said you can play this after your homework is done." I pick up the console and walk out of the room with it.

"Carly!" She lets out a little shriek. "You can't do that! You can't!"

I hate this. I hate her being mad at me. But this is my job, and Nate agreed that he's okay with me disciplining her if needed because we both have similar ideas about behavior and consequences. He trusts that I'll do the right thing.

I hear the apartment door open and close and Nate's heavy steps walking in. "Hello!" he calls.

"Hey." I walk toward him down the hall with the game console.

His eyebrows raise seeing it in my arms. Then Quinn darts around me and bolts to her father.

"Carly took away my game!" she cries to him. "Daddy, she can't do that!"

He takes a steadying step backward as she throws herself at him. "What? What's going on?"

"She took my game away from me!" She's now crying dramatically.

I purse my lips and meet Nate's eyes over Quinn's head. "Do you want to tell him why, Quinn?"

"Because she hates me!"

"Oh my God," I mutter. "Quinn, you know that's not true."

She's working herself up. I've never seen her like this.

"Easy, pop tart," Nate says, rubbing her back. "Shhh. It's okay. Carly doesn't hate you."

"I don't feel good," Quinn sobs. "I think I'm sick."

Now my eyes pop open. Is that for real? Is that what's prompted this? Or is she lying again?

"What's wrong?" Nate asks. "Your tummy? Come on, let's go lie down." He turns to carry her to her room.

I'm just the nanny. Nate's her father. I guess I'll let him deal with it.

Now *my* stomach doesn't feel so good.

I go into the kitchen and start prepping vegetables for dinner. Nate's gotten back into eating healthy, so I've been trying to find recipes we'll all like that meet his nutritional needs. Tonight, I'm trying out a one pan chicken and veggies recipe. Mindlessly I cut chicken breasts and veggies into cubes and mix avocado oil with oregano, smoked paprika, garlic powder, salt, and pepper, thinking about what's going on with Quinn.

I hope she's not really sick. But then we have to deal with her behavior. I pout as I pour the oil mixture over the chicken and veggies then mix it up with my hands. I love her so much, and I don't want to be a "meanie" in her eyes, but I know love is tough sometimes.

Nate comes into the kitchen and props his butt on a stool. He shakes his head. "Rough day," he says.

I slide the pan into the preheated over. "Yeah, it appears so. What did she say to you?"

"She said she doesn't feel well."

"Does she have a fever?"

He frowns. "I don't know."

"Cough? Sniffles? Throwing up?"

"No."

I eye him. She's his daughter. "Did she tell you she didn't do her homework yesterday?"

"No." He frowns. "Last night she said she didn't have homework."

"She lied to you."

"She wouldn't do that."

My eyebrows fly up. "Do you think *I'm* lying?"

"What? No!"

I push Quinn's agenda across the counter to him and point at the teacher's note.

His face becomes a thundercloud. "Fuck."

"What's she doing right now?"

"Playing her game."

Now my eyeballs nearly pop out. "You gave it back to her?"

"Yeah. If she doesn't feel well, I thought she could play it quietly in bed."

I blink. Once. Twice. My chest tightens and my fingers grip the edge of the counter. I suck on my bottom lip as I consider how to handle this.

Frankly, I'm pissed at him.

But he's my boss.

I may feel like we're partners in raising Quinn. Lately, I've been feeling like we're partners in a lot of things. That's the problem with sleeping with your boss, I guess. I knew that, and yet I did it anyway.

I pull in a slow breath through my nose and let it out. "I feel like you've undermined my authority with Quinn by giving her back the game after I took it away."

His head jerks and he peers at me. I see him thinking as expressions flicker across his face. His mouth tightens. His eyes narrow. His eyebrows twitch together.

I await his response with a growing knot in my stomach but I keep my chin up and meet his gaze steadily.

He looks down and rubs the back of his neck. Then he lifts his head. "You're right," he says quietly. "I'm sorry."

Tension lets go of my shoulders. "Thank you."

"I didn't think. I just reacted. I should have talked to you first."

"I understand."

"Do you?"

"It's hard not be emotional about people we love. To let our emotions take over. I didn't want to take that game away." I make a face. "She thinks I hate her now. But she refused to do her homework and then I learned she didn't do yesterday's and then I realized she lied about it and...I had to do something."

"I agree. It's not easy."

"She's been going through a rough time lately. But that's not a reason to let her get away with stuff like that."

"You're right." He swallows. "Okay. Let's go talk to her together."

"Together?" I study his face. "Are you sure?"

His gaze is unfaltering, his presence solid and steadfast. "I'm sure."

21

NATE

I'm angry and disappointed with my daughter on several levels and I let her know that. I'm also grateful to have Carly at my side, quietly providing her support. I feel like shit that I let her down. I want to make it up to her by showing her I've got her back, too. That we're a team.

We *are* a team. Boss/employee, yes. But it's more than that. I care about her as much as...whoa. That path throws me off, and I have to regroup. How I feel about her is different than how I feel about Quinn, but I care about Carly a fuck of a lot.

"Quinn, when I'm not here, Carly is like your parent. Whatever she says, you have to listen. Whatever she decides, I support. Okay?"

Quinn cries. She apologizes. Carly gets her to talk about what's going on with her.

"I'm scared," she says, her voice trembling.

"What are you scared of?" Carly asks gently. "Remember if we talk about it, sometime it's not so scary."

Quinn swallows thickly. "I don't think Mommy loves me anymore." She can barely choke out the last few words. "She went away because she doesn't love me anym-m-more."

Her stuttering anguish feels like a skate blade twisting in my gut. "No, Quinn. No. She loves you."

Quinn's just sobbing again now, so I gather her into my arms, and try to reassure, looking at Carly for help. She nods as I talk.

"Mommy loves you. She had to go to California because of her work."

"*You* have to go away because of your work," she sobs. "Then what happens to me?"

Jesus. That skate blade slices deeper.

"I'm here." Carly sets a gentle hand on Quinn's back. "I'm always here for you. And your dad will come back. And your mom will come back, too."

"Traveling is part of my job," I say. "You know that. I always come home."

Quinn nods, still weeping.

"Mommy hated leaving you, but she knew you would be with me. And Carly."

"She didn't call me to FaceTime last week."

Oh Christ. I meet Carly's eyes and she closes hers briefly. "Because she was busy. Do you want to try to call her right now?"

I pray Brielle is available.

"Y-yes."

Thank fuck we get hold of Brielle, who starts crying when Quinn asks poignantly, "Mommy, do you still love me?"

"Of course I still love you!" Brielle stares at the camera with wide, distressed eyes. "I love you more than anything. I miss you so much."

"I w-was afraid you left me because you don't want me anymore."

Brielle swipes at tears. "I do want you, honey. I love you. We'll see each other soon."

They talk more, emotions ebbing, and the pain in my gut subsides somewhat. Having a kid is hard because I feel her pain like my own, and it makes me feel helpless and angry. All I want is for her to be happy. But life's not like that.

After that gut-wrenching conversation, Quinn does her homework, including the missed assignment yesterday, while Carly putters in the kitchen getting our dinner together. Then we all eat together. I'm exhausted.

But grateful. Sitting here with Carly and Quinn, the drama over (for now?), I feel like we're a family.

It's what I've wanted for so long, but didn't realize. Of course Quinn's always been my family. Always will be, no matter whether I'm with a woman or not. But there's a kind of companionship and partnership I can't get from her. I get it from Carly.

Christ. I watch Carly eat, forking up chicken and veggies, listening intently to Quinn's rambling stories from school and the new Harmonia movie that's coming out around Christmas. She always listens to Quinn. She always listens to me. I can't wait to get her alone later and apologize profusely for my earlier screw up. I want her to know I've got her back as much as she's got mine.

I want so much and I feel like it's within reach. But there's a nagging worry that Carly's only here because of Quinn. When we're in bed, I can forget that. But sometimes those pesky misgivings poke their way forward and feed the self-doubts that have plagued me my whole life.

Quinn's game is off limits tonight, but she has a bath and we have some reading time, then get her into bed. Finally, I'm alone with Carly.

"You don't have to clean the kitchen," I tell her. I've told her that before, but she ignores me. "I can help. You cooked the meal."

She meets my eyes. "Okay. I'll hold you to that."

"Please do." Her cool calmness is unnerving. "I want to apologize again for earlier. I never meant to undermine you."

She nods. "Thank you. I appreciate that. And I appreciate you telling Quinn that she has to listen to me."

"She knows that." I rub my face. "She was just in a snit today."

"She gets scared."

"Yeah."

"It was...difficult..." she says slowly. "To challenge you on that. You're my boss."

I eye her. I can see shutters up on her face. "I'm glad that you did."

Her face softens minutely.

"Did you think I'd react differently?"

"I didn't know. You could have been pissed at me."

I'm floundering a bit here. I want someone in my life. More than just hookups and flings. But I'm not used to having these kinds of discussions. It's uncomfortable. But I don't want to be that guy—who can't admit a mistake, who gets angry at being called on something.

Nobody likes screwing up. I do it all the time on the ice and I'm used to my coaches holding me accountable. Most of my coaches have been good guys who want me to play my best and I trust them.

Is that what it's like off the ice? Trusting that someone wants better for you and that's why they call you on your bullshit? Not to belittle you or hurt you, but to make you better?

I look at Carly and her staunch, immovable goodness. She's *good*. I want to trust her.

"I was pissed," I admit in a low tone. "At first. It didn't last, because you were right. I fucked up. And I'm so, so sorry, Carly."

Her lips quiver and her eyes brighten. "Thank you." She pauses. "But maybe we've made a big mistake...getting too involved with each other."

Shit. I search around through my jumbled thoughts. "I don't agree."

She waits.

"You want me to explain that?"

Her lips twitch up into a half-smile. "Yes, please."

"I was afraid of that."

She makes a soft sound of amusement.

I rub the back of my neck and look away. "Okay. I think we've just proved that it's not a mistake. We had a disagreement. We both got angry. Neither of us said something we regret. We talked it out."

Turning back to her, I watch as her eyes clear and soften and her mouth relaxes into a plush curve that I want to kiss so damn bad I'm almost shaking.

"You make a solid point," she whispers.

"Thank Christ." And I reach for her and pull her into my arms. "Jesus, Carly." I thread a hand into her hair, tug her head back and kiss her—hard, sweet, lustful, tender. I need her taste like my lungs need oxygen and I crush her to me as I feed on her sweetness and goodness and hope and faith.

She melts against me, soft tits against my chest, her tongue playing with mine, hands sliding over my shoulders and hanging on like she never wants to let go. I don't ever want her to let go.

I get the email from Quinn's school principal a few days later. At first I assume it's about her homework again, and I start to get annoyed, but it's not. It's because she called a kid on the playground an asshole.

Greeeaat. I knew the swearing was going to be a problem. We talked about not swearing at school and she said she understood. What the fuck?

I'm not the best role model when it comes to swearing, I know.

I arrange to meet with the principal Mrs. McDivitt after school, and I let Carly know that I'll be picking up Quinn today. I show up early and wait for my daughter outside the office. When the bell rings and she arrives, her little face is unhappy.

"C'mere," I say before we go into the office. "Give me a hug." I fold her into my arms and squeeze her gently. "I love you no matter what. Okay?"

She nods.

We enter the office and are soon seated in front of Mrs. McDivitt. Memories of being in the principal's office crowd into my brain. It happened more than once and always made me feel like a loser. I hate feeling like a loser. I don't want Quinn to feel like a loser. But if she misbehaved, she has to face the consequences of that.

"Quinn, did you call Brian an asshole?" Mrs. McDivitt asks.

"Yes." She lifts her chin and folds her arms across her chest.

"Why did you do that?" I ask quietly.

"Because he was bugging me. He kept pinching me and telling me I'm ugly. So I told him nobody talks to me like that and he's an asshole."

Mrs. McDivitt coughs. "I see. That language is inappropriate at school, Quinn."

"I know." Her chin sets and she kicks her feet. "But he was being mean to me."

"Sometimes boys do that to girls they like," Mrs. McDivitt says. "Maybe it's because he has a little crush on you."

The noise in my ears starts low, then grows into a roar that drowns out everything else, and the air in the office is literally tinted red. "Excuse me?"

She rephrases her sentence but it's the same bullshit.

"Where's the boy?" I demand. "Brian."

She gives me a blank look.

"Why isn't he here?" I ask. "I want him here."

"I'll be speaking to him and his parents," Mrs. McDivitt says.

I lean forward, both hands on her desk. "Okay. Good. Make sure you tell them that if their little asshole kid has a crush on a girl, pinching her and insulting her is not the appropriate way to behave. Violence and aggression are *not* the way to show affection. That is a toxic message and I hope you *never* tell that to another girl." I straighten. "Let's go, Quinn."

She stares at me and slides off the chair.

"We need to talk about discipline—"

"We can talk about that when you tell me what kind of discipline Brian gets. If his behavior is just brushed off, it gives him the idea it's okay to pick on someone to get their attention. This is an opportunity to teach him healthy ways to express his feelings, and also to respect girls."

I take Quinn's hand and stride out of the office.

"Am I going to be punished?" Quinn asks anxiously.

"Let's talk at home." I'm so furious I can't think straight.

When we get home, Quinn rushes in and tells Carly, "Daddy swore at the principal!"

She turns big eyes on me. "What?"

I've calmed down a little but I'm still agitated. We relate the story to Carly, and she listens with her usual intentness. When Quinn tells her what I said to Mrs. McDivitt, she covers her mouth.

"Oh my," she murmurs.

"Daddy told her Brian is toxic!" Quinn chirps.

"Not exactly," I correct gently, and I tell Carly more of what I said.

With bright eyes, she peers at me over the hand still covering her mouth. "Oh my God," she mumbles. "Oh, Nate."

"I kind of lost it," I confess, running a hand through my hair. "Now I probably made things worse." I look at Quinn. "And we do have to talk about swearing at school."

"I know. I'm sorry." She's clear eyed.

"Let's come up with some other words you can use if someone is mean to you," Carly says. "Okay?"

"Okay! Can I do my homework now?"

I blink. "Um. Sure." I meet Carly's eyes, which are still focused warmly on me.

Quinn skips off to get her backpack which she left at the front door.

"Why are you looking at me like that?" I ask Carly, confused by her heated expression.

"Because those are the hottest things I've ever heard you say," she whispers.

I start. "Uh. Wow. Okay." She does look like she wants to ride me like a bronco.

She leans closer. "Be ready later. I'm sneaking into your room. You are so getting laid tonight."

I grin, my shoulders going back. I open my mouth, but Quinn scampers in and sets her stuff on the table.

Carly enters my room quietly. I'm still awake, lying on my back in the dark, and so fucking hard. She steps out of her silky robe, slips under the covers, and moves between my legs, the duvet and sheet falling behind her. She finds my dick and wraps her hand around it just how I like it.

"God. So nice," she whispers. "You're already hard."

"I get hard just thinking about you."

"I like that." She slides her hand up and down, up and down. There's just enough light to see her face, the mesmerized expression on it. "I like how you feel. So hard, but soft." She bends her head to kiss the tip.

A groan climbs up my throat.

She flicks her hair back, then pauses to gather it behind her and do a few twists to keep it out of her way. She shifts position, pushing the covers further down the bed, and crouches, her bare ass in the air. What a view.

She presses my cock flat on my belly and licks my balls.

"Oh Christ." My hands curl into fists. "Yeah."

Her little tongue plays there, sliding and slipping, then she sucks so gently. Her fingertips caress me, and her tongue traces the seam of my sack. Heat runs down through me, over my abs, into my balls.

She kisses me there, then drops more kisses up the length of my shaft, lifting me and bringing the crown to her lips. She pulls back my foreskin, looking up at me with the sexiest, naughtiest smile, and lays a kiss on the very tip where I'm leaking. "Mmmm."

"Fuck." I love how appreciative she is, like she's in heaven doing this. *I'm* in heaven, spiraling, practically levitating off the bed as hot sparks crackle over my skin.

She teases me for a few minutes, her fingers circling my shaft, giving me tiny, closed-mouth kisses on the tip, rubbing it over her bottom lip, all the while looking up at me with bright eyes. "You're so smooth here."

I grunt.

She licks me, around the corona, over the glans, down the shaft, her tongue slippery, getting me wet.

"I like it wet," I gasp.

"Good." She flicks at the frenulum and my muscles quiver. Her fingers sliding wetly on me, she opens her mouth and takes me in. Not far. Just enough to blow my brains out.

"Jesus."

"Mmm." She uses both hands now, sucks a bit then draws back and gives me a wide, wicked smile.

"What are you smiling like that about?" I choke out.

"I like this."

"Fuck yeah. I like it too. Suck me, baby."

"Mmm."

Seeing her lips stretched around me, her cheeks hollowed, her eyes fastened on mine, is like the best erotic dream I've ever had. She's fucking gorgeous. And dirty. And I love it.

She takes me deeper and deeper, using her tongue to keep me wet. I bump the back of her throat and she pulls off for a moment, blinking. "I'm okay."

"Okay." My voice is hoarse. "You don't have to take me all."

"I don't think I can," she whispers. "You're too big." She wets me with her tongue again and then in the hottest thing I've ever seen, she slowly licks her hand to get it wet and wraps it around me again. She strokes me, sweeping over the head on her up stroke, sliding back down. She jacks me for a few minutes, switching up how fast, how hard, watching my face.

"Yeah," I mumble when she gives a firm squeeze. "I like that."

Then she takes me in her mouth again. One hand reaches up and brushes over my chest, then my abs, then teases through my pubic hair, making me shudder. I'm making noises of almost pain, my hips starting to lift, my legs shifting on the bed.

"Shhh. We have to be quiet," she whispers.

Fuck.

"I'm coming," I grate out.

"Yessss." She keeps her mouth moving on me, every stroke and suck and lick taking me higher. And she stays there when I come, jetting into her mouth in hard, weighty pulses, pleasure exploding in my center, flooding my veins with ecstasy.

She takes it all and it's so goddamn filthy and beautiful. When I'm spent, she gives me one last kiss and lays her cheek on my stomach. I'm breathing hard, heart pounding, thoughts obliterated. "Holy fuck."

I feel her smile.

"Pleased with yourself?" I tug at her loose bun and run my fingers through her hair.

"Yeah. Are you pleased?"

"Jesus." I stroke her hair again. "I can barely form words." I pause. "But here are a few words."

She lifts her head. "What?"

"Get up here and sit on my face."

She grins. "Yes sir."

I need to get Carly alone. We have alone time at home, after Quinn's in bed, or when she's at school, but I want more than that. I want to take her out. I'm falling for her ass over blades, and we've only gone on two dates.

I want to celebrate. Monday I got to ditch the no contact jersey for my skate with the team. The season opened with a three-game road trip, which I didn't go on, and it's possible I could play the first home game Saturday night. I'm excited and wired and I want to share that with someone who'll be just as excited and wired for me. Carly.

But how the hell do we do that? And would she even go on a date with me? Surely after we've been sleeping together for over a month, going on a date wouldn't be that inappropriate? That's bass ackwards.

My day—no, week—no, month—is made when Quinn gets an invitation to a sleepover at Hazel's, along with Jada, Friday night. The last time Quinn was invited to sleep over at a friend's, she didn't want to go. She was still attached to me like hockey tape. But this time she wants to.

"This means you have a night off from nanny duties," I tell Carly. "Do you have plans?"

"No." She smiles. "I could make some."

"How about with me? I would love to take you out for dinner." I wait for her objections.

She thinks about it. I knew she would.

Finally, she says softly, "I would love that, too."

"And then...how about going to an open mic night to listen to some music?"

"Sure!"

"Excellent." I rub my hands together. Now I'm even more excited. "It's a date. I'll pick you up at seven."

"Pick me up?" She smiles.

"Yeah. Outside your room." I give her a quick smooch.

Friday morning, the team doc examines me before practice. "You're good to go," he pronounces.

I leap off the exam table. I feel like jumping up and down like Quinn. "Hell yeah! Thank you, doc."

He does the paperwork stuff he has to do while I head to the dressing room to change for practice. It's up to Coach as to whether I'm in the lineup tomorrow, and I'll understand if he doesn't play me. They've been working without me, and he'll need to switch up the D pairs to fit me in to the lineup. So I don't want to get my hopes up too much.

But my luck is holding. After I practice like I'm trying to make the Olympic team, Coach calls me into his office to tell me I'll play. Now I'm ready to fucking dance on the ceiling. We have a team meeting and he outlines the D pairs for tomorrow's game. Things have been juggled since training camp, and he puts me with Barbie, which is cool. We're both veterans, we both know the systems, hopefully I can slide in and make an impact.

So Friday night is truly a celebration. And most of all I'm celebrating that Carly's going out with me.

2 2

CARLY

Nate takes Quinn to Hazel's place. While he's gone, I get ready in my room with the door closed, and I keep it closed when I hear him return.

I feel like a teenager. Nate and I have gotten to know each other pretty well living together. I know he likes his showers scalding hot, and doesn't always put his socks in the hamper, and leaves the peanut butter sitting on the counter with the lid off. But this is only our third date. It's weird, and I'm excited about going out with him.

Yes, I know we shouldn't. We shouldn't be banging each other's brains out any time we get a chance, either, but here we are.

I go for dressy casual, pulling on a gray sweater dress I love and I'm so happy to wear now the weather's cooler. I tug on my black suede over-the-knee boots that I bought in Paris, add a couple of bright-colored beaded bracelets with ribbon bows, and move a few things to a small black purse. I glance at the time on my phone. Don't want to keep him waiting!

I add a deep burgundy lipstick, rubbing my lips together to spread it and studying my reflection. A date!

At exactly seven I open my door to find Nate in the hall, leaning against the wall. My heart punches against my ribs at seeing him.

He's not a sophisticated-looking guy, with his long hair, bumpy nose, and chin scar. But in narrow dark jeans, a navy and beige patterned shirt left untucked, and a tan casual sport jacket—he's hot. He looks up from his phone and straightens, studying me.

I like how he looks at me. Nobody's ever looked at me with that much admiration and desire in their eyes. My skin flushes hot and I feel tingly all over.

"Those boots," he says roughly. "Holy shit, Carly."

"You like?" I pivot, hoping I don't fall over.

"I fucking love them. And this dress." He runs a hand down my back and over my butt, and squeezes through the knit. "So hot."

"You look hot, too." I kiss his jaw where his stubble is trimmed to barely a shadow.

"Thank you." He glances down at himself. "I forgot how to dress to go out. It's been a while."

"It has, hasn't it?" Our first date was early summer and neither of us has been on a date since. "Better make it good, Mr. Hockey."

"You can't call me that."

"Why not?"

"That's Gordie Howe. One of the greatest of all time."

"Would he mind?"

"Uh, he's dead."

"Then you're Mr. Hockey to me." I trail my fingers over his jaw and head toward the door.

He gives my butt a little tap that makes me hop, but also flips my belly.

We take a car to the restaurant where he made reservations—Plum. I've never heard of it let alone been there before and I gaze around at the interior as we're shown to our table. It's on the second floor of the building, with high ceilings and arched windows. One wall has a moody painted mural of a forest, the others are all creamy vanilla. My heels click on the pale oak floor as we walk to our table, and I slide into a mulberry velvet booth with a gold chandelier above us.

"Sexy," I murmur as we settle in.

"Me?" Nate asks. "Or the restaurant?"

"Both." I grin. "This place is like a European brasserie."

"Is it?" He looks around. "Is that good?"

"Oh yes! I miss Europe."

"Do you want to go back?"

"To visit? Or to live?"

"Either."

"Well, I think I'm done living there. But I'd love to go back and visit." I pause. "I'd love to show it to you."

He smiles. "I'd like that."

The menu is just as interesting as the décor, and we start with Pacific Blue shrimp to share, along with a bottle of champagne that Nate orders. After much deliberation we agree to share an entrée, too—a generous salt-crusted Porterhouse steak that's intended for two. We add potato purée and broccolini.

The music is European, too, lively and kind of bohemian, and I'm transported back to the place I love. But this time Nate is with me and it's even better This time I'm not reminded of the family I loved and lost. I have those experiences and memories and they'll always be with me. Now I have different things—different people in my life, different experiences.

I'm moving forward.

After we order and the server has poured the lovely wine, Nate holds my hand on the small table, his thumb tracing over the inside of my wrist. It's sultry and sexy, and desire pulses low inside me.

"Why the champagne?" I ask, lifting the flute to my lips.

"We're celebrating."

"We are?"

"You finally agreed to go out with me." He grins.

I smile back at him.

"And...I got cleared to play today."

My mouth drops open. "Oh my God! That's great!"

"Yeah. And...Coach is putting me in the lineup tomorrow night."

My eyes fly open wide. "Yay! That's fantastic, Nate!" My heart swells so big I think it might burst out of my chest. "I'm so happy for you. It's been a long road."

He picks up my hands and kisses my knuckles. "You've been with me for most of it. And I want to thank you for that."

"You're paying me," I say dryly, even though my heart is bumping unevenly.

"Phhht. I'm not paying you to sleep with me. Don't even joke about that."

"I know. Are you saying sex was the magic cure?"

He looks thoughtful. "I wouldn't rule that out."

I laugh softly.

"You're so beautiful." He smiles. "I wanted to bring you someplace like this and show you off."

"Show me off? Like I'm an object?" I'm protesting, but his words make me feel beautiful.

"Not like that," he says mildly, as if knowing I'm not really arguing. "You know that."

I smile. "I do."

"I want people to know how lucky I am someone like you is with me."

My chest heats. "Aw." I squeeze his hand. "Is this your idea of a perfect date?"

He tilts his head. "I don't know. This is pretty nice. But I like to do active things, too. I just haven't been able to for a while."

"True. What would be a good active date?"

"Skating in the park. A rowboat across the lake. Kayaking on the river."

"Those all sound fun."

"Even playing shuffleboard or pool is fun. Sometimes the whole team gets together at this place in the West Village, and it's tons of fun. That reminds me…"

I cock an eyebrow.

"The place we're going to after this—some of the team will be there."

"Oh. Okay." I sound casual, but this is actually kind of big. Dinner for two is one thing; meeting his friends as a date and not his nanny is a whole different game. I meet his eyes and I know he's thinking the same thing. But he arranged this, so he must want it.

He gives my hand a gentle squeeze.

"Cookie's girlfriend Emerie is a singer."

"I met her at the game, right?"

"Right. She used to be a busker. I don't think she's playing in the subway anymore, but she's doing open mic nights now. Last year she won a big competition."

"Cool. That's kind of wild, though, that a professional athlete would be with a busker?"

"Ha. It is, except that's not the whole story. Emerie is actually filthy rich. She's the step-daughter of the owner of the team. Vince D'Agostino."

"Who filed for bankruptcy."

"Yeah." He wrinkles his nose. "Maybe she's not so rich after all. Anyway, we like to go watch her perform sometimes and support her."

"That's nice." I pause. "So the team owner's step-daughter is dating a player."

"Yep. Just a bit awkward. But I guess he won't be the owner for long. We still haven't heard anything more about that."

"Does it bother you? I mean you, plural. All the players. The uncertainty can't be good."

"I think everyone has pushed it aside. It's out of our control. We just need to play the best we can."

"That's why you're pros."

"Yeah." His smile makes my chest warm.

The shrimp are delicious along with the sparkling wine, and we take our team eating, talking about all kinds of things—Nate's schedule, Quinn's swearing, my book.

"When do you think you'll finish it?" he asks.

"I don't know. I think I'm nearly done. Then I'll have a lot of revisions to do, to bring it all together."

"You impress me so much."

"Thank you." My inhalation is a little shaky. "You impress me, too."

"Huh? How?"

"Oh, come on. You were hurt. You had surgery."

"Arthroscopic."

"Still. You had to recover and it was a challenge for you. You've worked hard at your rehab. You're determined and dedicated. Those are things to admire."

Color hits his cheeks. "Thank you. That…" He swallows. "That means a lot to me."

"I also admire your body," I whisper, trying to lighten the mood since I seem to have struck a chord. "All that hard work pays off."

He gives me a dirty smirk. "I admire your body, too. I'm picturing you in your bra and panties and those boots—"

"Carly?"

We're both in a fog of lust, and slowly look up at the man standing next to our table.

Jeff.

Holy shit. My jaw nearly bounces off the table. I stare at him.

"I thought that was you," he says. "Wow. How are you?"

"I'm…good. Surprised. I thought you were…" I trail off awkwardly.

"I'm out," he says quietly. "A few weeks ago."

"Um. Good…for you." I have no clue what to say.

Jeff glances at Nate.

"Um, Nate, this is Jeff Mills." He recognizes the name and his jaw tightens. "Jeff, this is Nate Karmeinski."

"Holy shit, you play for the Bears." Jeff stares at Nate.

"I do." Nate gives him a taut smile. "Are you a hockey fan?"

"Yeah, I love hockey." Jeff shakes his head. "I didn't know…" He looks back at me. "I actually didn't know you're back from Paris."

"Yeah. A few months ago. You knew I moved there?"

"I heard, yeah. Not from you." His reproachful look makes my stomach tighten with guilt. It's true that I left without saying anything to him. "Carly…uh. Look, I…" He glances at Nate again, checks our ring fingers, which are bare, then says, "Could we talk sometime? There are things I'd like to say to you, and I have …questions."

I gaze at him, pinning my bottom lip between my teeth. Was it unfair to him to leave like that? But learning he was a criminal didn't make me feel like he deserved explanations. I thought he'd know how betrayed I felt. How deceived. How broken-hearted. "I don't know…"

"Really, I want to talk to you." He sounds more urgent. "It's important to me."

I suck briefly on my bottom lip. Maybe I do owe him that, at least. "Um. Well. Here's my number." I give him my cell number reluctantly. He enters it into his phone.

"Sorry to interrupt your dinner," he says. "We'll talk. Thanks, Carly."

He's so earnest and serious. It surprises me. I don't know what I expected if I ever saw him again.

He walks away and both Nate and I watch him, then turn to each other.

"You gave him your number?" he demands in a low tone.

I blink. "Yeah. I kind of feel sorry for him. And…a little guilty, honestly."

"*You* feel guilty?" He gapes at me. "After what he did?"

I grimace. "I know. At the time, I thought that was reason enough to take off. But I never talked to him. I never heard his explanation for what happened."

"Explanation? Jesus Christ! He stole from people."

I wince. "I know. But we were together for years. And I probably should have told him how I felt."

His eyes search mine. "How did you feel?"

"I told you. I felt betrayed. I don't know if he ever outright lied to me, but he certainly wasn't honest with me. My life was destroyed by that. Everything I thought I was going to have was gone. And I ran. Maybe...that wasn't the right way to handle it." I shake my head. "I may never hear from him."

"Oh, you'll hear from him," Nate mutters. "The way he looked at you? Jesus."

I gaze back at him. "How did he look at me?"

"Thirsty. And you're a big sexy drink of water." He tosses back the rest of his wine.

A server immediately appears and carefully refills both our glasses. We're silent amidst a new buzz of tension.

"Jeff and I are over," I say to Nate once the server leaves. "It was years ago."

"Then why see him?"

"I don't know if I will. And if I do, it doesn't matter."

A muscle ticks in his lean jaw.

I lean forward. "Nate. Are you jealous?"

He scowls. I'm sure he's about to say no, but he closes his mouth. He's silent for a drawn-out moment, then he mutters, "Yeah."

My heart throbs. I feel it through my whole body. I don't know what to say. I can see it was hard for him to admit that. That his instinct was to deny it. And he made himself vulnerable by disclosing that. Because...what are we? I'm his nanny. We sleep together. But he was brave enough to tell me the truth.

I want to throw myself across the table and into his arms and hug him and kiss him and tell him he has no reason to be jealous because I...

Oh my God.

I think I'm in love with him.

I press my fingers to my mouth.

Nate eyes me. "What?"

My breath lifts my chest, quickly, in, out. "Nate."

"What?" he says again, slower.

I glance around the restaurant. We're surrounded by people. I can't do this here.

I can't do this anywhere.

Terror suddenly grips my heart in scrawny, bony hands and squeezes. This isn't what I wanted. This isn't what I imagined when I came back to New York. I wanted it to be different this time. I want to have my own home, live my own life, not worry about taking care of other people, and do what I've dreamed of doing—write about things I'm passionate about.

How did this happen?

The server arrives with our steak dinner.

"That thing's huge," I murmur when we've been served.

"I know, but you said you like it." Nate glances at his crotch.

After a beat, I crack up laughing. That settles the vibe down, all right. He meets my eyes, his glinting with humor, and we dig into our steak.

Okay. I don't know what's happening or what to do about it, but right now I'm going to have fun on this date.

23

NATE

I definitely didn't want to run into Carly's asswipe ex-boyfriend. Jesus Christ. He went to fucking prison. He hurt her.

I want to hurt him.

Okay, now I understand violence. I want to do violence to that guy. I wanted to stand up and drive my fist into his pretty face.

But I'm a mature man who doesn't need to resort to violence to express my emotions. Which Carly correctly called me on when she asked if I was jealous.

Oh fuck yeah, I was jealous. The way he looked at her...the way she looked at him...fuck me.

I have an ex, too. I don't want to get back with Brielle. I understand that Carly and Jeff are done. I understand that in my head. But my goddamn heart still thumps with a hot, angry beat. It's those goddamn insecurities that keep popping up.

I settle down as we eat our meal, focusing on Carly. I want her so fucking much. She makes everything in my life better. The thought of losing her, of her going back to her ex, makes me enraged. I try to calm down about it.

"Is the open mic place near here?" she asks after we decline dessert.

I check the time on my phone. "Yeah. I picked this restaurant because it's close. And it's good."

"It was amazing."

I settle up the bill after a short squabble over her paying half of it and shepherd her out of the restaurant. If Jeff Jerkoff is watching, good, let him see me take care of her.

We walk a couple of blocks to the Mystic Nomad and find a bunch of people already there with seats saved for us. Emerie and Cookie are seated, too, and she looks excited and glowing as she sips a cocktail. I introduce Carly to Cookie, then to the others—Hellsy and Sara, Morrie and Kate, Brando and Lola, and Lola's friend Kaylee. Hopefully they all like Carly and maybe we can go out together sometime. I see the looks the guys are giving Carly and me, the question in their eyes—*are you fucking your nanny?* Not just fucking her, my dudes, I'm dating her.

Carly and Sara immediately strike up a conversation of mutual admiration. It turns out Carly has listened to Sara's podcasts and Sara also reads Carly's blogs. Sara's a pretty well-known influencer with her vlog and podcasts about all kinds of weird shit. I don't know how else to describe it.

"You need to be a guest on my podcast!" Sara says excitedly. "That would be so cool. I would love to talk to you about some of the things you write about."

"Oh, I would love that too!" Carly seems just as excited. "Let's do that!"

They pull out their phones and start looking at calendars.

Murph arrives then, without his girlfriend. When he has a beer in his hand, I move over to him. "Where's Charlotte?"

"We broke up."

"What? Jesus. You okay?"

He looks weirdly unaffected. "I'm fine."

I don't think he's fine. They've been together a while.

I squeeze his shoulder. "I'm here if you wanna talk."

He shrugs and chugs his beer.

Lola's baby bump is getting bigger and she and Carly launch into a discussion about due dates and gender reveals (Jesus, please, no) and how Lola's been feeling. Then Nadia and Barbie arrive, throwing their hands in the air as they're greeted with cheers from us. Nadia sashays toward us through the tables like a supermodel on a runway.

"Vat songs you play tonight?" Nadia asks as she hugs Emerie. "I love the one about sunrise."

Emerie smiles at her. "I'll sing that one just for you."

"Yes! And Igor likes the sexy one about sex." Igor is Barbie; we call him Barbie because his last name is Barbashev.

Emerie laughs. "He *thinks* it's about sex."

"It's totally about sex," Cookie says dryly.

Emerie gives his shoulder a little push, but grins.

Millsy and Lilly arrive then and they're both wearing weird smiles on their faces. As we shift around to make room for them at the tables we've pulled together, Sara shrieks.

Startled we all turn to her. She grabs Lilly's hand and holds it up. "When did this happen?" she cries.

A deep pink flush runs up into Lilly's cheeks. "This afternoon!"

I spy the flash of a diamond on Lilly's left hand.

"Shut the front door!" Sara jumps up and down, literally. "Oh my God!"

"Dude!" Hellsy slaps Millsy's back. "Congrats!"

Everyone—except Carly, she hangs back, smiling—crowds around the couple admiring the ring, wanting to know how the proposal happened, when the wedding will be. Millsy pulls Lilly against him, arm around her waist and they look ridiculously ecstatic.

"It was in the park where we met," Lilly explains. "Otis escaped and attacked the dog I was walking."

"He didn't attack her," Millsy says patiently about his dog. "He just wanted to meet her. She was cute."

"Right," she says with an eye roll. "But he knocked me down and then Easton came running up and started flirting with me."

He grins. "I thought you were hot."

"Well, I thought you were a jerk. Anyway, this afternoon we took Otis for a walk in the park—such a gorgeous day and the leaves are just beautiful right now—and when we got to the spot where that happened, he proposed."

Everyone makes noises of approval.

"So romantic!" exclaims Nadia.

Finally we all settle down and order drinks, and then it's Emerie's turn at the mic. She has her guitar and takes her place on the stage beneath the spotlights. We all stop talking to listen. I mean, you can't help but listen because her music is mesmerizing. Between songs, though, we applaud wildly, whistle, and cheer.

"She's so good!" Carly says, beaming while clapping enthusiastically.

"She really is."

Then Emerie's done and returns to sit with us.

"That was amazing!" Lilly says.

"You are so good!" Nadia grabs her shoulders and kisses her on each cheek. "You are a rock star!"

Emerie's cheeks flush and her eyes shine.

"How can I listen to more of your music?" Carly asks her.

"I have a SoundCloud," Emerie says. "Thanks!"

Carly pulls her phone out and a moment later says, "Hey! You're a trending track!"

"Really?" Emerie leans closer.

Carly shows her the phone.

"Wow!" Emerie's eyes are as big as hockey pucks. She sits back in her chair as if floored.

"Which one?" Cookie asks.

"Hidden Love."

"Oh yeah. Congrats, baby." He leans over and kisses her cheek.

She turns to him and the look they share is so full of love and affection, I feel like I'm intruding.

Carly's watching them, too, a sweet smile on her face.

I look over and see Murph talking to Lola's friend Kaylee. He's flirting up a storm.

I don't know what happened with him and Charlotte, but this seems like a recipe for Trouble. I catch his eye and give him a look.

He ignores me.

"Hey, Brando." I motion to him.

We move apart from the group. "Check out Murph and Kaylee."

He lets his gaze slide casually over to them as he takes a sip of his drink. "Where's Charlotte?"

"They broke up."

"What? When?"

"I don't know. It had to be recent."

"He's hitting on Kaylee."

"Yeah. I mean, she's a grown adult, but maybe she should know he's probably not in a good space right now."

He nods. "I'm on it." He moves, then stops. "Wait. Why is your nanny here with you?" He narrows his eyes at me.

"Uh." I wet my lips. "She's not just my nanny."

His smile is as wide as a hockey rink. "Ah. Things changed."

I smile, too. "Yeah."

"She got rid of the no banging the boss rule?"

"Jesus, keep your voice down." I shake my head.

"She did. That's great." He slaps a hand on my shoulder. "And I really like her."

Warmth spreads through my chest. "Good. I really like her, too."

After baby talk, wedding talk, and music talk, conversation turns to the financial situation of the team.

"Still no news," Morrie says.

"It takes a while for big deals like that to happen," Kate says. She's an agent and represents a bunch of hockey players. "But I've been hearing some buzz about it. Something's happening."

"We might hear more soon," Hellsy says.

Kate's head whips around. "How do you know that?"

He blinks. Then squints. And scratches his neck. "Someone said something...I can't remember."

She purses her lips.

"What?" I ask her. "Do you know something?"

"Maybe." She gives me a cheeky grin. "But I don't like to spread rumors."

"Go ahead," I say. "I want to hear the rumors."

But she's a vault, locked up with the key hidden away.

"What did *you* hear?" Morrie asks Hellsy.

"That's it." He shrugs.

Gah. Even though they've said it won't change anything, I want to know what's going on. I hate not knowing.

As if she senses this, Carly squeezes my arm. "Hang in there, big guy."

"I'm trying," I say. "Patience isn't one of my strong points."

She leans in with her lips close to my ear. "Sometimes you're patient."

Heat flows through my veins. "Sometimes. And sometimes...I'm trying to listen to you and be patient but I'm really just picturing you naked."

She laughs softly.

"Like right now." I nuzzle my nose against her hair.

"We have all night," she reminds me. "Quinn's sleeping over."

"Oh God. The things I want to do to you tonight. All night."

"Stop."

"We could leave right now."

"Do you want to?"

"I've had enough dating. Now I want you to put out."

"I was a pretty sure thing." She laughs. "Okay, let's go."

I'm back. Back on the ice, back on the team, back in the arena in front of a sold-out crowd of die-hard fans. The season home opener is always a special game. Sure, there's pressure. The expectations of the fans are huge. We expect a lot of ourselves, too. The fans are hungry for hockey after the summer, and the players are itching to get back to it, also. The possibilities of the season stretch out before us.

For a moment before I skate out onto the ice, I'm beset with doubts. My knee feels good, but playing an actual, hard-hitting game is a whole different thing.

Fuck that. I worked my ass off for this. I've got this.

It's the home opener and there's a big production at the start of the game. They introduce each of us as we skate onto the ice in a cloud of fog, flashing lights and pumping music. When it's my turn, I step onto the ice lifting my stick to the crowd, and join the other guys to form a circle around the Bears logo at center ice. The crowd is cheering, the stands in darkness other than the red, gold, and white spotlights shifting over them.

"Ladies and gentlemen . . . yooooour New York Bears!"

Standing in the circle, we lift our sticks to salute our fans.

My biggest fans are up there watching—Carly and Quinn. They're sitting with the other Bears WAGs and I want to play well for them. And for myself. And for everyone, really, but having them here for my first game back is pretty damn special.

Then the Aces players come skating on. We leave center ice and do a few laps around our end while they announce the starting lineup, then I head to the bench for the national anthem. I'm not starting, but it'll only be minutes before my first shift. I shift from one foot to the other, adrenaline coursing through my veins. I need to harness the energy but not let it take over. I visualize myself on the ice, focused, alert, but relaxed.

Morrie wins the opening faceoff, a good sign, and we're off. I watch the action as we head to the Aces net and get our first shot on goal. The Aces get the rebound and head the opposite way with slick tape-to-tape passes, but Jammer and the rookie Lavoie do a good job of keeping them to the outside and negate their chance. They turn back the other way with lots of jump, but maybe a little too much jump and Axe is offside.

I vault over the boards, ready for my first shift. The knee feels good. I take my place for the faceoff, jockeying with Aces D man Tanner Bennet with some mild shoving and swearing. JBo wins the faceoff and snaps the puck to me. Bennet almost steals it but I hang on and dump it into the O zone. Benny and JBo battle along the boards, the puck pops free, and Millsy gets it to me at the point. I see it coming, pull my stick back, and one time it at the net.

Fuck yeah!

The lamp lights, the horn blares, and arms go in the air. Jesus Christ, my first shift and I fucking score! I'm almost too astonished to cellie but my teammates come at me with big grins.

"Hell yeah!" Millsy yells.

"Snipe!" JBo says.

"You're baaaaack, baby!" Barbie shouts.

I head to the bench to knock gloves with the other guys, my heart pounding, a smile stretched across my face, and I can't help glance up to where I know Carly and Quinn are likely cheering like crazy along with the rest of the crowd.

I fucking love this.

24

CARLY

I'm having lunch with Jeff today.

I'm anxious about it. But not so much about seeing him—because honestly, I'm over him and whatever he has to say isn't going to change my life—but because I haven't told Nate.

Why haven't I told him? I guess I'm just avoiding conflict, because I know he doesn't want me to see Jeff. Also I'm confused about our whole relationship. I work for him. That doesn't give him the right to control who I see or what I do. But it's more than that. I don't just work for him, but...what am I to him other than his nanny? Do I want to be more to him than that? I keep reminding myself of my goals for coming back to New York, but I feel like everything has changed since meeting Nate. And I don't know if that's good or bad.

When I'm with him, it's good. So good. Everything. And that's all I want. Him. To be with him. But then my brain starts analyzing stuff and telling me I'm caving to patriarchal beliefs that a woman needs a man. I don't need a man. I want to be my own person, succeed on my own merits. The fact that I am succeeding is fantastic and magical and awesome, but it's not lost on me that the reason I can write my article and blog posts and work on my book is because Nate offered me a job.

Is my whole life going to be taking care of other people? What about *my* dreams and goals? Maybe this decision to see Jeff is a little act of rebellion against the fact that I still don't feel I'm in control of my own life and this is a way to take charge.

It's not that big a deal. It's closure, for both Jeff and for me. I never had a chance to tell him how I felt, and maybe it wasn't fair to him to leave without giving him a chance to tell me his side.

So here I am, at a little bistro on 35th Street, scanning the restaurant to see if he's here yet. He is. He lifts a hand and I take a breath as I start toward him.

Jeff is objectively good-looking, in a way I thought was my "type"—short, styled dark hair, clean-shaven, even features, and a tall, lean build. But now I look at him and feel zero attraction.

I like Nate's rough edges. His long hair that hangs in his face. His scar and bumpy nose. His rough hands, thick thighs, and strong muscles. I liked his appearance before I even saw him play hockey, and—call me superficial, I'll take it here—when I saw him on the ice for the first time the other day, I was actually turned on.

Jeff stands and greets me by taking my hand, but he tugs me closer and kisses my cheek. I stiffen, fasten on a smile, and take the seat opposite him.

"I was so glad I ran into you the other night," he says, sitting again. "I've wanted to talk to you for so long."

I eye him as I lay my napkin on my lap. "Well, now's your chance."

"That guy you were with—Nate Karmeinski—are things serious?"

Well, that's jumping right to it. "I'm not sure yet," I say with a smile, which is the honest truth. It's also the honest truth when I add, "I care about him a lot."

"Ah." Jeff's eyes dim, the corners of his mouth turn down, and he nods. "I guess I shouldn't be surprised."

"Did you think I'd wait for you?"

He gives a huff of amusement. "No. I mean, I guess I had that hope at first but after you disappeared, that kind of faded away."

"How could you…" I stop. I don't want to make this antagonistic. "All I can really tell you is how I felt at the time, Jeff."

We're interrupted by a waiter filling water glasses and telling us about the special, some kind of chicken salad that I go ahead and order even though I don't really hear what it is. Jeff gets the same.

"Okay," he says. "Let me have it. Tell me how you felt."

I gaze at him for a moment as I take a sip of water. "Okay. You broke my heart."

He flinches. "Fuck. I'm sorry, Carly."

I want to question that but I don't. I just keep going, tell him how hurt I was, how betrayed, how humiliated. "I questioned our entire relationship," I say. "I questioned *myself*. How could I have misjudged you so badly? Someone I cared about? It felt like everything that had happened between us was a lie. It felt like you were someone I didn't even know. I felt like I'd lost everything—my relationship, my hopes and dreams for the future, my lover, my friend."

"I'm sorry I hurt you," he says quietly. "I wish I could have talked to you and explained things."

He sounds remorseful. But I'm skeptical. I trusted him once. "Are you going to tell me what happened? Why you did…what you did?"

"I didn't do anything wrong."

My jaw drops. "Jeff…"

"Will you listen?"

I swallow. "Okay."

He tells me a story of the things his boss asked him to do. I don't really understand much of it. He tells me about being approached by FBI agents who wanted him to cooperate in their investigation of the company. But he wouldn't, because he honestly didn't think he was doing anything wrong. "I was offered a chance to plead guilty and cooperate against the higher ups at Affiniti. *They* weren't arrested," he adds with an edge of bitterness. "I told the feds I would cooperate if I felt they'd done something wrong, but I didn't. I would have told them whatever they wanted to know. But I believed I was innocent. I plead not guilty. And ended up in prison."

I can only stare at him as I take this in. "So you're still saying you did nothing wrong? Even after a trial and a conviction?"

"Yes."

"I...don't know what to say."

"You felt betrayed and heartbroken," he says in a low voice. "But so did I. I wanted you there, supporting me."

Our meals arrive and we take a couple of minutes to arrange things. My mind spins like a termite in a yoyo. I pick up my cutlery and stare unseeingly at my salad. This was so not what I expected to hear.

"You went to prison," I finally say.

"Yeah." He grimaces. "Minimum security, but still not fun. I missed a lot of things. Most of all, you."

"Don't do this," I whisper.

Everything I've told myself over the last three years is being smashed to pieces. Except, I still don't know if I believe him. He may be certain he was innocent, but a judge and jury convicted him. How do I disregard that?

Was I wrong to not talk to him then? I was completely sure he'd been indicted for good reason. I mean, innocent people do go to prison, but...my temples throb and my jaw aches from clenching my teeth.

"I missed fresh fruit," he says with a wry smile. "Wearing my own clothes. Driving my car."

I nod, still trying to make sense of it all. "What are you doing now?"

"Remember James Vale?"

"Yes..."

"I'm working for him. He started a health insurance software company."

"Oh, that's good." Again, not what I expected.

I try to eat, forking up a piece of spicy chicken and chewing it, while Jeff talks more.

"James stayed in touch," he says.

I get the unspoken message. *And you didn't.*

I'm so confused. I feel like shit, and yet...I don't know what I even feel. Obviously one of those mix of emotions that's hard to sort out, like we talked about with Nate's teammates that day. So many emotions. It's going to take me days to sort them out. Weeks.

"I'm sorry, Jeff," I say. "I did owe it to you to listen to you. I don't know if that would have changed what happened, but you're right. I ran away without giving you the chance."

"Thanks." He nods, pushing a tomato around his plate. He's as enthusiastic about eating as I am. "I know you're with someone else now, and I'm happy for you. I wish things could have been different, but thanks for talking to me and hearing me out." He swallows. "I loved you."

My eyes and nose sting and my throat thickens. "I loved you, too."

His smile is sad. "Shit happens."

"Yeah." I squeeze my eyes shut briefly. "C'est la vie."

"Ah. Tell me about living in Paris."

We talk more and manage to eat some of our lunch, then say goodbye. It's sad and sentimental and regretful. We have a lot of good memories together. I did care about him. I was heartbroken, and I blamed him. But also I'm still cynical. And now maybe a little guilty.

We hug, an embrace that we both know will be our last. This time we both know it's over.

And when I turn to walk out of the restaurant, I see Nate coming in.

25

NATE

What in the blueberry fuck muffins is going on here?

That's Carly. And her asswipe ex-con ex-boyfriend. And they're holding on to each other tighter than the tape on my stick.

I feel the pressure in my veins erupt, blasting up to my head so fast I think it might explode. My hands curl into fists and I have to blink away the red haze in front of my eyes.

They let go of each other and Carly turns. She sees me. She stops short. "Nate."

She's fucking gorgeous, as always, wearing high waisted jeans and a cropped pink sweater. I hope she's showing Jerkwad Jeff what he's missing. Not trying to entice him back.

I'm not thinking clearly, I know it. "Carly. What the fuck."

She frowns, glances beside her where Jeff has followed, then back at me. There's a moment that feels about ten years long.

"Are you here for lunch?" she finally asks me.

"Yeah." I jerk my head at Brando, standing behind me.

"I thought you had practice today."

"We did. But it was here at the Apex Center." Only two blocks away from this place.

"Oh." She darts a smile at Brando. "Hi, Brandon."

"Hi." He's looking back and forth between Carly, Jeff, and me.

Jeff gives me an assessing look that pisses me off. I scowl at him. I take a step toward him, but Brando grabs my jacket.

Carly's eyes widen.

"You didn't tell me you were having lunch with him." I glare at her. "Jesus, Carly."

Her frown returns. "What?"

I am so fucking stupid. Okay, not stupid. Maybe I'm a sucker. I should have known that someone as smart and beautiful as Carly would lose interest in me. Just like every other woman who spent more than a night with me.

She was hugging her ex.

I told her I was jealous of him. I close my eyes briefly as pain corkscrews through me. *So fucking stupid.* No more of that bullshit. I'm locking that shit down. I give her a long, dispassionate look. "Well. Hope it was a nice lunch. See you later."

I move around her to talk to the hostess about a table, ignoring Carly.

"Two, please," I say.

The hostess smiles at me and picks up two menus. "This way."

I follow her without looking back, hoping Brando's with me. I take the seat with my back to the door and Brando sits opposite me.

"Are they gone?" I ask tightly.

He flicks a gaze up front. "Yeah."

"I fucking knew this was going to happen." I set my fists on the table and work at uncurling them.

"Knew *what* was going to happen? What *did* just happen? Who is that guy?"

"Her ex-boyfriend. He just got out of jail," I say bitterly.

"Wait, what? Jail?"

"Yeah."

"Uhhhh…we're gonna need a drink for this."

"No shit."

A pretty waitress arrives with a bright smile for both of us. "Hi guys. You look thirsty."

I give her a sour look and her smile dims. "I'll have a shot of Jameson. Make it a double."

"Sure thing." She bats her false eyelashes at Brando. "How about you?"

He orders a beer.

"I'll give you a few more minutes with the menu," she says.

I ignore the menu, my appetite vanished.

"Okay, what's going on?" Brando asks.

I pick up a cardboard coaster and turn it. "Fuck. I don't even know. Things have been going great, and I thought...shit."

"That didn't tell me much."

"I know." I sigh. "It's complicated."

"Maybe banging your kid's nanny isn't such a good idea."

"You seemed to think it was, before."

"You're right. I have no idea what I'm talking about."

"It was a genius idea. It's worked out perfectly for both of us."

"Then why are you currently having kittens?"

I wince. "Like I said, everything *was* going great."

"Until the ex showed up. You think she wants to go back to him?"

"She says they're over. We ran into him the other night." I tell Brando the story, as much as I know, anyway. "He's a fucking criminal. How could she want to go back to him?"

He lifts his hands. "But does she?"

"She had lunch with him and hugged him."

The waitress arrives with our drinks. I toss back mine and ask for another.

"Do you want to order food?" she asks warily.

"Not really."

Brando closes his eyes then blows out a breath. "Come on, man. Eat. He'll have a double cheeseburger with fries. I'll have the chicken salad special."

I stare at him. "A cheeseburger?"

"Sometimes you need it."

"Fine." I don't even care. "The ex said he wanted to talk to her. And I was jealous. I admitted it. What an idiot." I shake my head. "It doesn't matter."

He looks at me like I just told him I never want to win the Stanley Cup.

"It doesn't," I insist. "We're just banging. Like you said."

"Then why were you jealous of him?"

Fuck. "Okay, fine. I may have fallen for her." Christ. That's not even accurate. I can't fucking imagine my life without her. I've fallen alright, hard, so hard I'm seeing stars and thinking about weddings and happily ever afters. Bonehead.

"I should have known," I say again. The waitress brings my second drink and I take a mouthful of it, going slower this time. "I finally meet someone I actually want a relationship with, and of course she's more interested in the suit guy. Just like Brielle." I roll my eyes and take another gulp.

"Whoa, hey. You're being awfully hard on yourself."

"She'd rather be with a criminal than with me!"

"You don't know that. Come on, man, get a grip."

My blood heats all over again. "You saw them! They were glomped onto each other."

"Yeah." He purses his lips. "Do you really think this is like what happened with Brielle?"

"Feels like it." I remember her telling me she'd fallen for someone else and how gutted I'd been. Actually, this feels worse. Somehow when Brielle and I split up it wasn't a big shock. Our marriage had been coasting for a while before that. We were together for Quinn.

But Carly...it felt right. It felt real. And that makes it hurt even more.

"You need to talk to her about this."

"That sounds fun."

He rubs his forehead. "Probably not fun. Those conversations never are. Believe me, I know. But you gotta do it."

"We leave on a road trip tomorrow. No time."

He gives me a long look. "Lots of time for you to think about it though."

2 6

CARLY

Nate acts like nothing is wrong when he gets home. I've been waiting anxiously so we can talk, but he stays busy with Quinn all evening and then says he has to pack for their trip and disappears into his bedroom.

Is nothing wrong? Maybe? He seemed upset when he first saw me and Jeff at the restaurant, but maybe he thought it over and realized it didn't mean anything. But then why won't he talk to me? Something about his cheeriness seems off.

He'll be gone for six days. They play three games in Seattle, Vegas, and Phoenix. How am I going to survive six days, wondering what's going on and if we're okay?

We're not okay. I mean, this is the first road trip he's gone on since we've been together, and I'd expect some goodbye sex the night before, at least. And maybe a kiss in the morning, when Quinn's not around. I don't get either of those things, just a quick rundown of Quinn's schedule for the coming week, which I already know about. We also plan times for FaceTiming with Brielle.

But that all fades away when Quinn wakes up crying in the night. "Daddy!"

Nate and I meet in the hallway outside her room, in the shadows.

"Daddy!" Quinn cries again, then appears in front of us.

"What's wrong, pop tart?" He turns from me and scoops her up.

"I don't want you to leave tomorrow!" She wraps her arms around him and hangs on like a little monkey. "I don't want you to go."

His eyes meet mine over her head and I bite my lip. I move closer and set my hand on her back. "I'll be here, Quinn. Remember? And I love you."

She buries her face into her father's shoulder.

"I know it's scary," I say again. "You'll miss your dad when he's gone."

She nods.

I rub her back again. "Are you afraid Daddy won't come back? Is that what your worries are telling you?"

She nods again.

"I'll always come back to you," Nate says to her, his tone gentle but firm. "Always. I love you."

"Do you think those worries are worth listening to?" I ask her. We've talked about this before. "How real is it that your dad won't come back? Do you think it's true?"

She's silent, taking in hiccupping, shaky breaths. Finally, she says, "No."

"I agree," I say softly. "What can you say to your worries?"

After a moment, she says, "My daddy loves me and won't leave me. It's just for a few days."

"That's right. Don't let those worries boss you around. They're wrong."

"Get out of my head, you dumbass worries!"

I press my lips together. It's the right sentiment but the swearing isn't exactly appropriate. Oh well.

"Dumbass worries!" Nate repeats. He gives me a helpless look and again I try not to smile. "Come on. Let's get you back to bed. I'll stay with you for a few minutes." He meets my eyes. "Thank you."

I nod and watch him carry Quinn to her bed and set her down so gently. He stretches out next to her and I back out of the room and go back to my own.

I'm worried about the morning, but Quinn seems to have dealt with her fears and emotions. Nate takes her to school on his way to the airport, and she leaves happily enough with him. Hopefully there's no meltdown at school.

The apartment is quiet after they leave. A good chance to get some work done. But my mind is darting around like a squirrel on meth. I'm replaying my conversation with Nate that night we ran into Jeff. I'm replaying yesterday. I still have a gnawing feeling things aren't right.

I should have told Nate I was going to see Jeff. Maybe that's what's wrong. He admitted he was jealous, and then seeing me with Jeff and hugging him, without knowing I was going to do that probably made him mad. I get that. I screwed up. Should I call him? Text him? Apologize?

I don't know what to do.

Do I really need to tell him everything I do? What are we even doing together? The other night I was so scared at the idea of falling in love with him. I keep reminding myself that we're just fooling around, having sex when his daughter's not around. We're not getting involved, like, emotionally involved.

I don't need to make this into a bigger deal than it is. I saw my ex. We talked. We got closure on our relationship. Done. If Nate has issues with it, he needs to bring them up to me. And he hasn't.

With that settled in my mind, I focus on my book. I'm so close to finishing. The excitement of being done gives me an adrenaline rush that has my fingers flying over the keyboard. I stop to grab a yogurt for lunch and sort through some ideas, then keep writing until it's time to pick up Quinn. All that's left now is the last chapter, which will summarize everything else and pull it all together. So close!

The leaves are turning in Central Park so we go for a walk there after school. The sun illuminates the amber, pumpkin, and scarlet leaves against the perfect azure sky, the still-green grass carpeted with similar shades. Quinn kicks through the rustling leaves, chatting as we walk. "I'm still afraid," she confides. "But Daddy says he'll call me every day while he's gone."

"Of course he will. He's going to miss you, too."

"It's good that he'll be busy playing hockey so he won't have time to miss me."

I smile. "Right."

I make us macaroni and cheese for dinner, watch Quinn do her homework. Then we play a few rounds of Old Maid.

"What even is an old maid?" she asks, studying her cards.

"It's an old-fashioned expression," I say. "They used to call unmarried ladies old maids."

"Even if they weren't old?'"

"Yeah. Dumb, huh?"

"Yes." She picks a card from me, grins, and lays down a pair. "I don't want to be an old maid."

"You can be a happy unmarried lady. Like me." I pick a card. No match. I'm getting my butt kicked here.

"Yes. I want to be like you. Maybe I'll write books." She matches her last pair. "You're the old maid!"

"I think we should rename the game. Let's call it…bachelor girl."

"Okay. But wait. Then you would be the winner, because being a bachelor girl is fun."

"That's right! I won! Finally."

"Noooo!"

I grab her and squeeze her and we're both laughing and then I snort laugh and that makes her laugh even more. Then she has her bath and we get ready for bed.

"I love you, Carly," she murmurs when she's tucked in. "I'm glad you're here."

"Thank you. I love you, too, sweetie." I smooth her hair off her forehead, my heart aching.

Dammit. I've done it again. I've fallen in love with another child who's not mine. A child I'll lose some day.

And I've maybe fallen in love with her dad, too.

27

NATE

In an amazing feat of compartmentalization, I manage to focus on hockey for our games and forget about what's going on at home. But in my hotel room after the games, I can't stop myself from replaying that moment—seeing Carly hugging her ex, the way he looked at me, and how my gut seized into a piece of granite.

I'm pissed, to be honest. Why didn't she tell me she was going to see him? Why was I such an idiot to admit I was jealous? Good thing I never told her I think I'm in love with her. Has she been using me, like every other woman I've been with longer than one night? She had a perfect setup—good pay, free time to write, a nice place to live. Have I been taken once again? Goddammit.

I pick up the remote for the TV in the hotel room and flick through channels, trying to find something to distract me. Nothing's doing the trick.

What do I do when I get home? Should I fire Carly?

I can't do that. I still need her. Quinn loves her. And the truth is, I do love her and I can't do that to her. So, I don't know what I'm going to do when I get home. Fuck.

Noise in the hall outside my room has me lifting my head. Someone is swearing up a storm. What's going on? I roll off the bed, drag my weary body to the door and fling the door open. Barbie is standing in his open doorway, an empty waste basket at his feet, surrounded by a wet patch of carpet.

He looks at me. "Kids."

I hear muffled laughter from down the hall.

The "leaner" is a tired old practical joke. You fill up a container—sometimes an ice bucket, sometimes a waste basket, or one time a team used a big garbage can and flooded three floors of the hotel—lean it up against a teammate's hotel room door at an angle, knock, and run down the hall. When the guy opens the door, water dumps from the bucket into his entryway.

The new guy, who we call Flip, appears, along with Beave and Dutchy.

"What the fuck?" I stare at them.

"Come on, boys, you gotta be more creative than that," Barbie yells down the hall.

They're all laughing. Having fun. My frustration level is already at DEFCON 2 and this sends me over the edge. "Shut the fuck up, you assholes. Some of us are trying to sleep."

They shut up and stare at me, open-mouthed.

These young pups are way too zippy.

"Hey, easy, man," Barbie says. "They're just having a little fun."

I feel about a hundred years old. "Not in the hall, they're not. Jesus. Come on. There could be guests on this floor other than us."

They all exchange baffled looks. I'm being an asshole. I know that. I don't care. I resist the urge to slam my door as I return to my room, but I want to. I want to punch something.

I'm on my way home from the airport when I get a call from Brielle. My gut is all twisted up, thinking about seeing Carly again and how that's going to go. I take the call using Bluetooth and keep driving. "What's up?" I ask, still grouchy.

"Look, I've been thinking."

"Okay. About what?"

"About Quinn. After that incident with her homework, and her crying on the phone to me…I can't do this."

"Okay," I say again with a little edge. My patience is meager right now. "Do what?"

"I can't live apart from Quinn." Her voice thickens. "It's too hard. I miss her. She misses me. She needs her mom."

Well, yeah. "You're the one who moved away."

"I know, I know. And I really want this part. So…I want Quinn to come here and live with me and Parker in L.A."

My vision goes dark for a moment and I have to jerk the wheel to keep from drifting into the lane beside me. My entire body flushes hot. "You want her there."

"Yes. That's okay with you, right? I know it's hard for you during the season, so this should help out."

"Help out? Taking my daughter away from me is helping out?" My hands grip the steering wheel so tightly I nearly snap it.

"I'm not taking her away from you!"

"Uh, yeah, that's what it sounds like."

"You don't see her that much during the season."

"I still see her! Christ. This is fucked up, Brie."

"I'm sorry! But you know it would be better for her."

"No, I don't know that!" I pull in a deep breath and try to calm down. Maybe I need to pull over for this. "She's doing better. Carly's been great with helping her deal with her anxiety."

"She needs her mother."

"What about her father? What if she misses *me* once she gets there and this starts all over again?"

She's briefly silent. "I hope that won't happen."

"You hope she won't miss me."

"That's not what I said!"

I flick on my turn signal and head for an exit ramp. "That's what it sounded like."

"Of course she'll miss you! She loves you. But if it causes problems, we'll deal with it. I'll deal with it. Not a nanny she doesn't even know."

I feel like bugs are scrawling over my skin. "She knows Carly. She loves her." And I was thinking of firing her.

This would solve that problem, I guess.

But that doesn't sit well with me. And not seeing Quinn…at all…what the fuck. I can't even comprehend that. Sure, I'm busy during the season, but not to the point I never see her. I don't know how many games we play in California but that would be the only time I might get to visit her, if my schedule allows.

"You know it would be better for her," Brielle says, her tone gentler. "Think about Quinn, Nate."

I pull into a gas station parking lot and stop. I'm still clenching the steering wheel and my back molars grind together. "I *am* thinking of her. What about school? Her friends? She's familiar with my place. You're going to uproot her for somewhere totally new where she knows nobody. That's not going to help."

"But I'll be with her." Her tone becomes pleading again and I can tell how emotional she is about this. "I didn't realize I'd miss her so much."

"Is this about you missing her? Or about Quinn?"

"Well, both. But it just broke my heart to hear her crying like that, and her thinking I left because I don't love her anymore." Now Brielle is sobbing.

"How often would you see her when you're shooting? I hear there can be long days."

"I'll figure that out. Parker can bring her to the set, maybe."

I feel like I'm being strangled and my heart is crammed in my chest cavity. "Could we figure out something else?" I choke out.

"Like what? She's too young to fly on her own, and it's a long flight. I've tried to think this through, and this is the best option."

I can't argue with what she's saying. My head is too fuzzy to think clearly; maybe there are other ways we could handle it, but none are coming to mind right now. I'll try to fit in trips to L.A. as often as I can, but that's not easy during the hockey season. Pressure builds behind my burning eyes.

My baby girl. My Quinn. She's so precious to me. I love her so much. How am I going to bear this?

I guess the same way Brielle did, at first. That didn't last long, though.

I rub both hands over my face. "Okay," I croak. "Fine. How are we going to do this?"

Brielle can fly here tomorrow to get Quinn and take her back to L.A. "I'll be a wreck, but oh well," she says. "I'm sorry, Nate. I know this is hard."

I still have a noose around my neck, strangling me. "Yeah. It is."

I sit there for a while after we end the call. Brielle's going to text me flight details. I stare into the distance, trying to figure out what I'm going to do. I guess the first thing to do is tell Quinn. I check the clock on my dash. I can pick her up from school if I go right now.

I quickly text Carly to let her know I'm picking up Quinn. And try to get some armor in place so I don't breakdown into a puddle in front of my daughter.

CARLY

"Carly! Guess what!"

Quinn blows into the apartment in a tempest of excitement, followed more slowly by her dad.

"What? Tell me, tell me everything." I smile at her.

"I'm moving to California!"

My smile ebbs. What? Did I hear that right? I lift my gaze to Nate.

The look on his face tells me I did hear that right.

"Um...wow." I try to gather my wits. "How did this happen?"

"Brielle called. She wants Quinn there with her. We discussed it, and I asked Quinn how she feels about it and she wants to go see her mom."

"Of course you do." I feel frozen. Numb. But I stretch my lips into a smile. "This is amazing. When is this happening?"

"Tomorrow! I have to pack! Do you think there's room in my suitcase for all my Harmonia toys?" She dashes down the hall.

"We might have to ship some things," Nate follows her, casting a glance my way as he walks away. He pauses. "We'll talk."

"Sure."

I sink onto a stool at the counter and gaze sightlessly at the kitchen, fingers pressed to my mouth, a sudden chill in my core.

This is why I didn't want to work with children again. I knew this would happen. I tried to protect my heart, but it's not that easy. Once again, someone I love is leaving me.

And...even worse...now that Nate doesn't have Quinn, he doesn't need a nanny. He doesn't need me.

Nobody needs me. The one person who maybe needed me was Jeff and I left without a word. My sister. Ayla. The Maddens. Now Quinn and Nate.

But wasn't that what I wanted coming back to New York? To be independent, make my own way, pursue my own dreams for once?

What I *thought* I wanted.

I don't know what to do. My impulse is to go to my room, pack up my own things, and leave. Nate said we'll talk, but I'm terrified of what that's going to be like.

Somehow this time I know it's going to hurt even more to lose Nate than it did to lose Jeff. I thought at the time I was heartbroken, but God, my entire body is hurting as if my heart was torn from my chest and my insides shredded.

I should never have let myself care so much.

Okay. I have to do this. I have to be an adult. Standing, I wipe my palms on my jeans. I walk to Quinn's room where a giant suitcase is already half full of things. "Need any help?" I ask cheerfully.

Nate looks up. His eyes are distant, his jaw tight. I can tell that he, too, is putting on a happy face for Quinn. This must be so hard for him. Now my heart hurts even more, because my own misery is one thing, but seeing Nate so demolished is even worse.

I swallow, my throat thick and tight, and move to Quinn's closet.

"I think you can take some of these," Nate says to Quinn, toys in his big hands. "But some we'll have to send you."

She sucks her bottom lip unhappily. "Okay," she grudgingly agrees.

"Does this have to be so fast?" I ask quietly.

"Apparently this is the only break Brielle has for a while."

"Ah." Brielle may be a good mom, and she may love her daughter beyond anything, but I'm pissed at her again. She's disrupting Quinn's life again. Maybe her intentions are good, but the effect is still messy.

I just did laundry so I fetch that and we go through it for Quinn's things. I help them pack, then return to the kitchen to get dinner ready. Chicken tacos is one of Quinn's favorites, so that's good. It's also a good meal for Nate because he can add avocado and tomatoes, and I use whole wheat tortillas. I try not to cry as I prepare the meal, then call them to come eat.

Quinn's full of chatter about the plane ride (she loves planes) and maybe going to Disneyland and the beach with her mom. "I'll have to miss a couple of days of school," she says, finishing her meal. "But that's okay. Mom said she already knows a good school for me to go to and she's making arrangements."

I nod, frequently glancing at Nate, who's quiet, although he does eat three over-stuffed tacos.

"I talked to her school when I picked her up," he says. "So they already know."

"Let me know if there's anything I can do," I offer. "I know it's a lot, all at once."

"Yeah." He rubs his forehead. "It is." He meets my eyes and gives me a regretful smile and lift of his shoulders.

I let him put Quinn to bed. In my own room, I text Gianna.

CARLY: *Hey. Might need a couch to sleep on again.*

It takes a few minutes for her to reply.

GIANNA: *WHAT??? What happened*

CARLY: *Quinn is moving to LA to be with her mom*

GIANNA: *Noooooo how can this be*

A few seconds later...

GIANNA: *Are you okay*

CARLY: *Not even a little.*

Gianna sends kisses and hugs emojis.

GIANNA: *When are you coming*

CARLY: *Tomorrow?*

GIANNA: *Oh wow, okay, that's fine. I'm so sorry.*

CARLY: *Me too.*

Too good to be true, I guess. That's how the saying goes. Ah well. C'est la vie.

Since we're in packing mode, I gather my things. I haven't accumulated much since moving in here, but I did buy a few things to decorate the room. I gaze at the cushions, framed prints, and small plant with sadness and indecision. I guess I'll just leave them.

I get ready for bed early. I'm so, so tired. I feel heavy and weak as I slide under the covers. In the dark, I lay awake for a long time, trying to talk myself out of this dejection. At one point I hear Nate's footsteps in the hall. He pauses outside my door.

I wait, my breath suspended, my muscles tense. Does he want to talk now?

I can't do it. I just can't. I need some time to pull myself together. We'll talk tomorrow.

No knock comes on my door and I eventually relax and fall asleep. It's a terrible sleep with crazy dreams that make no sense, me taking Quinn to the airport and losing her there and running all over JFK looking for her. I see her on a baggage conveyor belt surrounded by suitcases and I run for her but she disappears into the bowels of the airport. So I don't feel much better in the morning. In fact, I think I feel worse—now I'm even more tired and irritable on top of sad.

Brielle's flight arrives at eight-thirty and she's taking a car service here. Their flight back to L.A. leaves later this afternoon, so they'll have some time. Nate has a practice this morning and he's ready to leave for the practice facility when I get up.

Not our usual routine as of late, when he wasn't playing and we'd get Quinn to school and jump into bed for some adult fun. My chest tightens.

So I'm here to greet Brielle when she arrives. Quinn throws

herself into her mom's arms and they share an emotional embrace that lasts minutes. Brielle tears up but Quinn, surprisingly, is all smiles. I wonder if she even realizes what this means. My heart constricts even more.

"I'm going to have a shower," Brielle says when their greeting finishes. She picks up a carryon. "I feel gross from being on the plane all night."

"I'll get a couple of towels for you."

"Oh, I know where they are." She waves a hand and heads down the hall.

Okay.

While Brielle uses the bathroom, I get Quinn's breakfast.

"There are palm trees in California," Quinn tells me between spoonsful of cereal. "And it's sunny all the time."

"I've heard that."

"I've never been there! Have you been there?"

"I went there once, for a vacation. It was really nice."

"I want to go to the animal park."

"The zoo?"

"No, it's not a zoo. It's an animal park. In San Diego."

"Right. I've heard of that."

"The animals are not in cages and you ride a train...or a bus? And you see them just like wild animals."

"That sounds amazing. Make sure you send me pictures."

I hear the sound of a blow dryer humming and soon Brielle appears, all fresh and gorgeous and in different clothes, expensive-looking athleisure wear. Her blond hair hangs straight down her back and her lips gleam with pink gloss.

"Would you like coffee?" I ask. "Or something to eat?"

"I would love coffee, and I'm starving." She sidesteps me and helps herself to coffee then opens the fridge door to peer inside.

Again, okay.

She pulls out a carton of eggs and sets about making herself scrambled eggs—two whole eggs, one egg white—and slices a grapefruit in half. She knows where everything she needs is.

"Are you done with your cereal, honey?" she asks Quinn.

"Yeah."

Brielle picks up the bowl and slides it into the dishwasher, then swipes a cloth over the counter.

I move aside so she has room and then wonder why I'm hanging around here like it's my place. Brielle is Quinn's mom and she's definitely taken over. A tingling sensation runs up the back of my neck and I resist the urge to flee to my room.

"I want to wear my mask and my cape on the plane," Quinn says. "In case I need to rescue someone while we're in the air."

"No, honey, you can't wear that on the plane," Brielle replies.

"Why not?" Quinn crosses her arms and frowns.

"I...well, security at the airport might not let you."

I have no idea if that's true. "What if you wear it to the airport, but then if security tells you to take it off, you have to, to be able to get on the plane."

"Okay."

"No," Brielle says firmly over top of her. "You can't wear that to the airport."

I'm pretty sure Nate has never told Quinn she can't wear her cape. I bite my lip, seeing Quinn's disappointed face. Brielle overruled me pretty quickly, there.

"We're going to go out and pick up a few things for the trip," Brielle says. "You can have the day off, since I'm here. In fact, I guess your employment is done."

Oh. "Okay," I say slowly. This makes me feel as small as a mustard seed. But she's right. I'm not needed here anymore.

"I'm sure Nate will pay you two weeks in lieu of notice," Brielle continues. "It was short notice."

"Right." I squeeze the word out between my pinched lips.

"I can give you a check, if you need it? He'll pay me back."

"No, that's fine. I'm sure he'll transfer the money. I'm not worried about that."

Jesus. My paycheck is the least of my worries right now.

Brielle clearly has no idea that Nate and I have been sleeping together. And it's not as if I can tell her. How weird and awkward would that be? She thinks my employment is done, and…it is.

Why am I even here?

My things are all packed. I guess I can go.

"Come say goodbye to me," I say to Quinn when she has her shoes on to go out. "I'll be gone when you get back."

She runs at me and gives me a tight squeeze. I wrap my arms around her small body, breathe in the scent of her strawberry shampoo, and scrunch my eyes closed against the tears stinging there.

"I'm going to miss you," I whisper to her.

"I'm gonna miss you too. But you can come visit. Right?" She pulls back and stares at me.

I smile. "Maybe sometime, yeah. That would be fun."

I know it will never happen.

She and her mom head out.

I'm left alone in the apartment with my intense feeling of melancholy. Covering my face with my hands, I drop onto the couch and let the tears flow, covering my face with my hands. "I hope she's happy," I blubber into my hands. "I just want her to be happy." I sob until I'm drained. I drag myself into the bathroom and wash my face with cold water. I look hideous. Who cares.

I haul my suitcases downstairs and out onto the street and lug them all the way to Gianna's place. I still have the extra key and I let myself in.

Nothing's changed here. I bet the other girls are thrilled to have me back. I roll my eyes as I park my cases in a corner of the living room. Then I lie down on the couch and fall asleep.

29

NATE

When I get home from practice, Quinn and Brielle are in her room getting her backpack ready for their trip. She has snacks, coloring books and other activities, her handheld game console, and her beloved Clover and Storm.

"Are you all set?" I ask her, trying to be chipper about this.

"Yes!" She's clearly excited. I'm glad. But I'm crushed. My daughter is moving across the country and I don't even know when I'll see her again. I looked at the schedule and we have a trip to Vegas, L.A., and San Jose mid-December. Nearly two fucking months away.

"Where's Carly?" I ask, thinking she's in her room.

"She's out," Quinn says. "We said goodbye."

"Oh. Okay."

I keep my game face on as I drive them to the airport and stay with them until they go through security. Then emotions inundate me. I drop my head, my chest suddenly hollowed out, my bones aching.

At home, I walk in and drop my keys on the table. Silence.

"Hey, I'm home."

I walk through the small foyer. Kitchen and living room are

empty and no lights are on. Frowning, I stride to Carly's bedroom. Also empty.

Huh. Is she still out? Maybe she's picking up food for dinner?

Then I realize the room is more than empty. It's...devoid of anything. No clothing, no computer on the small desk, no toiletries on the dresser.

I feel like I've been smacked in the face.

She's gone? What the fuck?

I check my phone, although I would have noticed a text from her. Nothing. "Oh, Christ." I sit on her bed and look around.

Okay. I lift my phone again and tap in a message.

NATE: *Where are you?*

After about five minutes, I give up. I walk into the kitchen and open the fridge door. I inspect the contents for possible dinner options. Then I grab a beer and shut the door. I wander to the window overlooking the city. The sun is setting and lights are coming on, the sky streaked with pale clouds.

My phone buzzes and I grab it.

CARLY: *I'm at Gianna's.*

That's it? That's all? I glare at the phone. My patience is thread-like, my irritation level is high, and I'm kind of pissed at the world right now.

NATE: *Are we going to do this on the phone?*

CARLY: *Do what?*

NATE: *Have this fucking conversation*

It takes a while for her next message. I finish my beer and grab another one.

CARLY: *You mad, bro?*

I'd burst out laughing if I wasn't so goddamn angry.

She just left.

I'm not going to open myself up to more hurt. I'm not even going to admit how pissed I am right now.

NATE: *Nah I'm good*

CARLY: *Okay*

What else do I say? She left.

So is this it? We're done?

I slump on my couch. I just put my daughter on a plane to go live on the other side of the country. And Carly's gone. I'm fucking alone. Again.

I think back to the start of the off season when I was so goddamn lonely. I was fucking around with a bunch of women and that didn't help. I wanted more. I thought I had finally found it. Her. The one. Then she left.

"Who crapped in your Corn Flakes?"

I give Brando a quelling look. We're warming up on stationary bikes in the training room before our game. "I don't eat Corn Flakes."

"You should. They're delicious. What did you have for breakfast this morning?"

"I didn't eat breakfast."

"Ah ha. That's the problem. Not enough fiber. Also you might be hangry."

I sigh.

"Did you have your game day snack?" he asks.

"Yeah."

"Nap?"

"Sort of. I haven't been sleeping great."

"Another problem." He pauses. "I'm sorry, man. It must be rough having your daughter move across the country."

I grunt my agreement.

We pedal on for a minute, then Brando says, "Did you talk to Carly?"

"Nope." I pedal like I'm Lance Armstrong in the Tour de France.

"Easy, man, save your energy for the game. We're just warming up."

Right. I slow down.

"I told you, you have to talk to her."

"I don't want to."

"Fuck off, yes you do."

"I really don't."

He heaves an exaggerated sigh.

"Look," I say crossly. "I got the message. I'm not the kind of guy women want long term with. Carly is brainy and talented and beautiful. I don't know if she wants to go back to her convicted felon ex, but clearly she doesn't want to be with *me*. As soon as Quinn was gone, she took off."

"Maybe she wouldn't have, if you'd told her you wanted her to stay."

"I told her I was jealous of her ex and what did she do? Rubbed it in my face. She went out with him anyway."

"She didn't rub it in your face. She didn't even tell you about it."

"Okay." I have to concede that. "But that is also a problem."

He grunts. Because he knows I'm right. If it was no big deal, she would have told me about it. But she didn't.

"I give up," Brando says. "Just don't let your bad mood fuck up your game."

"It won't." I grit my teeth.

If anything, I play better. I'm pissed. I'm hitting hard, chasing the puck, joining the rush. I get three assists and we win.

As I shower after the game, I rub soap over some tender spots— my hip, my ribs, my shoulder. Christ, I'm going to hurt tomorrow. All that energy turned me into a fiend on the ice. Some of the guys are going out, but all I want to do is lie down on my bed.

I have a voice message from Brielle. They tried to video call me but didn't get through. Duh. Didn't she check my schedule? She asks me to call in the morning because Quinn misses me.

Well. I hope she's not too sad, but the fact that someone misses me is a tiny bright spot in my shitty life right now.

I don't care. I'll find someone to have sex with. No commitment, like before. I don't want any attachments. I don't need anyone else.

CARLY

I'm back to sleeping on the couch, applying for crappy jobs, and trying to find a place of my own.

The good news is, three of the agents I queried about my book are interested. They want to read it! I'm definitely excited about that.

I miss Nate and Quinn so much, I feel like there's a gaping hole inside me. I miss the life we had together. I wasn't really part of their family, but I felt like it. And it wasn't as if I was just there for a ride—looking after Quinn was a challenge at times, especially with the anxiety she felt after her mom left. But I love her. I wanted to care for her and make sure she was okay.

And I wanted Nate to be okay. In every way. His knee. His career. His family.

I hope he's okay.

I miss him. I miss how much fun we had together, doing little things like making a lunch for Quinn, watching a movie, or the hot times we had in bed, because I'm pretty sure I'll never find another man who's so generous and thoughtful not to mention strong and ripped and...

I can't even think about that stuff or I'll start crying.

I keep busy writing, since it's all I have now. I put up some blog posts, write another article, and it doesn't take long before I hear from one of the agents that she loves my book and wants to offer representation.

I let out a shriek of delight when I read that email. Luckily, I'm home alone.

I don't know what to do, because I'm still waiting to hear from two other agents and one of them is my dream agent. She represents a few authors I admire. I do some google research and apparently I can contact those other agents to let them know I have an offer.

So I do that.

I get a quick response. One agent passes, but my dream agent asks for a day to finish reading the book. Okay. I don't want to wait, but I calm myself down and send an email agreeing to that.

When Gianna gets home, I tell her my news.

"Oh my God!" She opens her mouth wide. "That's amazing!"

"Yeah, it is."

Her forehead creases. "You don't seem excited."

"No, I am. I'm just…well I don't want to get too excited until something happens for sure."

Also, I'm sad.

"Oh, Carly. I hate seeing you like this."

"I'm fine."

"You're not happy."

I give a half-hearted smile. "I am happy. You know…just not with my whole heart. But I'm okay. It'll just take time."

I'm such a drag. I came back from Paris all depressed about losing the Maddens, and now I'm doing it all over again. In fact, it feels even worse this time, because not only did I lose my family, I lost the man I'm in love with. The best man I've ever met.

"Have you talked to Nate?"

"No. What's there to talk about? He sent me my last paycheck."

She rolls her eyes. "I think there's a lot to talk about. I think he cares about you."

"He doesn't love me—he just used me because I was there looking after his daughter."

"Do you really believe that?"

I'm too hurt to really think about that. I toss my hair back. "Isn't it obvious?"

"No. It's not." She gives a frustrated sigh. "Okay. Take some time. I'm here for you."

"Thanks."

My dream agent offers me representation the very next day.

I can't believe this is happening. For real! I actually burst into tears of happiness and relief. And the first person I want to share this fabulous news with is…Nate. A sob escapes me that's not exactly a joyful noise.

Anna and I talk on the phone and she's awesome, easy to talk to, smart, knowledgeable. She mentions a few publishers she already has in mind and says she's going to touch base with them right away. But she cautions me that publishing moves slowly and it could take months.

Ugh.

Fine. I'll just keep on keeping on.

I already have another idea for a book. There was so much I could have included in "Be a Man," and I have a premise that could bring those things together. So I start working on that.

A few days later, I get a job offer from a marketing firm as a receptionist. I know I can't afford to turn this down. Although my bank account is fat thanks to Nate's generous pay and not having to spend money on rent and food, I need to be employed to get an apartment. So I accept the job. They give me a start date three weeks away. I mark that Monday on the calendar with glum satisfaction.

I'm getting what I want. A job. Possibly a publishing contract. Hopefully my own place. What more do I need?

30

NATE

We're playing against the Golden Eagles. They're a good team. I'm struggling with focus but I'm determined to play as well as I can. I was worried about losing hockey when I had to have surgery. It's important to me. And right now, it's all I've got left. But it hasn't been my best game.

We down two-one and it's halfway through the third period. We're getting ready for a faceoff in the O zone. The linesman thought their goalie had the puck and blew the whistle but the puck was loose and I could have had it and I'm pissed. Now we have to be sharp here to keep them from scoring.

Morrie's taking the faceoff. I'm on his right, Barbie on his left, Axe and Bergie on either side of me. The Eagles player with us, Hopko, is jousting for position with Axe. "Come on, dummy," he says. "Outta my way."

I fucking hate that word. I heard it too many times as a kid. I bet Axe did too. I bite down harder on my mouth guard. "Shut up, Hopko," I snarl

Axe bumps him back. Hopko grins, shoving Axe again. "Big dummy."

They're elbowing and pushing in a familiar dance but what's not familiar is Hopko continuing to call Axe a big dummy.

I happen to know Axe is dyslexic. I also know that like me, he was often told he was a "dummy." And I'm already short-tempered and irritable, because of life, because we're losing, because the fucking blind ref didn't see the puck.

"Say it one more time, asshole," I mutter to Hopko.

He laughs. "Dummy."

That's it. The second the linesman drops the puck, I throw down my gloves and go at Hopko.

The element of surprise is on my side and I land a couple of good punches and have him down on the ice in seconds. Of course I stop hitting him when he's down and I don't resist when the linesmen pull me off him. My guys are milling around me, the Eagles guys prepared to go after them. The crowd is cheering for me although they have no idea what's going on. I'm sure it looks like I jumped him for no reason.

Cooler heads prevail and it doesn't turn into a bench clearer, but I'm off for five minutes. I don't even give a shit.

I skate to the box, shaking back my sweaty hair. My knuckles throb. Oh well.

Morrie delivers my gloves and helmet. "What the hell man?"

I shake my head, my heart still racing.

After my penalty is served, Coach benches me for the rest of the game, which is only six more minutes. I'm going to hear about this after the game. I'm still buzzing with adrenaline and feeling reckless.

The score stays the same and we lose. Fuck.

I tramp down the tunnel to the dressing room with the rest of the guys, the vibe subdued.

Morrie repeats the question when we're in there. "What the hell, Nate?"

Axe speaks up. "He was sticking up for me."

Everyone looks at Axe.

"What the hell was going on?" Brando asks, sitting in front of his cubbie.

"He was chirping him," Bergie says, but he's frowning. "But it wasn't that bad."

"It *was* that bad," I snap. "He called him a dummy."

Everyone exchanges glances.

I sigh and drop my head, elbows on my knees. "Fuck."

To make things worse, I'm on the list to talk to the media. I know exactly what they're going to ask me.

Axe comes up to me. "It's okay, man. Tell them."

I meet his eyes. "Really?"

"Yeah." He shrugs. "I'm sick of this shit. Tell everyone. I don't fucking care."

Do I?

Nope. After everything I've just been through, telling the world I have ADHD doesn't seem like the worst thing that could happen to me.

"Okay," I say throwing back my shoulders. "Let them ask. I'll fucking answer."

And I do. I feel the censure from the reporters because of how it looked. So I let them have it.

"Hopko called Axe a dummy," I say. "Repeatedly. I know a lot of chirping is good-natured, and nobody takes it seriously, but what people don't know is that Axe has dyslexia."

That shuts everyone up.

"And I have ADHD," I continue. "Both of us have been called a "big dummy" too many times in our lives to count. Also lazy. And stupid. Sometimes it gets to you. Dyslexia is a learning disability, but it doesn't mean you're not intelligent. A lot of smart people just learn differently."

It feels good to stand up and say these things. People don't know I have ADHD because I've worked hard on strategies to overcome it and I'm taking medication. I've been ashamed of it most of my life and I shouldn't be.

"Calling people with learning disabilities names is not acceptable. Kids. Adults. Anyone. As kids, Axe and I had hockey, thankfully. I believe I'm a better hockey player because of my ADHD. Nobody wants kids growing up thinking they're stupid or not getting the kind of attention they need to learn because people think they are. That's just not right."

I can tell this is all unexpected and I get a bunch more questions thrown at me that I do my best to answer.

"I reacted, I defended my teammate, I took my penalty, and that's all I have to say about that." And I'm done.

I skip my usual post-game cool down and hit the shower. Letting the water stream over my face, I close my eyes. I don't know what will come of this, but I'll handle it whatever it is. Maybe it'll be a big nothing burger.

As I think more about it, though, I don't want it to be a nothing burger. I don't want it to go away. I got all fired up talking about it, and now I think maybe there's more that I can do. Maybe Axe would want to help me. We could help kids with learning disabilities and ADHD, especially ones who play sports. Lots of the guys adopt organizations that are meaningful to them. I bet I can find one to work with.

This gives me a sense of purpose I haven't been feeling for a while and gives me the confidence to walk into the locker room with my head up.

"We're going to the Amber Horse," Brando says. "You coming?"

My first impulse is to say no, but I shrug. "Sure." What the hell.

As we're walking to the bar, Brando says, "I didn't know you have ADHD."

"I don't talk about it much."

"It's not that big a deal."

I slant him a look. "It was to me."

"Yeah, yeah, I get it. I don't mean to dismiss it. But Jesus, it seems like everyone has ADHD these days."

I frown. "I don't think so."

"I mean, I don't think so either, but people are a lot more open about it and open to taking medication, I think. My brother and my cousin—both in their late twenties—just got tested and now they're on medication for it."

"Huh."

Maybe he's right. Maybe people are more open about it now. For me, it's always been a source of shame.

"How did you know about Axe?" he asks.

"We talked about it when we were rookies. We were roommates on the road. He saw my meds and we started talking about it. We went through a lot of the same things."

"It was a dumb fight…"

"Dumb."

"Fuck. Sorry. Uh…"

"Irresponsible. Foolish. Ill-advised."

"Yeah…"

I smile. Oh, the irony. I'm the worst offender when it comes to ableist language about myself.

"But I get it," he continues. "And then talking to the press about it like that…that was pretty badass."

"Thanks. I've been a little short-fused lately. I just didn't give a shit anymore."

"You miss Quinn."

"Yeah."

"And Carly."

I don't answer.

"Do you seriously think she dumped you because of your ADHD?"

"What? No. I mean…" I stop. I rub my mouth. We're at the bar and we pause outside the door before going in.

"Did she make fun of you? Call you names?"

"Jesus. Of course not." I think back to my meltdown when I was helping Quinn with her homework. Carly was supportive. Understanding. Non-judgmental. She explicitly told me I'm not stupid.

Brando eyes me. "Come on. I'll buy you a beer."

We find the others already there—Morrie, Hellsy, Axe, and Cookie—and join them at the table. There are always hockey fans at this bar after a game, and they're usually respectful of us, but tonight I get some cheers and high fives as I walk through the tables. I'm knocked off balance a bit, but I respond with smiles and thanks.

"Respect, man," Cookie says, clapping a hand on my shoulder.

"Yeah, totally," Hellsy adds, lifting his beer to me.

Warmth spreads through my chest. "Thanks."

In the morning I get a call from Tim Headley, the communications director for the Bears.

"Asher Wynn from The Athletic wants to interview you and Nils. He wants to do a piece on hockey players with learning disabilities."

"Whoa. Asher Wynn writes for the Athletic now?"

He chuckles. "Yeah. Are you up for that? We'll make sure we have the right to read the article before it's published."

"Is Nils in?"

"Yes, he is."

"Okay," I say slowly, forking my fingers through my hair. "Yeah. I'll do it."

Being interviewed by a sports journalist about this scares the shit out of me, but fuck, I decided last night this was going to be a way to make my life mean something more. I have to sack up and be a man.

Be a man.

When we end the call, I think about Carly's book and her talking about being a man and what it means. I just told myself I have to "man up." What the fuck does that even mean?

I remember being told as a kid to "man up" when I got upset about something, which happened often out of frustration and

233

anger. That meant not feeling upset. Or, hiding my feelings. I learned to do that. But that's not really what being a man is about, like Hellsy and those guys have talked about.

My ADHD doesn't define me. I'm a good hockey player. I want to be a good guy. I think I am. But yeah...I fucked up. I fucked up with Carly. I turned to violence when I punched Hopko. After I was all, *I don't believe in violence.*

I guess I have some work to do.

31

NATE

I'm video calling with Quinn. It's a great way to stay in touch, thank you technology, but not the same as having her here. She's chilling in a bunch of cushions on the couch, showing me her new socks and telling me about her new school and how she wishes she had friends there.

That sucks.

"You'll make new friends," I assure her.

"Can I talk to Carly?" Quinn asks. "She probably knows how to make friends."

And I don't?

I hear Brielle in the background. "Why would Carly be there, Quinn? She's gone."

"Because Carly is his girlfriend, duh," Quinn says to her mom.

I freeze. And blink at my phone.

"What?" Brielle's voice comes closer. Her face appears in the screen. "No, she's not."

I blink a few more times. "Well, we, uh, were…" Fuck it. "Yeah, we were dating," I say carefully to Brielle.

Her mouth opens. And closes. Her eyes widen. "Oh shit."

"Mommy! That's a bad word."

Brielle barely glances at Quinn. "I didn't know that, Nate."

"Uh…I guess I should have told you? Sorry. But it was really new and…well, things didn't work out."

Brielle bites her lip. "I, uh, told her to go home," she says. "The day I was there to pick up Quinn. I thought she was just your nanny! And the job was done. I offered to pay her what was owing to her, since we gave her short notice of the job ending, and I told her she could take the rest of the day off."

A solid lump of granite forms in my gut. "Oh."

Fuck me.

"I'm sorry," Brielle says again. "Did that cause problems?"

Oh no. Not at all. Carly just fucked off like she'd been told to fuck off and never come back and Jesus Christ, I'm about to lose my fucking mind. I cough. "Uh."

"Are you okay, Daddy?" Quinn asks, nudging her mother aside. "Are you sad?"

I swallow. "I'm fine."

"I think you're sad." She narrows her blue eyes at me. "Remember Carly said we're supposed to talk about how we feel. Are you sad? Afraid?"

I stare at my little girl's image.

"If you talk about it, it can help," she urges me, clearly having learned her lessons well.

"Yeah. That's right. And yeah…I am sad. I miss Carly."

"But you could get her to come back," Quinn says. "You just have to tell her you miss her."

Sure. That's all. So easy.

So why don't I do that?

"I guess I am a little afraid," I say, my voice scratchy.

Quinn nods. "What are you afraid of?"

Christ. I remember Carly asking Quinn that exact question. Getting her to open up about her fears and deal with them and tell them to get lost. Something hot and sharp pierces between my ribs.

What *am* I afraid of?

I'm afraid that if I go to Carly and tell her how I feel and that I miss her and want her back, she'll say no. Because I'm not good enough for her.

I'm afraid she wants her ex back. Or someone like him.

She's fucking perfect. I mean, nobody's perfect, but she's perfect for me. I love her so much. Pain spreads further through my chest.

"Tell your dumbass fears to go away!" Quinn says.

I choke out a little laugh. I know I should correct her language, but goddammit... "You're right. I need to do that. I need to kick them out. Take a hike. Get lost."

"Yes. That's it! But if you're afraid of Carly, you shouldn't be, because she's very kind and she loves you."

My throat squeezes. "How did you get to be so smart?"

She tosses her hair back. "I just am."

"Yes, you are. I love you."

"I love you, too, Daddy."

We end the call.

I think about Carly. About her unconditional support. About the fact that I trusted her enough to open up about my ADHD and how she reacted. She never once made me feel stupid, despite how smart she is. When we talked about her research, she always talked to me like I was an equal, even when explaining things.

I trust her.

Why did I freak out when she saw her ex? Yeah, I was jealous. Also, I was *scared*. I was scared she'd want him more than she wanted me. Some big portfolio manager, a guy who had to have brains. Of course, he *is* a criminal. And he hurt her. Those are not points in his favor.

I miss her. So fucking much. Not as a nanny. As my friend, my partner, my lover. We got to know each other in a different way than if we'd just dated. Living together for those months showed us each other in a whole different light—a real light. And she's *real*. Fun. Smart. Kind.

I need to apologize to her for being such an idiot. Er, bonehead. Whatever. I fucked up. I can admit my mistakes. Everyone makes them, right? I made a mistake. I need to tell her that.

I need to do it big. But I need help.

32

CARLY

I get "the call" when I'm sitting on the toilet. Of course.

Anna calls to tell me that there's so much interest in my book that we're going to auction. I don't even know what that means, and she explains the publishers will bid on my book, and we'll take the best offer.

Holy shit.

This is unreal.

"There's a lot of current discourse around toxic masculinity and male entitlement," she tells me. "Your timing is bang on with this book. And your approach is so positive. You're not making men out to be evil; you focus on how ending toxic masculinity will help men."

By the time our conversation is finished, the toilet seat is imprinted on my butt. I don't even care. Excitement bubbles inside me. This is really happening!

Once again I wish I could share my excitement with Nate. I know he'd be proud of me.

I watched him on TV last night. I told myself I didn't need to watch the game, but I did. I sat with my hands over my mouth when he got in a fight, which the announcers said they didn't know why he jumped that guy.

Then he came out after and the media asked him about it and he told them why.

I was so proud of him.

I watched in amazement as he brusquely talked about his ADHD and Nils Axelsson's dyslexia and how it's not okay to call people names because of that. Pride swelled inside me until I was nearly bursting with it, my hands shaking, a trembling smile on my lips.

I'm having a hard time focusing, so I go for a run in Central Park. The trees are mostly bare now, the ground covered in leaves that crunch beneath my trainers as I run. The air is the perfect temperature for running, fresh and cool, and I enjoy the feeling of breathing the coolness deep into my lungs. Running is a good time for my brain to work through things.

Nate.

I think about some of the things he said. When I commented that he doesn't like reading... *No. But I'm not stupid.*

When he said, *I don't think I can help Quinn with her homework.*

He told me, *Being good at hockey helped with my self-confidence, when it got trashed because people thought I was stupid.*

He told me about his ADHD. And that honestly and bravery meant so much to me. But I don't think he told me everything. My heart hurts for what he went through as a kid, being thought of as stupid or lazy. Fuck those people. He's right. Nobody should be made to feel they're stupid.

He's the best man I know. But I can sort of see that there could be some insecurity there. It seems absurd—he's so talented, so successful at what he does, playing hockey in the best league in the world, and also a good father, loyal friend, determined athlete.

When I hear again from Anna, she has fantastic news. All the deals being offered for my book are over a million dollars. Again, she brings me down to earth by explaining how the payments will be made. I haven't just won the lottery. But...I did it. I fucking did it.

She counsels me on which deal I should accept and then it's done!

We later speak to the editor at the publishing house who says she's thrilled to have acquired my book. I'm thrilled, too!

When Gianna gets home, I immediately lay my news on her. I'm bouncing on my toes, so excited I almost can't get the words out.

"Oh my God! That's fantastic!" She grabs me in a tight hug and we sway together for a moment, both of us laughing. "Let's celebrate!"

"Yes! I'll take you out for an expensive dinner! And champagne."

"Okay! I'll make a reservation," Gianna says. "Tomorrow night. Somewhere fancy."

"Perfect!"

When we arrive at the restaurant, I'm taken aback. Plum. This is where Nate brought me on our third date. Where we ran into Jeff.

"I didn't know we were coming here," I say slowly.

"You said it was great." Gianna leads the way in, seemingly oblivious to my disquiet.

Yes, it's lovely with the big flower arrangements and arched windows and chandeliers. I just have to suck it up and enjoy it without being reminded of Nate.

We splurge on a bottle of Bollinger, although my stomach clenches a bit at spending so much money on wine.

When it's been poured, we toast.

"To you," Gianna says. "To all your hard work and perseverance. You're a talented writer and now the whole world will know it."

My cheeks warm. "Thank you." I touch my glass delicately to

hers in a tiny clink, then sip the bubbly. "Although I think a lot of the credit has to go to Nate."

"What?" She frowns. "What are you even talking about?"

"He gave me a place to live and a job that gave me time to write. I couldn't have done it without that."

"Bullshit. You wrote that book. You would have written it no matter what."

I grimace. "I don't know."

"Of course you would have! Stop with thinking that! You were lucky to get that job, yes, but he was also lucky to have you."

I wrinkle my nose. "Right." I pause. "I've been thinking about Jeff."

She squints ay me. "Why?"

"He said he wanted me there, supporting him. I'm a shit girl-friend." I sigh. "I abandoned my boyfriend without talking to him, when he needed me most."

She watches me. "Nate needed you. He just lost his daughter."

I pull in an unsteady breath. "Oh my God. I did the same thing to him." I close my eyes on a wave of shame. "He was devastated about Quinn. I should have been there for him instead of protecting myself by running away again." I open my eyes and stare at Gianna. "I have to tell him that. I have to tell him I'm sorry."

She nods. "Yeah. You probably should."

I fight for control of my emotions. "We should order."

"No rush." Gianna sips her champagne. "So, I decided to get the boob job."

I blink. "Really? Oh good."

"Yeah. I think I'll feel so much better about myself."

"When is that happening?"

"Next month."

"I'll be there to help you after."

"Aw, thank you. I'm not looking forward to it, but I'm being brave. You're a good friend." We toast again.

Gianna checks her phone.

I pick up the one-page menu and scan it. "So French! I love it. It brings back memories. Hey, maybe I should move back to France. Maybe I can support myself with my writing, and I can do that anywhere."

"Whoa. Seriously?"

I shrug. "Maybe? Let's order. I want this steak with spinach puree and glazed cipollini onions."

"Hold on." Gianna tosses back the rest of her champagne. "I have to go to the ladies' room."

"Okay."

I peer down at the bubbles dancing in my wine. How am I going to talk to Nate? Should I text him? Try to see him? My chest constricts with remorse.

Gianna returns and takes her seat. I look up at her and my mouth falls open wide enough to drive a Zamboni into.

Nate is sitting across from me.

33

CARLY

I blink rapidly. "Whuuuu…"

Nate's face is drawn tight, but his lips curl into a half-smile. "Hi."

"What are you doing here? How…?"

The waiter appears. He gives Nate a startled glance. "Should I bring another glass?"

"Um…" I give Nate a perplexed look.

"Please," he says calmly.

My forehead tightens. "What's going on?"

"I asked Gianna to set this up. So I could see you and talk to you."

My jaw drops. "You're kidding me."

He smiles. "Nope."

"Wow. She's good. Where is she? She's got some 'splainin' to do."

He laughs. "On her way home."

"Oh my God." How is this happening?

"I had to talk to you." He meets my eyes. "Quinn told me to tell my dumbass fears to take a hike, so I did, and here I am."

I gaze at him, then ask slowly, "What are your dumbass fears, Nate?"

He swallows. "Women I've been with have never wanted me for

myself. I was a hockey player they could show off. I was the big dumb jock with the IQ of sunscreen."

My eyes widen. "Someone did not tell you that!"

"I overheard her say it. In high school." His mouth twists and he shrugs.

"Oh, Nate. That's terrible. She was a terrible person. You are *not* a big dumb jock."

"That's why I was so pissed about you seeing Jerkoff Jeff. Okay, I was afraid. He's the kind of guy you should be with and I was afraid that was who you wanted."

I raise my eyebrows. "A convicted felon?"

His lips twitch. "No. Educated. Sophisticated."

My eyebrows shoot up.

"He reminded me of Parker," he admits. "Brielle's husband. Except younger."

"Ohhhh." Now I get it.

"I wanted to come after you, when you left. By the way, Brielle apologizes."

I frown. "For what?"

"She didn't realize that we were in a relationship. That last day… she basically told you you were fired, and to go away."

My throat thickens, remembering. "Yeah. She did."

"She had no idea. She's really sorry."

"Oh. Okay." Wow.

"I wanted to come after you. I was pissed that you left like that. I didn't realize you'd been 'dismissed.'"

I lean forward, filled with urgent need. "I'm sorry I left. You were losing your daughter. I should have been there for you."

"Ah, hell," he murmurs. "I didn't deserve that."

The waiter arrives with a flute for Nate and fills both our glasses. "Are you ready to order?" he asks.

"No," we both say.

I smile distractedly at the waiter. "Just a few more minutes. Thanks."

He nods and disappears.

Nate sips his wine. "Hmm. I've never been into champagne, but this is good."

"It's expensive."

He grins.

"We were celebrating."

"Celebrating what?"

I break into a huge grin. "I sold my book! It's going to be published!"

His jaw slackens, then he grins, too. "Hey! That's fantastic! Congratulations." He holds out his glass to me. I pick up mine and do another gentle clink. "That's really great, Carly. I knew you could do it."

I gaze at him. "You did?"

"Yeah." His eyes warm and I feel it seep into me, right to my bones. Only then do I realize how cold I've felt. "Of course. You're so smart and talented. Hard-working."

I feel like champagne bubbles fill my chest, effervescent and golden. "Thank you. I think the exact same of you."

Our eyes meet. And hold. Energy shimmers between us, heat and light and sparks.

"Yeah?" he asks roughly.

"Yeah."

After a charged moment, he says, "I didn't come after you because I was afraid you would tell me to get lost. And...that would fucking kill me, Carly."

"Oh." I stare at him, my chest expanding. "Really?"

"Yeah." He leans forward and takes my hand across the table. "I'm in love with you."

"Ohhhh." I start trembling, even on the inside. "Oh, Nate." I'm afraid to believe it, but I want to. "I love you, too."

He closes his eyes briefly. "Okay, wow. Okay."

I huff a small laugh at that. "I was afraid, too."

"Yeah?" He opens his eyes and gazes at me with intent interest.

"Yes. I was afraid of trusting the wrong person again. Afraid of not being loved for myself."

He gazes back at me. "How could you be afraid of that?"

"Because all I've ever done is look after other people. I was afraid to believe that you wanted me as more than just a nanny for your daughter."

"Fuck." He closes his eyes, looking like he just took a butt end to the solar plexus.

"I never told you what happened with my sister," I say. "Wait. Let's order, so the waiter doesn't keep bugging us."

"I don't even care what I eat," he mutters, but picks up the menu. "Steak. There. Done."

We get that taken care of and I pick up my champagne again.

"Okay, tell me about your sister." Curiosity shines in his eyes.

I tell him about her pregnancy and my niece and what happened. "I took two years of my life to help look after them and then they just left."

He makes a rough sound, his eyes darkening.

"It hurt so much. I love them both, and Ayla...she was so precious to me. I don't think I tried to take over as her mom, but I guess it doesn't matter because Sophia felt that way. So I haven't seen them much since then. Of course, I was in Paris for three years."

"You should go visit them."

I bite my lip and look at him. And the love and reassurance on his face gives me courage. Another thing I've been afraid of. But... maybe I could do it. "And I spent nearly three years with the Maddens, and got so close to the kids, and then they just ended things. Like it was just a business arrangement. Which I guess it was. But I loved those kids."

"And that's why you took off after what Brielle said."

"Yes." My voice is a whisper. "It felt the same."

"I'm sorry. She's sorry."

I nod.

"It was *never* just a business arrangement," he says quietly. "For me. I wanted you from the minute I fell at your feet in the park. It was killing me when you lived with me and we had to keep things platonic. I'm sorry I didn't tell you how I was feeling."

"I mean, I sort of knew…I was falling for you, too. I loved being with you. I was just afraid to believe it, and then…"

"Yeah. I know. I fucked up." He squeezes my hand. "It was you who gave me the courage to be honest about my ADHD."

"Oh! I saw you on TV. That was amazing, Nate."

He smiles. "Thanks. I did it because I told you about it and you didn't judge me. Or think less of me."

"Then why were you so worried about Jeff? Jeez!"

"I don't know! Those old insecurities crept up on me again."

"Well, tell them to go away. Like I told Quinn to deal with her worries."

"I'm trying to learn that."

"At first, I tried to hold back and not care about you. Or Quinn. But that was impossible. I love her, Nate."

"I know you do. And that's not why I love you, but damn, it makes me love you more. Seeing you two together, having fun, playing in a blanket fort or making me a get well card…and she loves you."

"I miss her. Is she doing okay with Brielle?"

"Yeah. She had a few tears one night when we called, but overall she's fine."

"That's good. I'm sorry she's so far away now."

"Who knows. It may not be forever. Brielle could end up back here."

"I suppose."

"Or I'll ask for a trade to the Golden Eagles."

My head jerks around. "Would you do that?"

"I don't know. Maybe?" He searches my eyes with his. "Would you come to California?"

"I was just thinking about moving back to France," I say musingly. "Just before you got here."

"Fuck, no."

I smile. "I figured I can write anywhere. So...yes, I'd go to California with you."

Our meals arrive.

"I don't even want to eat this," Nate says.

"That's a hundred dollar steak. Eat it."

He laughs. "Okay.

We make it through the meal, which is delicious, and when the table is cleared, we forgo dessert.

"Is there anything else I can get you?" the waiter asks. "Coffee? Tea?"

"Just the check," Nate says, not looking at him, staring at me.

I smile. "I'm getting this. I have money."

"No, you're not."

"Yes, I am. You weren't even supposed to be here! Please. Let me pay. I've been making money and I want to do this."

His face softens. "Okay."

Sensing Nate's urgency, I quickly take care of the bill. I want to feel his arms around me, feel his strength, his forgiveness, his energy. I want to kiss him and taste him ad hold him, too, and tell him how much he means to me.

Out on the dark sidewalk, it has started to rain. We stand under the awning as traffic swishes past us on Park Avenue. He looks down at me. "My place?"

"Okay."

He hails a taxi and we slide into the back seat. He holds my hand and we're silent as we cruise up Park Avenue then zigzag over to Central Park West and to Nate's place. The city slides by in a blur of colored lights. But the whole ride, anticipation buzzes in the car. Sparks snap between us. My blood heats and my nipples tighten. I press my thighs together against the insistent ache there.

Nate sets a hand on my lower back as he ushers me into the elevator and up to his floor.

His apartment feels like home as we walk in. I feel such a sense of homecoming I almost cry. But I'm almost afraid to believe in what's happening.

I'm wearing a short black coat and Nate turns to me, unbuttons it and undoes the belt. He slips it off my shoulders and tosses it onto the chair. "I've missed you," he rumbles. "So damn much."

"Me too." I go on my toes to kiss him and his mouth meets mine in a hungry press.

A growl sounds in his throat and his arms wrap around me and pull me tight against him.

"This," I gasp against his lips. "This. I need you."

"I need you, too, baby."

I hang onto him as we press together and our mouths meet again, and again, lifting, clinging, tongues sliding. My hands slide into his hair as we eat at each other's mouths, my knees weakening, my bones melting.

"I want to take you to bed," he says. "But I want to be clear first."

"Okay." I brush my mouth over his beard stubble.

"I love you."

I draw back and meet his eyes. I see his emotions shining there, and they fill my heart and warm my skin. "I love you, too." I touch his cheek then kiss him again, a tender, melting press of our lips together. "Take me to bed."

34

CARLY

In his room, we hold each other again, so tightly, not kissing this time, just breathing together. He groans against my neck and I squeeze him more, loving how warm and solid and strong he is. He smells so good, that delicious sandalwood scent of his body wash and deodorant layered over the scent of his skin that makes me crave him.

"I could never get over you," he whispers. "Never."

My heart fills with joy and relief. "Me too."

He cups my face and kisses me until every thought has blown out of my head and I can only feel him and taste him. I grip his shirt and hang on in case I float away, I'm so light and frothy. His firm lips move on mine in silken licks and tender sucks and he tastes like lust and longing.

I take his hand and set it on my hip, then move it up to my breast. His big hand covers it, molding it, and heat sizzles through my veins. He looks down at me and the expression in his eyes is such naked ardor and fondness and relief and I have a sense of falling, like the floor has disappeared beneath my feet and I'm tumbling down and down, and I know it's love.

We kiss again, long kisses, slow kisses. "We have all the time," he whispers.

"Yes." My fingers start to work at his shirt buttons. I'm eager to feel his skin, sleek in places, rough with hair in others, hot and alive. I rub my hands over his pecs, trace his collarbones, drag my fingertips over the pulse at his throat, then brush them over his nipples, hard little nubs.

He sucks in a breath. I do it again.

"I like this dress, but I don't know how to get you out of it." He touches the bow at my waist.

"Yes, undo that." I reach behind my neck to unfasten the single button as well. Then he lifts the hot pink fabric up and over my head.

"Let me look at you." He sets his hands on my waist and his gaze moves over me with such a covetous expression I feel it everywhere, tingles over my skin, deep inside me. "So beautiful."

He traces the lace edge of my pink bra, slipping his fingers beneath it to trace the full curve there, and my breasts swell, my nipples tight and tingling. Then he drags his fingers down my stomach and does the same at the edge of my panties, teasing me, making me ache.

"I need you," I whisper.

"Yeah." He's watching his fingers move on me with an intent expression. "Look at you in pink lace and heels. Better than any fantasy." He licks his bottom lip, his eyes blazing.

"Did you think about me?" I suck that lip into my mouth.

"Fuck yeah."

"I thought about you, too." I palm his erection through his pants and he groans. "All the time." I undo his belt and then his pants.

He steps back and shrugs out of his shirt, then shoves his pants down. He's naked now, so beautiful with his strong bone structure, hard packed muscle, dark hair falling over his eyes, his full lips parted. He strokes himself, and he's thick and hard and ready.

So am I. My panties are wet.

I kick off my hot pink heels and climb on the bed, giving him a view of my ass in my thong and he makes another rough, desperate sound. He follows me, moving between my legs, gazing down at me with adoration and I'm so full of emotion I can't breathe.

He reaches for my panties and slides them down my legs, then caresses my legs on the way back up, all the way to my bra. He spies the front opening and flicks it, and my breasts spill free, aching to be touched. "Gorgeous." He leans down to kiss me between my breasts. "You are so fucking gorgeous."

I'm floating, dreaming, watching him as his eyes drift closed and he kisses me, then tugs a nipple into his mouth. Sensation streams straight down to my womb. I'm already aching for him and I need more. "Please…"

"Mmm. We have all the time," he says again. Then he lifts his head and meets my eyes. "Forever?"

My throat clogs. I reach a hand up to him to touch his jaw. "Yes. I want forever."

"Good." He turns his head and nips a fingertip.

I get rid of the bra and he moves to the nightstand.

"Wait." I put a hand out. "Do we need that?"

We gaze at each other, open and honest. "Do we?"

"No." He knows I'm on birth control. "I haven't been with anyone else."

An expression moves over his face I can't quite interpret. "I haven't either," he says. "Not since I met you. And I got tested before our first date."

I smile. "Oh ho. Sure of yourself, were you?"

"Hopeful." He bends and kisses me, his lips sweet and gentle on mine. "So fucking hopeful."

He fills me with such completeness, such beauty, tears form in the corners of my eyes. I tip my hips up to him to take him as deep as I can and he moves on me, slow at first, watching my face, gliding in, withdrawing, then in again. My orgasm is building already, heat twisting, sensation coiling. I watch his face tighten, his eyes darken, and he moves his hips faster. He settles his fingertips over my clit and rubs in tight circles, giving me exactly what I need, and I'm done. I'm starlight and moonshine, glowing and shimmering, pleasure searing through me so intense I almost can't bear it.

Nate arches his back, tips his face up, and groans through his own orgasm, filling me with liquid heat, so intimate and special. I hook my ankles at the base of his spine to hold him closer, my body still throbbing and tender.

"Christ," he gasps, lowering himself on top of me. He kisses my mouth, my cheek, then drops his head onto the pillow. His chest inflates against my breasts, his heart thudding against mine. I kiss his shoulder and hold him. And hold him.

Finally, he says, "Are you okay?"

"I'm so good."

He raises his head and gives me a wicked look. "Yes, you are."

He cleans me up and I fall even deeper for this man, and then we snuggle into his bed, wrapped in each other's arms and the sheets.

35

NATE

We're drinking coffee in bed the next morning, both of us naked, tired, and happy.

"I'm sorry I didn't tell you that I was going to see Jeff."

My muscles tighten briefly, but I relax. "I wish you had."

"I knew after I should have told you. It really didn't seem like that big a deal to me. And maybe it was a way for me to feel like I was in control of my own life."

"Shit."

"I wanted to hear him out and get closure. And...well, it turns out I learned something about myself."

I frown. "Like what?"

She shifts to face me more directly. "Like...Jeff still says he's innocent. He pled not guilty. He wouldn't cooperate with the FBI and implicate his bosses. He still believes they didn't do anything wrong."

"Holy shit."

"Yeah." She shrugs. "I believe him. I mean, I believe that *he* believes that. But...he was convicted. So..."

"Yeah."

"He's paid a price, but I don't know if he's learned anything from it. But that's not my problem. Anyway, he told me how he felt when I took off for Paris. He didn't know where I was for a long time and he felt like *I'd* betrayed *him*."

"Jesus."

"And I get it." She bites her lip. "I did run away, without even listening to his side of things."

"He's a criminal. He doesn't deserve that."

"I don't know. What if he is innocent? What if I abandoned him when he most needed support?"

I stare at her, my gut twisting. "What are you saying?"

"I'm saying that running away was kind of cowardly. And then I did the same thing to you." Her voice dwindles to a near-whisper. "Just when you lost Quinn, and I know that was hard for you, I ran away. Again."

"We talked about that." I reach out and smooth her hair off her face, letting my fingertips linger on her soft cheek. "You were hurt."

"Yeah. I thought you didn't want me anymore."

"I should have told you I didn't want you to leave."

"Even though you didn't need a nanny anymore?"

"That's not why I need you." My voice is low and raspy. "I could find another nanny, if I needed to. But I can't find another you."

"Oh." She gives me a tremulous smile. "I was also still a little mad at you for being all passive aggressive and pretending nothing was wrong. You were hiding your feelings! After all we talked about."

"I know." I hang my head briefly. "I'm sorry. I'm working on doing better at being a man."

Her smile is luminous. "I think you're a great man."

"I can do better." I lean over to kiss her mouth.

"I thought I wanted to be on my own, when I came back to New York," she says. "I wanted to find out who I am on my own, responsible solely for myself. I was afraid that taking that job from you and living with you wasn't really me being on my own, and I was afraid that the only reason I could write a book was because of what you did for me."

"Well, *that* is bullshit."

"That's what Gianna said. And you're right. I wrote a book!"

"Yes, you did."

"But then, when my dream came true and my book was going to be published, I just wished that you were there to share all that with me. What I wanted doesn't mean as much without people I care about."

"Did I tell you I'm proud of you?"

"You did. Did I tell you *I'm* proud of *you*?"

I chuckle. "It's good that we like each other."

"We just have to be brave enough to be honest with each other."

"Yeah."

I tell Carly about the interview happening next week with Asher Wynn. "He's apparently working on an article about players in the NHL with learning disabilities. Well, ADHD isn't technically a learning disability, but lots of kids have it. I don't know who else he's talking to besides me and Axe, but he wants to explore links between that and our success."

"That's interesting. And good for you."

"I hope it helps other people. Especially kids. And…I also got hooked up with this organization called LDF—Learning Disabilities Foundation. They're really interested in working with athletes. They don't have anything like that in their program, but they're aware of how beneficial sports can be for kids."

She turns wide, shiny eyes on me. "Wow. I love that."

I nod and give a little shrug. "I hope it's something I can do to make a difference."

"Oh my God, I love you so much." She launches herself at me and luckily my coffee mug is almost empty as she covers my face with kisses.

I laugh, get rid of the mugs and roll her under me.

"Look who's here."

Carly moves closer to me so Quinn can see her on her phone screen. She waves. "Hi, Quinn!"

"Carly! Hi!" And she bursts into tears.

"Oh no!" Carly and I exchange quick, concerned looks. "Don't cry, sweetie!"

"I miss you!" she sobs.

Brielle moves in behind her and hugs her from behind. "It's okay. It's okay."

Quinn nods and wipes her tears. "I remember what you told me, Carly," she says. "I try not to worry."

My heart kicks against my ribs.

"That's so good," Carly says. "If you need reminders, you can call me any time. And I miss you, too. So much."

"Are you back?" Quinn asks. "Is that why you're there with Daddy?"

"Yes."

"I did what you said," I tell Quinn. "I stomped on those fears and I talked to Carly and told her how I feel."

Quinn beams. "I'm so proud of you, Daddy!"

I laugh.

"And I was brave, too," Carly says. "You know what Clover's strongest superpower is?"

"Bravery!"

"That's right! What does she say about that?"

"It's okay to be scared because that just means you're going to do something brave."

"Exactly."

"It's good you won't be alone," Quinn adds. "Both of you."

"Right."

"That makes me happy." Quinn rubs her eyes again, but she's smiling.

We hear more about Quinn's new school and the surfing lesson she took and how one of the amusement parks is building a Harmonia world and she can't wait to go there.

"Ohhhh that would be amazing," Carly says. "I'm jealous."

"You have to come!" Quinn says. "We could go together."

"I would love that!"

She *will* see Quinn again. Somehow. Both my girls are the best things in my life and I'm going to spend the rest of my life taking care of them and making sure they're happy and being the best man I can be, even if it means letting people see my weaknesses and showing my emotions. The only way to build real connection and intimacy is truth and vulnerability. And love is worth the risk.

NATE

"We wanted to meet with you to get ahead of the news," Mr. Julian says. "You've probably heard there's a press conference scheduled for one o'clock this afternoon. We're going to make an announcement about the new team ownership."

The team is gathered in our meeting room and we all exchange looks. It's happening. The team has been sold.

"So I'll introduce you to the new owners. They want to say a few words to you and they'll answer some questions." He turns. "Come on in, guys."

Five men walk into the room, all wearing suits and ties.

We all recognize them. Or rather, we recognize four of them—the four biggest guys.

Tag Heller. Jase Heller. Logan Heller. Matt Heller.

My jaw drops and I swivel my gaze over to Hellsy. That's his dad and his uncles up there. He's got his bottom lip caught in a crooked hold and the way his eyes dart around tells me...he knew this was coming. Bastard.

Mr. Julian introduces them, although they need no intro to most of us. The fifth man, however does. "This is Gordon Harris, Junior.

He is the chairman and CEO of Harris Industries, which is a group of business with global interests primarily in food and clothing businesses."

Wait. I *have* heard of this guy. He's one of the richest men in the world. Holy shit.

"Good to meet all of you," he says casually when it's his turn to speak. "I'm a huge hockey fan, but the hockey business is new to me and the Heller brothers will be making the decisions about running the hockey organization, so you can rest easy knowing that this team is being run by some men with deep hockey roots and a lot of knowledge of both the game and the business."

Jesus Christ on a cracker. I'm pretty poleaxed right now.

But I think this is good...?

They talk about how no changes will be made, at least right away, that they have confidence in Mr. Julian and the assistant manager Dale Townsend, that want to get to know the team and the hockey operations side of things and figure out what's working and what's not working. The Hellers are all relaxed and open, making jokes with us and putting us at ease. "We hope we can run the hockey club without killing each other," Tag jokes with a wry glance at his brothers. "Sometimes we have differences of opinion but we'll try to keep those between ourselves and make decisions that are best for the team. Anyone have questions for us?"

"Hellsy?" Barbie pipes up. "You got any questions?"

Everyone roars with laughter.

Hellsy shakes his head.

It must be weird for him. Maybe for us, too. Will we have to watch what we say around him? I guess we'll see.

I go home and tell Carly the news. She thinks it's a good thing that someone with deep pockets has bought the team, and also guys who really know hockey.

"How was your day?" I ask.

"I got my tattoo changed."

I frown. "What? Your ankle tattoo?"

"Yes. Do you want to see it?"

"Of course."

The skin around it is still red where she's added some words in the same script. It now says "C'est la vie j'aime."

"What does it mean?" I brush my fingers over her delicate ankle bone, away from the fresh ink.

"It's life I love. Or, I love life."

I look up and meet her eyes.

"It's subtle, but it's different," she says. "I thought 'c'est la vie' sounded a little defeatist. I mean, shit does happen, but…we work to overcome it. And I do love life. I love *my* life. I love you."

My heart bursts into an explosion of heat. "Yeah. I get it. I love my life, too. And you. I love you."

"Has your life motto changed?"

"Nope. I still like, 'I licked it so it's mine'."

"Mmm. I like that one, too." She says it in a throaty, sexy voice.

I grin, although my groin tightens. "Actually I still like, 'life is an adventure, take the risk.'" I lean over and smooch her lips. "I wouldn't be here with you if I didn't take the risk of telling you how I feel. Or telling the world about my ADHD."

"Same. That is an excellent life motto. I wasn't sure about living a risky life, but you are definitely worth the risk." She kisses me back, her lips curved. "Let's have lots of adventures."

"Together."

"Yeah."

Thank you so much for reading Scoring Big! Want to read a BONUS EPILOGUE? Sign up for my newsletter for exclusive access to it!

. . .

And Bears Hockey continues with...

Roughing the Player

Watch for more details

AUTHOR NOTE

For all you eagle-eyed, sharp-memoried readers who noticed that the excerpt of Scoring Big that was in that back of Good Hands is different than this version of Scoring Big --- you are correct. I wrote that excerpt which was supposed to be chapter one back before Good Hands released. When I got back to writing the rest of the story...it didn't work. I tried. I tried so hard. I broke my brain. I really wanted it to be a "nanny next door" story but I just couldn't do it and I ended up ripping it apart and rewriting it. In the end, I'm super happy with how it turned out and I hope nobody is disappointed! It took a while, but I fell in love with Nate, Carly, and especially Quinn, and I hope you did too!

It was a rough ride getting this book done and I have to give huge thanks to editor Kristi Yanta. She saw what I was trying to do and helped me do it. Your comments and suggestions are so valuable. Thank you so much!

Thank you also to my author friends, especially PG Forte, Jami Davenport, and Kat Mizera, who listened to me whine about this book for months. Your support means so much to me.

Also thanks to my Sweet Heat Reader Group who always come through for me when I have questions like, "What does a seven year old girl like to do?" (I had a seven year old girl once, but that was a while ago. Ahem.) You guys are the best!

And as always, thanks to my readers. This year has been a bit of a struggle but you are why I hang in there. I am always honored that you read my books – thank you!

OTHER BOOKS BY KELLY JAMIESON

Heller Brothers Hockey

Breakaway

Faceoff

One Man Advantage

Hat Trick

Offside

Power Series

Power Struggle

Taming Tara

Power Shift

Rule of Three Series

Rule of Three

Rhythm of Three

Reward of Three

San Amaro Singles

With Strings Attached

How to Love

Slammed

Windy City Kink

Sweet Obsession

All Messed Up

Playing Dirty

Brew Crew

Limited Time Offer

No Obligation Required

Aces Hockey

Major Misconduct

Off Limits

Icing

Top Shelf

Back Check

Slap Shot

Playing Hurt

Big Stick

Game On

Last Shot

Body Shot

Hot Shot

Long Shot

Bayard Hockey

Shut Out

Cross Check

Wynn Hockey

Play to Win

In It To Win It

Win Big

For the Win

Game Changer

How Sweet It Is

Screwed

Firecracker

ABOUT THE AUTHOR

Kelly Jamieson is a best-selling author of over forty romance novels and novellas. Her writing has been described as "emotionally complex", "sweet and satisfying" and "blisteringly sexy." She likes coffee (black), wine (mostly white), shoes (high heels) and hockey!

Subscribe to her newsletter for updates about her new books and what's coming up.

Find out what's new...
www.kellyjamieson.com

Contact Kelly
info@kellyjamieson.com